KNEELING AT THE ALTAR

Jim Lusby is Waterford-born, and now lives in Dublin. A former Hennessy award-winner for his short stories, he has also written for the stage and radio. His previous novels are *Making the Cut* and *Flashback*.

By the same author

MAKING THE CUT
FLASHBACK

JIM LUSBY

Kneeling at the Altar

VICTOR GOLLANCZ
LONDON

First published in Great Britain 1998
by Victor Gollancz
An imprint of the Cassell Group
Wellington House, 125 Strand, London WC2R 0BB

A Gollancz Paperback Original

© Jim Lusby 1998

The right of Jim Lusby to be identified as author of
this work has been asserted by him in accordance with
the Copyright, Designs and Patents Act, 1988.

A catalogue record for this book is
available from the British Library.

ISBN 0 575 06606 7

Typeset by SetSystems Ltd, Saffron Walden, Essex
Printed in Great Britain by
Guernsey Press Co. Ltd, Guernsey, Channel Isles

All rights reserved. No part of this publication may be
reproduced or transmitted in any form or by any means,
electronic or mechanical including photocopying,
recording or any information storage or retrieval system,
without prior permission in writing from the publishers.

This book is sold subject to the condition that it shall not,
by way of trade or otherwise, be lent, resold, hired out, or
otherwise circulated without the publisher's prior consent
in any form of binding or cover other than that in which it
is published and without a similar condition including this
condition being imposed on the subsequent purchaser.

98 99   5 4 3 2 1

To my mother,
who first convinced me that a pen
was the lightest thing to carry through life

one

The small, dark-headed man sitting in front of McCadden in the Accident & Emergency waiting room seemed to have lost his place in the queue.

And even more uniquely, it didn't seem to bother him.

Sentimental drunks with minor injuries who'd shuffled in an hour or more behind him were placed on a list and seen by doctors and sent back home clutching packets of Anadin, while the little man just went on sitting there, pretending to read his *Irish Times*. Never quite reaching the end of the page he was on. And never turning over to the next.

The man was alone.

He might've been waiting for someone to come back from X-ray or a long consultation, McCadden conceded. Except that he never raised his head from the newspaper when patients returned to the waiting room. They had no interest for him.

And yet, whenever the front entrance doors were opened and another casualty stumbled in from outside, he always peered around the side of his newspaper, checking on the newcomer.

He was in his mid-thirties, McCadden reckoned. And

he was dressed in expensive casual clothes. A heavy wool sweater over a check shirt and light blue designer jeans. A green wax jacket had been draped over the back of the plastic chair to his right. By his side he had a shopping bag filled with exotic fruits that he occasionally ate. On the seat to his left he'd placed a neat bunch of fresh red roses, still wrapped in protective plastic and brown paper.

This was Thursday night. A little after nine o'clock. And early in October.

The hospital's visiting hours had long since ended for that evening.

Bored with the long wait for his injured colleague, McCadden began to speculate . . .

Two hours earlier, speeding along Michael Street in an unmarked car, Detective Garda Rose Donnelly had skewed into a lamp-post on the opposite side of the road after swerving to avoid a child who'd broken from his parents and darted out in front of her. The kid himself was fine afterwards, apart from the expected hysterics. McCadden, strapped tightly into the front passenger seat, had also escaped injury. But Donnelly, they thought, had broken or dislocated her right shoulder.

The man with the exotic fruit and the bright flowers had already been sitting in the waiting room when the two detectives reached Accident & Emergency. But it wasn't until Donnelly had been taken to X-ray that McCadden, bored with his own company, had developed an interest in him.

That was about eight forty-five.

And less than thirty minutes later, at nine fifteen, McCadden's curiosity finally wore his patience down.

Leaving his own overcoat and Rose Donnelly's handbag behind, he stood up and walked through the rows of plastic seats and up the aisle between them to the reception counter.

The young nurse behind the perspex screen was very attractive, he'd already decided. Dark black hair that was barely visible under the white cap, deep brown eyes, and very full and colourful lips. But she also seemed to resent her own beauty, as if it prevented her from doing her job properly. And she'd developed a curt manner as a defence.

'Inspector McCadden,' he reminded her quietly when she came to attend him now.

She stared at him resentfully.

Initially, she hadn't really believed that he and Donnelly were detectives. Not that McCadden looked as rugged as usual. In fact, he was clean-shaven and his hair had been recently cut and styled. But he was wearing a tuxedo. Rose Donnelly had on a blue evening dress. And the nurse had thought at first that they were a pair of party-goers flying high on drink or drugs.

The embarrassment of her mistake had made her even more abrasive.

'Yes, yes,' she said now. 'Detective Inspector *Carl* McCadden. As you were told already, Inspector, your colleague is currently in X-ray and you—'

'No, no,' McCadden interrupted. 'I don't want to talk about that.'

'What do you want to talk about?'

McCadden leaned confidentially forward. The nurse smelled invitingly of a faint lavender perfume. 'See that man reading the newspaper ... No, no, don't look at him now.'

'How can I see him,' she demanded, 'if I don't look at him?'

'This is a valid point,' McCadden conceded. 'It's clear the nursing schools still have rigorous standards. But what I mean is, don't look at him *immediately*.'

She actually smiled slightly. Although it was more that her cheeks caved in to two dimples than that her lips fully relaxed. But still . . .

'I understand,' she said.

McCadden nodded. 'Do you know if he has presented himself for examination?'

She shook her head. 'No, he hasn't.'

'Sure?'

'I fill out a record card for each patient. They pay a fee, so I also issue a receipt. I remember every one tonight. He's not among them.'

'How long has he been here? Longer than me, I know. But much longer?'

'I don't think so, no. Ten or fifteen minutes maybe.'

'Do you remember him coming in?'

'Not really, no. I noticed him later, when he was sitting down.'

'Looking at him now, and at the things he has with him, and with your knowledge of hospitals, what would you say he was doing if he wasn't in this waiting room?'

'Visiting a patient.'

'Right,' McCadden said thoughtfully.

Rose Donnelly showed up at that point, pushing backwards through the swing doors into the waiting room and noticing immediately as she turned that McCadden was at the counter. Her right arm was in a heavy sling.

'What's the damage, Rose?' he asked her as she approached.

'Nothing broken, anyway,' she told him.

'Good.'

'I've got torn ligaments in the shoulder joint. A couple of sessions in physiotherapy will clear it up. I didn't think you'd still be here, though, sir.'

He waved away her concern. 'Oh, I rang in and told them we both needed treatment.'

They'd been on their way to the Tower Hotel when the accident had happened. As one of the minor spin-offs of Ireland's current presidency of the EU, the head of the German Bundesbank was in town tonight, lecturing the formally dressed local entrepreneurs at a five-hundred-pound-a-plate dinner.

McCadden turned as he spoke and looked back down the waiting room. The little man, he saw, was still concealed behind his newspaper. He pushed away from the counter and walked down to collect his overcoat and Donnelly's handbag. When he came back, he said goodnight to the nurse and slipped the coat over Donnelly's shoulders before going out into the night.

But he did everything slowly. Reluctant to leave the puzzle unsolved. Detained by a vague feeling of unease and a characteristic tingling along the nape of his neck.

Their car was parked about a hundred metres away. The night had cooled since their arrival and a biting wind was rising. They walked crisply along the footpaths.

Two rows down from them in the car park, a stocky, crew-cut man, wearing only a light denim jacket over jeans and T-shirt, was standing by a white Honda Civic and obviously starting to get extremely cold. He was stamping his feet and furiously rubbing his hands together as he waited.

'I bet his wife has the keys, Rose,' McCadden joked.

She didn't laugh. Even after a year working with him, she was still uncomfortable with his irony.

The driver's door of their Ford Sierra was bent awkwardly inwards and wouldn't open any more. McCadden unlocked both doors on the passenger side.

'Better sit in the back,' he advised. 'It'll make it easier for me to get in and out if I don't have to climb over you as well.'

A little sleet started slanting against them as they drove through the hospital grounds towards the exit. McCadden flicked on the windscreen wipers and said suddenly, 'He could've been waiting for a member of staff to come off duty, you know.'

'Who, sir?' Donnelly asked.

'Someone with a birthday today. Hence the flowers. Or a patient about to be—'

He broke off to swerve slightly as the car's headlights picked out four men striding towards them in single file along the edge of the road, their heads down and shoulders hunched against the wind and the rain. McCadden didn't recognize any of the three who were walking behind. But their leader interested him.

'Well, well,' he said. 'Joey Whittle. A long way from home.'

'Do you know him, sir?'

'A bad man with drink taken, Rose. He ruined a promising football career because of it. He was only seventeen when he won an FAI Junior Cup winner's medal. Wouldn't think it to look at him now, would you? Leeds United, over in England, signed him afterwards. And they let him go just as quickly again when they saw his intimacy with the booze. You follow soccer, Rose?'

'No, sir. Boxing.'

'Boxing? Right.' McCadden glanced in his rear-view mirror at the receding figures. 'You reckon Joey's been drinking tonight?'

'I don't know. I thought he was working here.'

'Why did you think that?'

'He was here earlier.'

'Was he?'

'In the car park. Like an attendant, you know.'

'When was that, Rose?'

'When we arrived and parked ourselves.'

'Hm, right.'

McCadden drove on in silence, up to the main exit. There he stopped. The road to the left led to the fishing villages of Dunmore and Passage. The road to the right would bring them back to the city. Both were free of traffic. Behind them, a red Fiesta had pulled up. And was waiting.

But McCadden didn't move.

In the rear seat, Donnelly started getting a little uncomfortable. 'The car behind us, sir,' she said. 'It's flashing its lights at you.'

McCadden glanced in the rear-view mirror, but without actually seeing anything.

'Right,' he acknowledged absently. 'Not that nurse from reception, by any chance, is it?'

'What nurse, sir?'

McCadden laughed. And then he suddenly depressed the accelerator, released the clutch, and swung the Sierra in a wide arc, until he'd managed a U-turn and was driving back again through the grounds of the hospital and heading at speed for Accident & Emergency once more.

'I bet you a fiver, Rose,' he called behind him, 'that he's driving a white Honda Civic.'

'Who, sir? Whittle?'

'No, no, not Whittle. The little man in the waiting room.'

'What little man in the waiting room?'

McCadden pulled up outside the entrance to Accident & Emergency. In his eagerness, the damaged driver's door defeated him for a few moments, until he remembered again that it was jammed shut. He slid across and out the passenger side.

'Wait for me, Rose.'

The young nurse looked up at him expectantly as he burst into the waiting room. He smiled at her quickly and turned away, searching across the rows of dulled faces staring back at him. The red roses were gone. The bag of exotic fruit was no longer on the floor. Between them, the seat the little man had occupied was now empty, except for the folded newspaper he'd been reading.

'He left,' the nurse said. 'A few minutes after you.'

'Was he alone?' McCadden asked her.

'Yes.'

'Did anyone call for him?'

'No, he just stood up and left.'

McCadden swore. As he went back outside, an ambulance with its siren wailing pulled into the bay to deliver a patient on a stretcher. He ran past it, across to the car park. The white Honda Civic was still there, but no one was standing beside it any more.

He looked around after noting the car's registration number. Against the fluorescent glare from the waiting room and the flashing red light of the ambulance, the driving sleet was visible. Otherwise, he could see nothing in the darkness. And it was only when the siren was switched off and the wind gusted favourably that he was able to discover what was happening.

The sounds came from his right, in the green area to the side of the car park. They were the noises of a frenzied chase. The high-pitched whimpering and desperate breathing of a terrified quarry. The savage grunts and shouts of an eager pack behind it.

McCadden ran from the car park, through a border of shrubs, and on to the grass. Paper snagged in his shoes as he went. Something firm but brittle crunched under his feet. When he looked down he saw that the grass was strewn with long-stemmed red roses and passion fruit and kumquats.

Ahead of him, in the dim light that was spilling from the nearby wards, the little man weaved and ducked as he sprinted away from his heavier opponents, like a hare pursued by five overweight, lumbering greyhounds. Given open country to run in, he might've made it to freedom. He had more pace and stamina than his attackers. But he was running up a blind alley right now, towards a building whose shape was going to trap him. He had ten, maybe fifteen seconds of liberty left. And probably of health as well.

'Stop!' McCadden shouted from behind. 'Armed Garda! Stop!'

They all heard. Because they all glanced quickly back.

The three in the rear pulled up immediately and stood there awkwardly, with hang-dog expressions on their bowed faces. McCadden had a clear view of one of them. An anxious, middle-aged man with thick, untidy hair and a heavy moustache. But they were all the same, he guessed. Solid community men. It made him think of vigilantes. And, inevitably, of drugs.

Beyond them, the man who'd been watching over the Honda Civic stuttered a little, tugged equally by worry about the law and by his commitment to Whittle in front of him, and finally slowed to a compromising walk. But Whittle himself, a stocky, muscular man, drove relentlessly on.

McCadden ran on through the ones who'd stopped or slowed. 'You lot stay where you are!' he ordered humorously. Knowing they'd melt away as soon as he'd passed.

Against the pebble-dash wall of the building ahead, Whittle had now pinned the little man, his massive left hand encircling the other's throat, his right drawn back in a fist to smash the face he held as an immobile target.

The windows on either side had sucked in pallid figures in dressing gowns, abandoning the television sets in their wards for real excitement. Perhaps the spectators cheered as McCadden charged through shrubs to the rescue. But McCadden himself knew that he had no chance of reaching the struggle in time to prevent Whittle's blow. So he opted for the only lie that might confuse and delay the big man.

'He's one of ours, Joey!' he shouted. 'He's a guard!'

Whittle hesitated. His fist wavered behind his right shoulder while his mind slowly processed the information. And by the time he'd decided that it was nonsense or that the other's occupation was only a better justification for punishment, McCadden was up to him, barging into his left side and knocking him off balance.

Whittle's strike had already been launched. But the blow that had been intended for the little man's face now passed it by and Whittle's fist crashed into the wall instead. A second before Whittle's cry of agony sounded close to his ears and drowned out everything else, McCadden heard that distinct snap of broken bones.

The two went down together. The rough concrete tore through the knees of McCadden's evening wear and grazed the flesh underneath. Whittle lashed out in pain and fury with his flailing legs. A white sneaker flashed past McCadden's cheekbone without making any contact. A knee caught him in the stomach under his ribcage. Winded and bruised, he rolled a little away to safety before getting to his feet.

Whittle's face was screwed up in agony, he saw. The man was lying on his back on the ground. His left hand was propping up the other arm. The right wrist was dangling with unnatural limpness. Like the neck of a dead chicken, McCadden thought. And worst of all, perhaps, the little man, the mysterious object of all this unexplained violence, was no longer with them.

From behind, McCadden heard high heels clacking along the concrete. When he turned he saw the white sling first, and only afterwards Rose Donnelly's light brown hair.

'Rose,' he said gratefully.

'Can I help, sir?'

He nodded. 'Remember that white Honda Civic I was joking about in the car park? Go back and stand guard over it. If the owner approaches, arrest him. Disorderly conduct.'

As she left and he knelt to lift Whittle to his feet, two male orderlies and what looked like a young intern came from the wards to help. The intern took a quick look at his patient.

'Casualty!' he instructed decisively. 'Casualty!'

And after that, it was out of McCadden's control. He was given no chance to put his questions and no option but to tag along behind the hurrying group.

The same young nurse in Accident & Emergency looked out at him with weary indulgence when he turned up again. He thought she might've understood if he'd come back with the little man needing surgery. But to drag in yet another stranger who was injured...

Whittle was whisked off to X-ray. McCadden followed, waiting for him in the small seating area outside the theatre. And while he was there, Rose Donnelly found him again.

He didn't really have to ask for her report. He could see the disappointment in her face.

'No luck, Rose?' he said anyway. It was better to dump the blame on fortune instead of making her feel any worse.

She shook her head. 'It was already gone when I got there. I asked the hospital security to stop it at the exit if it's still in the grounds, but I think we've lost it. What's going on, sir?'

'I don't know,' McCadden admitted. 'I haven't a clue. I'm waiting to ask Whittle.'

She sat beside him and glanced at her watch. It was only ten fifteen.

'I've got the baby-sitter booked until after midnight,' she said.

But he couldn't judge her mood or discover her reasons for mentioning it. Regret? Resentment? Reassurance?

Like McCadden, Donnelly was separated from her spouse. Unlike McCadden, she hadn't agreed to the split and she had a small child to care for on her own. Cathy was eight years old, McCadden remembered. A lively, mischievous kid who was academically bright and good at sports. But Donnelly still worried about her.

'It hits them so hard, sir, when they don't have both parents,' she'd told him once. 'It really knocks their confidence. Cathy's always asking for reassurance.'

McCadden and his wife never had children. 'No, we're not ready for it yet,' Jenny used to say. 'I don't think you're ready for it. I know *I'm* not.' Earlier that year, three months after the legislation permitting it in Ireland had been enacted, McCadden and Jenny had been granted a divorce. A week ago she'd written him a letter, telling him that she was finally marrying Michael, the weekend gardener with a talent for dull attentiveness, and that she was pregnant...

Did a child need *that* much security, McCadden wondered. With *everything* regulated for its placid comfort? He doubted it. Although he'd responded to the news only with congratulations and good wishes.

Thinking about it now, he was on the point of telling Rose Donnelly to knock off and take a taxi home when a trolley, with Whittle stretched along it and apparently unconscious, was wheeled from the X-ray theatre by the young intern.

McCadden stood up. 'Hey, hang on. I need to interview this man.'

The intern looked aghast. 'This man is suffering from concussion.'

'I thought it was a broken wrist?'

'That, too. But concussion also.'

'You walked him across here.'

'He shouldn't have walked.'

'What do you mean, he shouldn't have walked? You marched him over here!'

'We didn't know.'

'*We?*'

'In any case, he'll be under sedation and observation until the morning. They're likely to operate on that wrist tomorrow.'

McCadden sighed and turned away. 'Come on, Rose,' he said wearily. 'I'll drop you home. And I suppose we'd better organize someone to let Whittle's wife and kids know where he is.'

They went back downstairs, through the corridors, into the Accident & Emergency waiting room again. The little man's *Irish Times* was still lying on the seat where he'd left it. But the young nurse was no longer behind the reception counter. Instead, there was a severe elderly woman, who looked without understanding or sympathy on McCadden's ill-treated evening wear and Rose Donnelly's sling and, misreading the signs, muttered something wistful about the sedate courtships of her own youth.

two

According to the records, the registered owner of the white Honda Civic was Denis T. Quaid, living on Water Park Road in the east of the city.

McCadden called there a little after eleven the next morning, on his way back to the hospital to interview Joey Whittle. No one answered the first time he rang the bell. Whoever was inside had the television on loudly, tuned to a children's cartoon, and he had to ring again, more insistently, before the door was finally opened. A well-dressed elderly man and a small boy stood in front of him. The child had thick curly hair and smears of chocolate on his plump face. The man was smoking a cheap cigar.

'Good morning,' McCadden said. 'I'm Detective Inspector Carl McCadden from—'

'McCallum?'

'McCadden.'

'There's a crime programme on the television called *McCallum*.'

'Right,' McCadden accepted. 'Are you the owner of a white Honda Civic, registration number—'

'Not any more, I'm not.'

'Don't tell me,' McCadden said wearily. He'd met the

obstacle too many times before not to know the twists of the story. 'You sold it over the last few weeks and the change of ownership hasn't been processed yet.'

'I don't know about the processing. That's not any of my responsibility.'

'It is, actually. But go on.'

'I sold it, all right. Well, what I did was, I actually traded it in on a newer model to a garage over in Ferrybank there . . .'

McCadden glanced at his watch. He was only a couple of minutes away from the hospital. Ferrybank was a longer journey, north across the River Suir. And there wasn't much point chasing over there immediately.

He thanked the old man, smiled faintly at the pouting kid, and left.

The hospital public wards were a lot worse than merely overcrowded that autumn, and Joey Whittle had been squeezed into a corner where a bed wasn't supposed to fit. He was without a cabinet, without a reading light and without a power point anywhere near him. His right arm, encased in plaster, was suspended in a sling attached to a free-standing frame beside the bed.

He looked extremely groggy, propped against stacked pillows with his head lolling to one side and his eyes closed. But the ward sister assured McCadden that it was only boredom and not the lingering effects of the anaesthetic since the operation.

'He's had no visitors, you know,' she whispered.

His wife and kids, apparently, hadn't yet filed in to cheer him up, even though they'd been notified before eleven the previous night. Some time that morning, when he was still weak from the operation, his mother had bustled along to fuss over everything and to complain about the decline in public health standards. Otherwise he'd been ignored by the outside world.

As McCadden drew up a chair to sit beside the bed, the noise of its legs scraping along the floor jolted Whittle from the light doze he was in. He half-opened his tired and bloodshot eyes, struggled to focus, and then stared out balefully when he recognized who it was.

McCadden took a single kumquat from his jacket pocket and placed it on the tray above the bedclothes. 'I brought you some fruit, Joey,' he said.

Whittle glowered at the little orange-coloured oval rocking back and forth across his tray. 'What is it?' he asked suspiciously.

'It's a kumquat.'

'It looks like a shit an orange might have.'

'I found a couple of them on the ground last night.'

'Some people have all the luck, don't they?'

'You remember the old apple market off Michael Street, Joey?'

'That's gone forty years ago.'

'Your mother would remember it.'

'What about it?'

'One of the women who had a stall there went on to open a fruit shop later,' McCadden explained. 'She was supposed to be the first to bring kumquats into Waterford. May Breslin. She was known as Kumquat May for a while. Except that very few people were familiar with the fruit and she got an undeserved reputation for being determined instead.'

'What the fuck are you talking about, McCadden?'

'Strong-willed? Determined? Kumquat May? No?'

'I don't know what you're talking about.'

'Are you in hock to someone at the moment, Joey?'

'What?'

'In deep, are you? Is that why you were trying to rip off that little guy last night?'

Whittle's mouth fell open so wide and so shamelessly that it was quite obvious robbery hadn't been the motive. McCadden persisted with the line, though. Fishing for the little revelations that objections always dragged along with them.

'How come you knew exactly what he was carrying in that—?'

'Hey hang on there!' Whittle interrupted. 'We never knew anything about any money.'

'Money? Nobody mentioned money.'

'You ask Christy...' Whittle glowered and looked confused and fell silent.

'I don't want any names, Joey.'

'I'm not giving you any names.'

'I take it they were friends of yours. Or neighbours of yours. All right? I'm happy enough with that. So what did he do to you?'

'Who?'

'The little guy you lot were chasing last night.'

'What do you mean? Don't you know?'

'I wouldn't be asking you if I knew.'

'You mean you haven't caught him yet?'

'No, I haven't, Joey. I don't even know who he is.'

Whittle struggled to pull himself forward in the bed. 'You've got to tell Corina, McCadden!' he shouted. 'You've got to contact my wife!'

'Your wife already knows.'

'Not about me! About Ryle!'

'Ryle? Who's Ryle?'

'His name is Ryle! The bastard we were after. John Ryle!'

'Okay. So his name is Ryle. What about him? You haven't told me what he's done to you.'

'He didn't do anything to me. He did it to Jason.'

'Jason?'

'My young fellow, Jason.'

'One of your sons, you mean?'

'He's only after starting secondary school this September.'

'How old is he?'

'He's thirteen. Ryle wanted to take photographs of him without his clothes on. Last Thursday. As far as I know, that's as far as the bastard ever got to. But that's one of the things I was aiming to find out when I caught up with him last . . .'

A nurse took that delicate moment to wheel in the mid-morning tea trolley. She saw from Whittle's chart that he wasn't allowed anything yet, so she smiled instead at McCadden.

'Would you like a cup, Inspector?'

'Got any coffee?' he wondered.

'Not in a hospital, Inspector,' she reproved.

When she'd moved on, McCadden drew his chair a little closer to the bed and leaned forward to lay a hand on Whittle's good arm.

'Joey,' he said, 'I need to hear the details on this. All right? When did you find out about it?'

'It was last night,' Whittle told him. 'We were having the tea. Around about six o'clock. Right in the middle of it, Jason started screaming. About Ryle taking photographs of him without any of his clothes on.'

'You said it happened last Thursday. How do you know?'

'That's when Jason said it was. A week before.'

'And this was the first you heard of it?'

'How many times do you have to hear of it, do you think, before you get it stopped?'

'I know.'

'If that was one of your kids—'

'I'm not *arguing* with you, Joey. I'm just trying to get everything straight. Okay?'

Whittle glowered, but nodded truculently. 'Yeah, okay.'

'How would this Ryle know Jason? What opportunities would he have for taking photographs? Is he one of his teachers?'

'Naw. He lives down the road from us.'

'Who lives down the road from you?'

'Ryle. He's a couple of doors away. He's one of our neighbours.'

McCadden stared. Whittle and his family lived in one of the older local authority estates. The last decade or so, unemployment had been high there. Most of the men read the English tabloids, stretched about as far as lemons on Pancake Tuesday when it came to exotic fruit, and couldn't afford anything better than department store clothes. Whichever way you looked at it, Ryle didn't seem to fit. But it wasn't good enough, of course, to be suspicious merely of difference.

'You'd better tell me how you came to be chasing him around a hospital, Joey,' McCadden asked.

'His wife's a patient out here.'

'That only explains what *he* was doing here.'

'The rest of the chaps, Christy—'

'I don't want any names.'

'They all have lads in Jason's class in school. They knock around together. The young fellows. We went to call on Ryle, anyway, last night, when I told the others what he was up to with Jason. He wasn't there. Someone said he'd gone to visit his wife in hospital. Someone else drove us out here. We found his car in the car park. He's only after getting it last week. A Honda Civic. But we couldn't find him.'

McCadden nodded. Thinking of the fury that the alleged molestation of children released in adults. Thinking of the terrors they harboured of homosexual advances. And of the strange, idealized visions of both childhood and sex that these feelings tapped into in a world where the realities were mostly grim.

'I'm going to have to look into this, Joey,' he said. 'I'll have to talk to the boy. You'll probably want to be there.'

'I'm not out of here until tomorrow.'

'Then I'll have to wait.'

Whittle shook his head. 'No. Get the wife to do that. Corina. Now that you're on to it, you'd better follow it up. I want the bastard pinned to the wall as soon as possible.'

McCadden pushed back the chair and stood up. 'I'll be back, Joey,' he promised.

'Hey.' Whittle summoned him. 'Are you going to charge me? You know. About last night.'

'You hadn't any drink on you, did you?'

'No. I wasn't out. I told you, I was having the tea. What's that got to do with it? Are you going to charge me or not?'

'Don't drink, Joey. And stay away from Ryle until I've sorted things out. Then we'll see. Do you still have your winner's medal, by the way? From the Junior Cup win?'

Whittle frowned suspiciously again. 'How do you know about that?'

'Remember the team you beat in the final that day?'

'I do, yeah. Why?'

'Remember the name of the player who played sweeper for them?'

Whittle shook his head. 'No. Why? What was it?'

McCadden smiled ruefully. 'No one ever remembers the losers, do they? Do you still have the medal?'

'No. I gave it to Jason a good few years ago. Him being the eldest and all. You know, pass it on, like.'

'Does he play?'

Whittle looked embarrassed by his inability to conceal an old disappointment. 'He don't, no. He's not, you know, sporty, sort of . . .'

When McCadden left, he walked across to the hospital's main reception to ask if a woman named Ryle was a current patient. A chirpy nurse breezily directed him to another ward and then enlisted an idling porter to guide him through the grounds.

But Miriam Ryle was sleeping just then and couldn't be disturbed.

McCadden stood at the end of her bed, looking down on her. She was a dark-haired, deeply tanned woman in her early thirties, very attractive, with fine, smooth skin and the kind of fresh appearance that suggested prosperity.

'But I'm afraid she's been quite distressed since last night,' the matron confided.

'Her husband?' McCadden appeared to guess.

The matron frowned.

'He didn't visit her as expected last night and she hasn't been able to contact him this morning.'

'How could you possibly know all that, Inspector?'

'Ah!' McCadden said mysteriously. 'Will you let her know that her husband is fine? Just a little delayed.'

'Of course, yes.'

'What was she admitted for in the first place, by the way? What's wrong with her?'

'Don't you know?' the matron enquired crustily.

'No,' McCadden admitted.

'She fell from a table at home while posing for a photograph and broke her collar-bone.'

'Right...'

'Who would want to stand on a table to have their photograph taken?'

McCadden nodded agreeably. 'That's a good question, isn't it?'

three

McCadden didn't drive immediately to Whittle's home after leaving the hospital. Co-operative parents or not, he wasn't walking in alone to interview a pubescent boy about an alleged sexual assault.

He rang Rose Donnelly first, ostensibly to enquire about her health, but really on the off chance that she might be interested in staying involved, despite her sick leave. He was lucky. He found her bored and exasperated. Her confinement to home had given unusual stability and confidence to her little daughter, who'd skived off to a fun fare on a day trip with the minder.

Once he'd side-stepped the Chief Superintendent's nervous lack of enthusiasm, he picked Donnelly up and filled her in while travelling.

'I don't know,' Cody had faltered. 'It's not as if Whittle has lodged a formal complaint, is it? It's all so *vague*. And this whole area of child sex abuse, you see. It's a potential minefield for us all. But we'll have to follow it up officially now, I suppose.'

'I'm going to interview the boy this afternoon.'

'No, no. I don't want you getting any further involved in it. You've done enough as it is. It's not that I don't trust your discretion, mind.'

'Right.'

'But we need someone with more experience of these matters. Hasn't Detective Sergeant Hyland just completed a course in headquarters . . .?'

'Paul Hyland is on holidays. Liam de Burgh is tied up on the drugs investigation. Frank Ryan is in Dublin, giving evidence in a case, and won't be back until tomorrow. I was thinking of asking Rose Donnelly along.'

'Detective Donnelly is on sick leave. I've just signed the form.'

'Her injury is minor. It certainly won't affect what I need her to do.'

'Yes, but I'm not entirely sure, you see—'

'She has training and experience in the area. Absolutely essential, as you mentioned. When she worked in Dublin, she was assigned to cases of rape and sexual abuse.'

'She's still quite new to the district. I'm not quite sure if this is the right occasion . . .'

'I'll go along with her,' McCadden volunteered.

Whittle's home had three bedrooms, seven boys under the age of fourteen, a noisy mongrel terrier and two bullfinches in ornate cages that were hanging in the front room. The birds looked plump, the dog was holding his own, the kids were undernourished, and the mother had the wrong end of the stick.

She didn't ask about Joey's condition in hospital. When McCadden volunteered encouraging news, she only snapped at him angrily. 'I hope they keep him in there until we're all dead and buried, the stupid fecker.'

With dyed blonde hair straggling around her face and a smoking cigarette always dangling from her lips,

Corina Whittle seemed to live on the edge of breakdown, constantly harassed and irritated. Inside her flapping jeans and limp sweater, she was painfully bony. About eight stone, McCadden calculated her weight. He thought again how there seemed to be a standard allocation of fat for poor couples. If the man, like Whittle, was big and brawny, the woman always shrank to feed him. If the wife was heavy, her husband was invariably slight.

'Is Jason home?' McCadden asked.

It was almost five o'clock by then, an hour since school had ended.

'He's out,' Corina Whittle told him. 'I'll go get him for you.'

'In a minute. I want you to fill me in on what happened last night first.'

'Didn't Joey tell you?'

'Joey's a bit woozy from the anaesthetic. He said to ask you.'

'I don't know.' She crushed one cigarette in the crowded ashtray on the hall table and lit another immediately. 'I was in the kitchen making tea.'

'But you must've heard something?'

'I heard Jason screaming his head off about Ryle wanting him to take his clothes off. Then I heard his father losing the head and screaming about getting Ryle. That's all I know.'

'Did Jason specifically mention Ryle?'

'I'm sure he did, yeah.'

'Had he been disturbed earlier that day?'

'Who? Ryle?'

'No, your son.'

'Jason? Disturbed? How do you mean? Disturbed at something he was doing, is it?'

'Was he upset?'

'He was quiet. But he's always quiet. You can't get a word out of him edgeways.'

'He hadn't been any different than usual, then?'

'Not that I noticed, no.'

'Right.'

'Can I go and get him now?'

McCadden and Donnelly waited in the cluttered front room. Until McCadden switched it off, the television relentlessly pumped out images of all the things the Whittles couldn't afford, from stylish clothes to peace of mind. But when the sound died, the two finches in the room suddenly became more agitated and started flapping their wings so violently against the bars of their cages that he had to turn the set back on again.

Corina Whittle was gone almost twenty minutes. Clearly, she had no idea where the boy actually was and only a hazy notion of where he might be. They heard her distinctly as the two of them returned to the house, verbally abusing her son for an absence she'd obviously encouraged. And she was still at it when they came into the room. It was an act, of course. Designed to demonstrate her maternal concerns. But the performance was too pathetic to do anything with but turn away from discreetly.

Jason Whittle was a short, scrawny boy for his thirteen years. He dressed tough, in a hooded sweat top, pre-torn jeans and black sneakers, but he hadn't either the height or the weight to carry the image. And he lacked confidence. His eyes dipped away from contact with others. Even indoors, he would've preferred to wear the hood to hide his face.

He couldn't have been much admired by his burly, aggressive old man, McCadden thought.

He had other problems as well. When his mother sat on the battered old settee opposite the police officers, she left a space by her side for the boy to take. But he openly rejected the offer, insisting on standing just inside the door instead, his head bowed, his hands twisting the cord of his sweat top around his fingers.

McCadden had asked Rose Donnelly to take up the questioning after the preliminaries. But it was a mistake, he realized quickly. The boy answered her queries, but only in grunts and monosyllables. And he kept glancing across at McCadden when he spoke. Recognizing only the male as a figure of authority.

He had a problem accepting instructions from women. Starting with his mother, and extending outwards to everyone else, he seemed to have a problem even communicating with women. All picked up from having Joey as a role model, presumably.

It was the wrong combination, McCadden decided. The two women and himself and the kid in the same room. It was going nowhere. So, he had a small dilemma. Should he let it drift? Should he indulge the boy's prejudices and take over, just to get some results?

Compromise, he decided. Get quickly to the essential question. Which was whether the boy had a specific complaint about Ryle or whether his parents simply had a grudge against their neighbour.

'Excuse me, Rose,' he said quietly.

'Yes, sir?'

'Do you mind if I ask a question?'

She frowned at him briefly, but then quickly caught on. 'No, go ahead, sir.'

'Jason?' he said. 'About those photographs—'

'Mr Ryle didn't take any photographs,' the boy cut in.

'That's not what you were saying last night,' his mother told him.

'It *is* what I said,' he growled at her.

'No, it's not.'

'Nobody was listening to what I said, were they?'

'Why would anybody be listening to you? All you ever do is tell lies, anyway.'

'What photographs was I talking about, Jason?' McCadden asked.

The boy switched instantly from the contempt he displayed towards women to the caution he had with men. 'What?'

'I mentioned photographs. You said that Mr Ryle didn't take them. But what photographs was I talking about?'

'I don't know. How would I know?'

'But there are photographs, aren't there?'

Of course there were, McCadden thought. Photographs existed. He could see it in the boy's face, the way an intense fury spread across his pale features at being caught out.

'Jason,' he said gently. 'If someone has injured you, you can do something about it. If someone is threatening you all the time, you can do something about it. If someone forces you to do something you don't want to do, even *asks* you to do it, like having your photograph taken, you can do something about it. That's the great thing. You can do something about it. All you have to do is mention it.'

'Nobody did anything to me. I keep telling you. You're the only ones doing anything. You won't believe me.'

'Okay. Point taken, Jason. Can you remember why you were upset last night?'

'You'd better ask them that.'

'Them?'

He jerked his head contemptuously towards his mother again. 'Them.'

McCadden raised his eyebrows.

Corina Whittle dragged on her cigarette, more desperately than usual. 'I don't know what he's talking about.'

'Okay,' McCadden said again. Soft ground, he thought. Shifting sands. And dangerous territory. 'You know Mr John Ryle, Jason, don't—?'

'No.'

'He's living down the road, Jason.'

'I don't know him.'

'You mentioned him yourself earlier.'

'He's a little liar,' Corina Whittle chipped in unhelpfully. 'He's always at it.'

McCadden struggled to hold his patience. He had to finish this, he decided. And quickly. He had to take it from another angle. 'I just want to clear up a last few points, Jason. Okay? You said that you don't know Mr Ryle. Have you ever been in his house?'

The boy's mood had turned stubborn. His stance was rigid. He wasn't looking at McCadden any more. And he'd already decided on his responses, regardless of the questions.

'No,' he grunted.

'Have you ever met him elsewhere?'

'No.'

'Have you ever talked to him?'

'No.'

'Maybe he gives you a bit of trouble, does he? You know, like a football going in his front garden and him coming out with a shotgun to chase you off.'

The boy lifted his head. The look in his eyes said quite clearly that McCadden was a lunatic. 'He doesn't have a shotgun.'

'Well, a brush or something, I don't know. Is he like that?'

'No, he's not. Ask any of the—?'

But Corina Whittle again disrupted the rhythm. 'Ryle!' she spat out. 'I'll tell you what Ryle is like! He's not one of us! That's what he's like! Not one of us!'

As a spasm of hatred and silent rejection twisted the boy's lips, McCadden stood up. He took another of his kumquats from his jacket pocket and tossed it over to Jason. Pure reflexes made the boy reach out to grasp it.

'Your father sent you that,' McCadden lied.

The boy was astonished. At the mere thought of his old man giving him a present? Or at the nature of the gift?

'You know what it is?' McCadden asked.

'It's a kumquat,' Jason told him.

'Right,' McCadden agreed. 'That's what it is.'

Shotguns and kumquats, he thought.

The boy knew enough about the interior of Ryle's house to be certain that there was no shotgun there. And although he could've become familiar with the exotic fruit elsewhere, it was most likely again that he'd learned about it from Ryle.

35

The boy, therefore, in lying about his relationship with his neighbour, was either trying to *protect* the older man or was too frightened of him to tell the truth.

'I'll tell you what,' McCadden proposed. 'You think over what we were asking you about and we might come back to talk to you again when we know a little more.'

four

But it took McCadden almost the entire weekend even to put a *shape* on the mystery.

And that against the stubborn, inexplicable resistance of the Chief Superintendent.

'Well,' Cody announced complacently on Friday evening, 'it all seems no more than a storm in a teacup now, doesn't it? Only the hysterics of an unhappy boy in a disturbed family. A cry for attention. No apparent crime. And no victim. I think we can safely close the file on it.'

The eagerness and the haste surprised McCadden. But he didn't share his wonder. Instead, he searched for an angle that would keep his own involvement alive. He said, 'John Ryle may be pressing assault charges against Whittle.'

Cody sighed with irritation. 'Hasn't anyone dealt with that yet?'

'Not yet.'

'Send someone out to talk to him.'

'He might be more inclined to let it drop if I saw him myself.'

'Then you'd better get it over with, hadn't you,' Cody snapped with sudden ill humour. 'And the sooner the better. My wife and I have planned a weekend in Dublin and I don't want it disrupted by any embarrassing developments.'

McCadden was in bed that night, finishing a last coffee while reading the collected essays of George Orwell, when the puzzle came back to distract him. Why would a chief superintendent's holiday be spoiled by a case involving a minor assault? He had no more idea now than he'd had earlier; but on the strength of the teaser he made another coffee, passed half the night flitting restlessly between work and Orwell, and managed only five hours' sleep before the alarm went off at nine.

Between eleven and twelve, after a late breakfast in town, he called twice at John Ryle's house, about thirty yards down the road from the Whittles. The place was empty and locked up on both occasions.

Early in the afternoon, though, he finally caught Miriam Ryle awake and largely unoccupied at the hospital. She had another visitor with her at the time, a tall, blond young man she introduced as George Ducy and vaguely described as a colleague of hers, but he left almost immediately, pleading a crowded schedule. Her elusive husband had also paid her a visit that morning, bringing a fresh bunch of flowers and a new basket of fruit, and staying chatting with her for almost two hours. Not the attitude, McCadden observed to himself, of a man desperately looking over his shoulder.

'No, Inspector,' Miriam Ryle said in surprise. 'He didn't seem anxious about anything. What should he be anxious about? Why are you asking about him?'

'He recently bought a white Honda Civic, didn't he?' McCadden improvised.

'Oh, that!' She laughed, with what seemed like relief. 'He did, yes.'

'We have some suspicions that the car may have been involved in a robbery before its sale.'

'Oh, dear.'

'Nothing to do with your husband, of course. He's driving it at the moment, I suppose?'

'He is. And he's gone down to Cork on business. He left after seeing me. He won't be back until Monday now.'

'Right. I don't actually have an occupation for your husband. What ah . . .?'

'He's a computer programmer. He designs games. Himself and his friend, who lives in Cork, have an independent company. A small one, really.'

'So he works largely from home?'

'Most of the time, yes.'

'And yourself?'

'I'm a secondary school teacher.'

'Right. So when you said that Mr Ducy was a colleague of yours . . . He's a teacher also, is he?'

'That's correct, yes.'

'You don't teach any of the Whittle kids, do you?'

'They're all boys.'

'So I've noticed.'

'All the boys on the estate attend the Christian Brothers' school. It's a traditional thing. I teach in a girls' secondary.'

McCadden didn't ask, because he didn't want John Ryle alerted to the angle of his interest, but the question plagued him. With an income at least in the middle bracket, no kids to gnaw holes in the bottoms of their purses or cramp their lifestyle, and a wide range of intellectual interests, why were the Ryles living in a poor housing estate?

'Thanks for your assistance, Mrs Ryle. Sorry to have bothered you.'

'No trouble at all, really.'

In the hospital car park, McCadden sat behind the wheel of the Ford Mondeo, considering his options. He didn't want to wait until John Ryle came back home on Monday. He wanted to keep chasing the leads. He had no clear notion of the actual offence that had been committed. Nothing but his own instincts to persuade him that something significant *had* happened. And not even a co-operative victim to help him out. But the thing had *bitten* him.

So what was he going to do? Drive back to the station and tell the Chief Superintendent, *My ex-wife has just become pregnant for the first time, I need to demonstrate the sheer madness of bringing kids into the world these days*? Cody wouldn't see the joke, of course. An earnest man, given to prayer and principles.

But Cody wouldn't see *anything*, it struck him, until he came back from his weekend break late on Monday afternoon . . .

McCadden reached across to the glove compartment, took out a booklet and checked names and addresses from his notes. Jason Whittle's teachers. The district health nurse. The social worker whose casebook included the family. The GP they'd nominated on the medical card scheme. The closest to him, he noticed, was also the most interesting. Sarah Wilson, the social worker, lived in one of the newer purchase estates less than a mile from the hospital.

She turned out to be a small, black-haired woman in her mid-twenties, very relaxed, and very much on top of her job. She'd just come home with the week's shopping when he called. She served him Bewley's Colombian coffee in the kitchen while she unpacked and carefully stocked the fridge and presses. And she didn't once have to check her data files to deal with his queries.

'Ah, Thursday,' she sighed, after he'd sketched the background. 'That figures.'

'Why?'

'Thursday night is crisis time in the Whittle household. Have you been in their dining room?'

'No. Only the front of the house.'

'There's a clock in the centre of the mantelpiece. One of those massive, ornate things, with gold plate. I think it was a wedding present. Every Thursday evening, Joey Whittle leaves his dole money under the clock. Or at least, the housekeeping portion of his dole. The money's always short. His wife always knows it's going to be short and that she's going to have to fight for her share.'

'So there's a row every Thursday night.'

'It's not as predictable as that. And this is what really disturbs the kids. These days, Corina prefers not to launch her attack before she's softened Joey's resistance. Sometimes she leaves the money untouched, with the edges of the wad just barely showing all the time under the clock, right through Friday and into Saturday, until someone's nerves finally snap. They play stupid games. I've watched them at it. Corina slowly dusts the mantelpiece, working closer and closer to the clock and the money. Joey stands up to flex his muscles, demonstrating *his* particular strengths. The tension mounts . . .'

'And you reckon that's what happened to Jason when

he screamed about photographs on Thursday night? He'd simply broken?'

'I think so, yes.'

'My Chief Superintendent suggests it was only a cry for attention. The boy wanted the focus back on himself. In which case, he could well have been lying about the photographs.'

'Maybe. But dancing up and down with multi-coloured handkerchiefs in no-man's-land isn't something even the dumbest of humans ever do. I think his nerves shattered. And whatever had been playing on his mind for the past week or so just burst through.'

'And the previous Thursday?'

'Same scene at the Whittle home, presumably. Same performances. Same tension. Why? What happened?'

'I don't know,' McCadden admitted. 'Not yet. You haven't come across any suggestion of Jason being sexually assaulted, obviously. Otherwise you'd have reported it.'

'Not at all, no.'

'Who does Jason hang around with, do you know?'

'He doesn't have a wide circle of friends. He's not really a very gregarious lad. There are only two others he's close to, both of them his own age and from the same estate. Luke Brady and Nicholas Hayden.'

McCadden finished his coffee and rinsed the mug in the sink. The flavour was a little light for his taste, but he'd enjoyed the novelty. 'Do you always drink Colombian?' he asked. 'I must introduce you to Java.'

'My husband already did,' Sarah Wilson told him. 'Five years ago.'

'Right,' McCadden accepted sadly. 'A man of taste obviously.'

His failed overture left the rest of the day uncluttered. Except for work.

Luke Brady turned out to be a tough, scrawny little street-wise kid, with spiky crew-cut hair and spooky blue eyes that already imagined they'd seen it all. One day soon, McCadden guessed, he'd find out that he wasn't half as clever as he thought he was and end up having to break out of what was known as secure accommodation just to save his reputation. But right now, he was convinced that he had all the angles figured.

His mate, Nicholas Hayden, a tall, long-haired boy with pallid skin and pale blue eyes, was much quieter than Brady, more reserved, and a lot more nervous. He'd bruised his ribs in a recent fall and was still heavily strapped under his threadbare clothes. Whenever he moved sharply, he winced with pain and cursed violently.

When McCadden caught up with the pair, a little after seven that evening, they were hanging around a street corner on the estate in a group of about twenty kids, ranging in age from six up towards fourteen or fifteen. Jason Whittle wasn't among them.

'Last Thursday week, lads,' he tried them after introducing himself and isolating the pair from the pack. 'Do you remember that?'

The two boys tensed immediately and glanced anxiously at each other, confirming McCadden's suspicions. Off-hand, no one really remembers what happened on particular days. And especially not kids. Unless they've been *dwelling* on something.

'What about it?' Luke Brady wondered.

'Did you see Jason Whittle that evening?'

'Jayo? Yeah, we saw Jayo. He came out about six, half six.'

'What did you do?'

'Just hung around. You know.'

'Did you stay on the estate all the time?'

'Ah . . . naw. We were down in the woods for a while. You know the woods across the other side, just a bit out the road?'

'Meet anyone?'

There was a silence. The two boys shuffled nervously and looked down at the ground.

McCadden waited, letting the quietness itself add to the pressure. Then he said softly, 'I've had a complaint, you see.'

The lie and the vague threat worked.

And Nicholas Hayden spoke for the first time. 'We only took his cane, that's all. We didn't do anything else.'

'Whose cane?'

'The blind fella's.'

'What blind fellow?'

'He was shouting at us,' Luke Brady offered. 'In the woods. Cursing at us, he was. We nicked his cane and threw it in the nettles. Then we legged it. We had to keep going. He followed us. Right back here, to the estate.'

'A blind man?' McCadden wondered. Chasing three kids across a busy main road, through waste ground and into the tight streets of the estate itself? Because of a cane? 'Do you know him?'

'Naw. Honest.'

But the denial was too frantic, too apprehensive.

'Come on, lads. I told you I had a complaint.'

'It's only aul Harris, isn't it?' Luke Brady said then. 'That's who it was. Ronnie Harris.'

'Harris?' The name had disturbing echoes for McCadden. He asked, 'Did he catch any of you?'

'Naw, not then.'

'Not *then*?'

'He didn't catch any of us when he chased us then. You know what I mean.'

'And what happened after that, when you all got back to the estate?'

'Nothing,' Nicholas Hayden said quickly. 'We all went home.'

'Jayo went home, too. It was real late, anyway.'

'We never did nothing after that. Honest.'

McCadden had his doubts. 'Right,' he said, leaving the uncertain tone hanging there to express his scepticism. 'I'll probably be seeing you again, then . . .'

Back at the station, before knocking off for the night, he pulled out the file on Ronnie Harris, familiar with the character's reputation as a former petty criminal, but not remembering precisely what shadowy aspect of it had disturbed him so deeply.

It wasn't difficult to locate.

Ten years ago, shortly after Harris lost his eyesight, but before McCadden was posted to the district, a young Waterford boy had disappeared on his way home from school. The boy's mutilated body had been found in a shallow grave in a nearby forest some months afterwards. The murder had never been solved, but among the main suspects for the crime had been Ronnie Harris himself. The investigating officer in charge of the case had been Detective Sergeant Frank Ryan.

five

On Sunday, early in the afternoon, McCadden and Frank Ryan sat in near-darkness in the otherwise deserted inspectors' office. The main fluorescent lighting had been switched off and only a small lamp on McCadden's desk illuminated the pair.

McCadden himself was leaning back in his tilted chair, his hands behind his head. Opposite him, on the other side of the desk, sat Ryan, who had dropped by in response to an earlier phone call. The big man was dressed in a dark grey suit that he'd twice described as his Sunday best. But the thing looked no fresher and no less crumpled than any of the others he wore on weekdays. He was eating a large pizza he'd just had delivered. And he was talking between the slices.

'Ronnie Harris,' he said thoughtfully. 'I've been breaking my balls in this city for fifteen years, Carl, and there are a few pieces of shit I still have to settle scores with. Harris is one of them. Did you read his file?'

McCadden shook his head. 'I didn't wade through the details, Frank. I wanted to talk to you first. I know you never had enough to bring any charges against him.'

'And that's what sticks in my gut. I don't think I'm ever going to shaft him now. Let me go back a bit, though. Ten or eleven years ago, Ronnie Harris was pulling in two or three hundred pounds a week from his scams.'

But Ryan stopped to chew another slice of pizza.

'Doing what?' McCadden asked impatiently.

'Robbery.'

'He has no convictions for robbery.'

Ryan vigorously shook his head while swallowing the last of the pizza. 'Harris never broke in anywhere himself,' he said then. He stuck a cigarette in the left side of his mouth and kept it trapped there while he sucked dough and mozzarella from between his teeth. 'He worked as an odd-job man around the city. In demand, too. But while he was at it, he checked out the houses that were vacant most of the day. And the ones with alarms. And the ones with a mutt barking in the back garden. And the ones with the best gear in the living room. He passed the info on for a cut.'

'So what happened to him?'

Ryan lit his cigarette. 'Very bright, our Ronnie was. You ask anyone who worked with him back then. But he's also as thick as a plank. You ask any of his old teachers. One day he was cycling home through Lady Lane. Someone stepped out of a doorway and put his hands on the bars of the bike to stop it. Someone whose mate had just gone into a house that Harris had promised was empty and who'd met an old geezer coming out of the kitchen with a shotgun. Harris had made a mistake. And he got acid thrown in his eyes because of it. Blind and bitter as a fucking bat ever since.'

'And the boy who was murdered?'

'The kid's name was Tommy Keating. The word I had

then was that his old man, Billy Keating, was the one who'd tossed the acid in Harris's face.'

'But there was no more retribution against Harris?'

Ryan shrugged. 'Billy Keating had a lot of enemies at the time. His kid's death finished him as a criminal, though. He lost his appetite, even for revenge. He moved to Cork afterwards with the rest of his family, where he got work as a barman. And he got old before his time.'

'You reckon Harris was capable of the murder?'

'Harris is a nasty bastard, Carl. Frustrated since he was blinded. Gone off the rails, I'd say. He had a woman, for instance, up to a few years ago. But he kept thinking everyone was laughing at him. And then he got to thinking that it must be because there was something wrong with the woman. He couldn't see her, of course. So he figured she must be ugly, or stupid, or diseased, or something. She spent a week in hospital after he tried to beat the badness out of her. And she wouldn't press charges afterwards. Sure. He was capable of murder.'

'Right.'

'What's he got to do with this other kid?'

'I don't know yet. It might be only coincidence. Harris lives in the estate opposite where the kids live. The woods are fairly common ground.'

'You want me to tag along when you go talk with him?'

'No, no, you head off to the match, like you planned. I'll keep you up to date. And thanks for dropping in.'

So four o'clock that Sunday afternoon, McCadden drove alone from the station to the local authority house where Ronnie Harris now lived by himself.

Harris's unpainted front door, newly hung by the

local authority to replace its abused predecessor, was already open.

It made some sense, McCadden accepted when he peered in, that a blind man might want fewer possessions and fewer obstacles in his home. But Harris's place was almost completely bare, like an illegal squat. As McCadden pushed the front door, it opened on to an empty hallway. There was no furniture. There was no covering on the concrete floor under his feet. And the only decoration on the walls were grubby finger marks.

McCadden didn't immediately step in. He stopped, alerted by voices. Reaching out, he caught the swinging door, in case its hinges creaked or its handle knocked against the wall.

The loudest and deepest of the voices was a man's.

'Toomey was never any good at all with a knife,' he was saying. 'He thought he was, like a lot of fellas you'd meet. But he had no more idea how to use it, now, than that aul' mongrel you sometimes hear howling out there...'

The other voices were children's. High-pitched. Excited.

'Cool!' they exclaimed. 'Deadly! Awesome!'

McCadden stepped in and stood in the doorway of the front room.

Ronnie Harris sat back in a dilapidated armchair in front of an empty grate. A single-bar electric fire near his feet was the only source of heating in the room. He was dressed as he must've been when he'd worked before his blindness, in jeans and a heavy sweater. But the clothes were worn and greasy now.

A heavy black beard partly concealed the shrivelled skin where the acid had hit his face. This was his only concession to appearance. And even that was the result of neglect. Above the beard, his hair was greying prematurely, giving a grotesque, two-tone effect to his head. All in all, he looked like a crudely drawn villain from a violent cartoon strip.

McCadden counted seven in the group of local boys standing in a cluster opposite the blind man. The contemporary storyteller, he thought sadly. And his rapt audience.

They came because they were fascinated by his condition and by his self-styled reputation for daring and ingenuity. And they stood just out of his reach because they were still frightened of him. He wore his violent past all too openly on his face.

None of the boys was that much older than nine. Harris would never hold his audience for long, McCadden knew. They grew too quickly and too predictably in this hopeless place. The night would come when they had to prove themselves by driving a stolen car or by carrying a stash of ecstasy or heroin under the noses of the police. And after that they were lost to him. After that the thrill and terror of real action killed off the excitement of his stories.

It was this fear of losing them that surfaced now as he sensed their distraction. He looked up and across towards the door. He wore no dark glasses to mask his scars, McCadden remarked. As if the lifeless eyes were also an essential part of the performance.

'Who is it?' he called. 'Who's there?'

'It's Inspector McCadden, Ronnie. From the Garda station.'

The kids became uneasy and searched for a furtive exit. But McCadden was blocking the only escape from the room. Until he stepped in and gave them a curt nod, they fidgeted nervously.

Harris raised his head as he listened to them scampering away. His lips wore the bitter smile that he'd obviously perfected over a decade of disappointments.

'They're gone, are they?' he said regretfully.

'They'll be back, Ronnie,' McCadden assured him. With equal regret.

There was a television, McCadden saw now, in the far corner of the room. It was turned on and tuned to one of the children's programmes, but its sound was muted. He wondered if some of the kids had been watching it while also listening to Harris.

'Are you getting out much these days, Ronnie?' he asked casually.

Harris took a crumpled packet of cigarettes from his jeans. His hands were trembling slightly as he opened it and pulled one out. When he put a flame to the cigarette with a cheap gas lighter, he drew the smoke in deeply and said, 'I don't like to be smoking in front of them when they're here.'

'Come on, Ronnie,' McCadden pleaded. 'Give us a break. Most of them are already heavier smokers than you ever were.'

'They're only young such a short time, though, aren't they?'

'Right. But you haven't told me, anyway. Are you getting out much?'

Harris turned his face away from McCadden. But only to properly position his left ear and to listen more intently. He drew again on the cigarette and quickly blew the smoke back through his lips.

'Where?' he demanded then.

It was the response of a man with something specific on his mind.

The thing about Harris, McCadden remembered Frank Ryan saying, was that he married cleverness with stupidity. He'd been maimed because of the mix. Like now, he sometimes concealed a thing ingeniously and then drew attention to it by standing guard over it.

'Where?' McCadden repeated. 'Anywhere, Ronnie.'

'I don't get out all that much,' Harris complained. 'Although I have to get a bit of air, I suppose.'

'Do you have a routine?'

'Like doing exercises, is it?'

'Do you shop locally, for instance?'

'I do my messages in the shop on the estate here, yeah.'

'Someone told me they've seen you in the woods below. Is that right?'

'Who told you that?'

'You know I can't let you have that information, Ronnie.'

'When? When did they see me?'

'You tell me.'

'Well, it wouldn't be any particular day, really, you see. I often go for a walk down there.'

'With who?'

'No one at all, really. Just myself.'

'In the woods, Ronnie? With all those trees to bump into and all those slopes to fall down? Are you kidding me?'

'There's pathways through it.'

'That's right. And in winter they're covered with wet leaves and fallen branches.'

'You get used to it.'

'No doubt you could. If you were down there every day. But as you said, you hardly ever leave the estate, do you, Ronnie?'

Harris, who had opened so cleverly, with such a smart imitation of concern for the young, had already become ragged with confusion and worry. He dragged heavily on the cigarette until the burning tobacco reached the filter. Then he searched around the fireplace with the fingers of his right hand, feeling for the empty grate to throw the butt into.

'What are the boys' names, Inspector?' he asked afterwards.

'Boys?' McCadden repeated. 'Did I mention any boys, Ronnie?'

'I thought you said . . .'

McCadden waited. He watched Harris mentally checking back through their conversation, searching for an occurrence of the topic, and then realizing that it was only in his own mind that he had been playing anxiously with it.

If Harris was innocent of any assault, McCadden thought, now was the time for him to tell his story. *Okay, I was down in the woods. I go there for a bit of peace and quiet. Some kids from another estate stole my cane. I chased them to get it back . . .*

But he pretended instead that the incident had never happened.

He laughed hollowly. 'I thought them young fellas were after saying something to you on the way out . . .'

For the moment, not wanting to reveal his own hand, McCadden said nothing about the vital Thursday night, either. It was always a topic he could return to. When he had more than uneasy suspicions to lean on Harris with.

53

He kept the interview vague. And it worked. Harris's uncertainty about the level of McCadden's knowledge forced him to tell as much of the truth as he could admit without actually incriminating himself.

'When was the last time you were down in the woods, Ronnie?'

'The last time? I was down there earlier today. Why?'

'Doing what?'

'I told you. I go for walks down there.'

'Meet any kids?'

'No, I didn't.'

'They use the place for playing in, Ronnie.'

'They were all in school. I don't go down there after school is finished.'

'Right. Where did you go to school yourself, Ronnie?'

'Me? I went to the Christian Brothers' school here in Waterford.'

'Did you? Do you still keep in touch with the place?'

'Would you ever fuck off for yourself!'

'When was the last time you were back there?'

'The last time I was there was the day I left the place for ever to go out and get a job.'

'So what, Ronnie? You didn't hit it off with the Brothers?'

'Them bastards!' Harris swore with sudden vehemence.

And McCadden knew that he'd struck a fruitful nerve. It was, quite clearly, a grudge of Harris's that was older and deeper than all the others. A wound and a sense of injustice that was quite distinct from everything else in his life.

'Mad fucking bastards!' he ranted. 'I remember one of them standing me on a chair once and beating me across the backs of the legs because I played soccer instead of hurling.'

'How do you feel about the boys who are pupils there at the moment?'

'You'd have to feel sorry for the poor bastards, wouldn't you? Same as we had it.'

'What about the ones who might be the favourites of the Brothers? You remember them, Ronnie. The teacher's pets. They're still around, aren't they?'

'What about them?' Harris growled. 'I don't care. I don't go back near the school now.'

'No, I don't suppose you do.'

'I don't.'

'Not to the school.'

'Not at all.'

'How about the woods, though?'

'What?'

'Are you planning on going back down to the woods again, Ronnie?'

'I don't know about that, do I?'

'Okay. If you do, and you see anything suspicious, you'll let me know, won't you?'

Harris, of course, didn't ask the normal questions that always occurred to the innocent. What was going on in the woods? What was supposed to be suspicious? What was McCadden hinting at?

Obviously, McCadden thought, Harris already had some answers to these.

55

six

At nine thirty on Monday morning, McCadden and Rose Donnelly sat in the crowded inspectors' office, dividing tasks between them.

'This is how it stands, Rose,' McCadden had opened cautiously. 'There's no official investigation. As far as the Chief Superintendent is concerned, the thing died on Friday night. The less said about it, the more comfortable he is. There's really only my own perversity keeping it going.'

'Surely someone else's perversity, sir?' Donnelly had supported him.

'You think so, too?'

'After meeting the boy himself, yes. I'm convinced of it. I had a look through the files on Friday. All cases of child sexual abuse and suspected abuse in the district, initially over the last few years. I wanted to continue this morning, if it's okay with you.'

'All right, Rose. But just this morning. Okay? Cody is due to return this afternoon, and you're supposed to be back on sick leave. How's the shoulder, by the way?'

'My daughter keeps swinging out of it. Otherwise it's improving. Will we meet back here for lunch?'

McCadden shook his head. 'I'm going out to see John

Ryle, but I don't think he's going to get home before noon. His wife isn't checking out of hospital until two or three o'clock, and I can't see him rushing back the seventy miles from Cork to sit by himself in an empty house in a hostile neighbourhood. I'll meet you in the Carnival Inn, let's say about...'

A uniformed guard came from the public desk, through the office, to stand awkwardly at the edge of McCadden's desk.

'Excuse me, sir?'

'Yes?'

'There's a young boy out front, sir, asking for yourself.'

'Oh? What's his name?'

'Luke Brady, he says, sir.'

'Right. Bring him in, will you?' McCadden requested. He turned to Donnelly to explain. 'One of the lads who was with Jason Whittle that Thursday night...'

Luke Brady, his spiky hair freshly gelled and his denim jeans and jacket newly washed, sauntered in a few paces ahead of the uniformed guard and casually dropped his school bag to the floor before sitting on the chair Rose Donnelly brought up for him.

'I said to the others I was going on the lam from school this morning so they wouldn't think anything, even if they heard I was in the cop shop,' he boasted.

'Sensible,' McCadden approved. 'What can we do for you?'

'You wanted to know what happened the Thursday night Jayo got in trouble.'

'I wanted to know that on Saturday evening, Luke. But you wouldn't tell me.'

'I couldn't then, could I?'

'Or more precisely, you insisted that nothing had happened.'

'I had to say the same as the others, didn't I? I couldn't be seen to be ratting to the cops.'

McCadden studied him. It was possible, he thought, that even at such a young age he already shared most offenders' uneasiness about sexual crimes. It was possible that he'd come in this morning to co-operate. More than likely, he was scared as well. And maybe he'd come to swagger a little, too, with his superior knowledge.

'Go on,' McCadden invited.

'Anyway,' Brady resumed, 'after, you know, after what we already told you, we bought some flagons of cider and went back down ... You know the woods I told you about, down from the estate and on the other side of the road?'

'Where you'd met Ronnie Harris earlier.'

'That's right. Where he chased us from, across to the estate, until we ran into the other crowd and they kind of scared him off.'

'What other crowd?'

'Ah, there was this crowd of characters knocking on all the doors, handing out leaflets. You know. To get people to vote for them.'

'The general election campaign,' Donnelly put in. 'Probably canvassers from one of the parties.'

'Right. You said you went to the woods, Luke.'

'Yeah. About an hour later. We went back and had a cider party in the woods there. And I'm not telling you where we got the flagons.'

'I don't want to know that, Luke.'

'I'm not telling you anyway. We were nearly caught and all as it was. One of the Bros from the school—'

'Bros?'

'One of the Brothers. The Christian Brothers. From the school. He nearly caught us.'

'Which one?'

'I don't know which one. We had to duck. I didn't see him. Only his skirts, you know. His habit.'

'What was he doing?'

'Out walking or something. I don't know. I didn't ask him, did I?'

'Okay. You bought the cider and dodged a Christian Brother. Then what?'

'Down in the woods, what happened was, Jayo got mouldy drunk. He always gets drunk. He's like his aul fella. Have you ever seen him when he's drunk?'

'Who?'

'Jayo.'

'No, I haven't, Luke.'

'Fucking spacer. He went off. He wouldn't listen to anyone. Told us all to fuck off and went off.'

'By himself?'

'What do you think?'

'Off where? What direction?'

'Into the woods.'

'Did you see him again that evening?'

'None of us did, naw. But he told me what happened the next morning in school, you see. He couldn't go home, could he? I mean, his old man would wallop shit out of him for drinking. It's a laugh, isn't it? So he went to Ryle's house instead, down a bit the road. And that's when it happened.'

'That's when what happened?'

'The business. Ryle, you see. He's fucking queer. He did the business with Jayo.'

Did the business, McCadden echoed to himself. No matter how foul-mouthed and street-wise they were, they always had this awkwardness with sex and with the language of sex. Between their euphemisms and their obscenities, there was only a terrifying darkness.

'Why would he tell *you*, Luke?' he asked. 'And presumably not anyone else. Didn't you all start out together that night?'

'Because I'm his best friend amn't I?'

'Did Mr Ryle ever approach you, by the way?'

'He wouldn't fucking want to.'

'No,' McCadden agreed. He wondered if the boy had some personal grudge against Ryle, or had been encouraged by his parents to blacken the name of a man they didn't accept as a member of their community. But probably not, he decided. It was all a touch too elaborate to be a set-up, all the mitching from school and the rest. If they'd wanted to shaft Ryle with the boy's testimony, they would've done it a lot earlier, and a lot more directly.

'I'll be talking to Mr Ryle myself in a little while, Luke,' he said. 'He won't have any stories to tell me about you, will he?'

'What do you mean?'

'Complaints, Luke. You're trying to get him into trouble. He might like to do the same for you.'

'I don't even fucking know the bollox.'

'Okay . . .'

They watched the boy get up and swagger back through the office to the corridor outside. The school bag was a heavy burden to him, they noticed. A badge of immaturity, of subservience, of everything that was stupid and degrading. A mark of conformity.

'If you get a chance in the afternoon, Rose,' McCadden said then, 'you might check out this political group that was canvassing in the area. See who they are. Get names and addresses. We'll want to talk to them as potential witnesses.'

seven

At twelve fifteen, McCadden drove alone from the station to John Ryle's home. Although it was only a short distance, the traffic was heavy, and it was almost one o'clock before he reached the estate. The house was along the fourth row, five or six doors down from the Whittles' home.

As McCadden turned in, a plastic football some kids had been playing with bounced from the footpath and rolled in front of him. He braked and stopped. The ball wedged itself under his number plate. He shifted the gear stick into neutral and pulled the handbrake on and sat there, waiting for someone to come and collect it. No one appeared. The kids who owned the football stayed where they were, arranged in a single file on the edge of the footpath, as if they'd been regimented.

Beyond them, along the length of the street, there seemed to be an unusual number of people standing on their front doorsteps, or in their front gardens, or at their front gates. Joey Whittle, discharged from hospital that morning and wearing his distinctive white plaster cast, was highly visible. As were two or three of the others who'd been involved with him in the chase on Thursday night.

But the neighbours weren't talking to each other. And they all seemed to be staring aggressively down at McCadden.

For a moment, as the atmosphere grew heavy with tension, he had that sickening feeling of having wandered into the wrong scene and of being vulnerable among predators. He thought he was about to be attacked.

But no one moved. Like statues, they held their poses and their hostile expressions.

Except for one small, balding man in a yellow jacket, McCadden noticed then, who was hurrying down the footpath, away from the stalled car.

McCadden wondered about him for a few moments. Thinking in terms of a fugitive being given a head start by the crowd. Or a vigilante scurrying for cover. Or a police informer seizing his chance to escape. Someone holding ground *between* the community and the cops...

And then it struck him.

Shit, he thought.

The man was rushing to John Ryle's house, he guessed. To warn others already there that a guard was approaching.

McCadden hit the accelerator and screeched away, puncturing the football under his chassis as he rolled over it. Luckily the road ahead of him was still free. He'd taken them by surprise. And no one had yet thought of driving another vehicle across his path.

As he gained rapidly on the running bald man and then easily overtook him, he worried about the scene awaiting him. He imagined the frail figure of Ryle being pounded with fists and baseball bats and iron bars...

But Ryle's white Honda Civic wasn't parked outside the house. The space was empty. McCadden swung sharply into it and pulled up, his front right tyre mounting the footpath and his bonnet making light contact with a metal electricity pole.

Opening the door and jumping out, he saw that the bald man in the yellow jacket had stopped about ten yards away, knowing now that he wasn't going to win this particular race. He'd started whistling instead. Loudly signalling to others inside Ryle's house. Warning them of danger.

Behind him, as if drawn along invisible tramlines, the other residents were being sucked in towards him and slowly forming themselves into a crowd.

But McCadden decided against radioing for help. A wagon of uniformed officers blundering in on this could spark a tense stand-off into a violent riot.

He vaulted the garden wall, not bothering with the closed gate. The front door, varnished instead of painted and therefore noticeably different from all the others on the row, was slightly ajar. Its lock had been forced.

McCadden pushed it fully open in front of him. The smell of petrol fumes hit him immediately. Jesus, he thought. Some fools were going to torch the place. Not appreciating that if this one went up, the houses on either side were also in danger.

McCadden instantly found his bearings. Even if the decoration was radically different, the layout of the interior was the same as in the Whittles' house. A front room and then a dining room on the left. A small kitchen straight ahead. A stairway leading to three bedrooms above.

It was from the front room, closest to the street door,

that the man came as McCadden entered. A young man, with long, untidy black hair and a patchy beard carrying a jerry can in his right hand.

'Dad?' he was calling.

But his reactions were quick when he saw McCadden. Screaming abuse, he raised and threw the petrol can, and then turned and ran down the corridor, into the kitchen and out the back door he'd already opened as an escape route.

McCadden had twisted away to protect his eyes from the liquid. The can hit his left shoulder. The petrol splashed down his black leather jacket and on to his jeans.

By the time he'd recovered, the last strands of the young man's long black hair were already disappearing through the rear door.

McCadden chased. But the back garden, designed by someone with a passion for split levels and miniature waterfalls, was empty when he got there. Footmarks in the flower beds and a disturbed stone at the summit of one of the falls indicated which way the intruder had escaped. To the right, into the neighbour's plain lawn garden. Where a heavy, middle-aged woman, with three clothes pegs in her mouth, was casually hanging out washing to dry on the line.

No need to ask her anything, McCadden could see. Her whole attitude insisted that no, she hadn't seen a thing. Nevertheless, he went across to lean over the dividing wall and called in.

'Excuse me,' he said.

The woman seemed to be startled by his presence.

'Jesus, Mary and Joseph,' she gasped. 'You put the heart across me.'

'Right,' McCadden accepted. 'My name is McCadden. I'm a guard.'

'Is there something wrong, guard?'

'Not particularly, no. But would you do something for me? Would you contact an official from the Tenants' Association and ask him or her to meet me in your house, say, in about half an hour. You wouldn't mind doing that, would you? It's important.'

The woman frowned. 'I don't know about that, now.'

'Look,' McCadden said. 'I didn't see anyone running into your garden, either.'

'I don't know what you're talking about, guard.'

'And I probably won't have to call on his dad, who wears a yellow jacket. Not if I can meet someone from the Tenants' Association instead.'

Going back into the house, it struck him then how *contemporary* in style the interior was. The estate had been built in the fifties, he knew. But nothing was left in Ryle's house now of the original fittings. The plain tiled fireplaces he'd seen in Whittle's home had been replaced with pine surrounds and hand-painted tiles drawing on William Morris designs. The floors had uncovered varnished boards and expensive rugs. Kandinsky and Bacon and Munch featured among the well-mounted prints on the walls.

Ryle's photographic equipment was in the front room, which was being used as both a studio and a library. But curiously enough, it wasn't the cameras or the lights or the VCR or the multi-media computer system that the long-haired intruder had broken in to damage. In the centre of the room, a pyramid of books, pulled at random from the surrounding shelves, had been doused with petrol and was ready to burn.

Funny, McCadden thought, how the old books were still considered the symbol, and even the source, of cultural difference. Ironically, one of the volumes on the floor was an Oxford dictionary and across the room's chimney breast, over both the pale blue wall and the framed Edvard Munch print, someone had written with a spray can of black paint the accusation PERVORT!

McCadden heard the street door being pushed open again while he was crouching to examine the pile of ruined books. He swivelled as he stood up, and found that the little man with the roses and the exotic fruit from Accident & Emergency was already standing in the doorway of the room.

He was holding a supermarket shopping bag in his left hand and his now useless latch key in his right. The plastic bag was rustling slightly because his whole body was shaking with fear. He obviously didn't recognize McCadden.

'Get out!' he ordered in a trembling voice.

'Are you John Ryle?' McCadden asked him.

'It's none of your business who I am. Get out before I call the police.'

'I'm a Garda, Mr Ryle. Detective Inspector McCadden. I was coming here to talk to you and I found an intruder in your home.'

Ryle's expression changed as he accepted the introduction and then checked around the room. A brief flicker of contempt showed on his lips as he considered the insult over the fireplace. He saw with relief that the computer and photographic equipment were untouched. But he lingered long and sadly on the damaged books.

'You'd better open some windows, Mr Ryle,' McCadden suggested. 'It's petrol. Most of it will evaporate. And then could we go somewhere to talk, please?'

eight

They went upstairs, where one of the original bedrooms had been decorated and furnished as a living room. Since the smallest of the three bedrooms was also converted, to a study in this case, it was clear that the Ryles had no immediate plans for cots and Babygros.

McCadden lost himself in a deep pink armchair. Ryle, shocked and subdued, sat on the edge of a futon couch, leaning forward with his head down and staring dully at the floorboards under his feet.

'You've got unwelcoming neighbours, it seems,' McCadden opened.

Ryle shrugged. 'You get bad ones everywhere, don't you?'

'No doubt,' McCadden agreed. 'I hear you work as a computer programmer. Is that right?'

'Yes.'

'Successful?'

'Moderately, yes.'

'And your wife is a secondary school teacher,' McCadden mused.

'That's right, yes. She teaches English.'

'Do you mind a personal observation? I like the interior of your house. I think you've done something with it that I wouldn't have thought possible with a three-bed estate house. But I also think—'

'That it's out of place.'

'No. That's a value judgement. But it's *noticeable*. It strikes a distinctive chord. Which might be pleasing in itself or as part of a phrase. But if you keep striking it alone, it's bound to become a little wearying.'

'Are you a philosopher, Inspector?' Ryle demanded sourly.

McCadden shook his head. 'No,' he smiled. 'That would be too noticeable in a police force, wouldn't it?'

He stood up and walked across to the front window to look down on the two cars outside. Both were safe. And the crowds had melted from the street.

Still looking outwards, he asked bluntly, 'Why do you live here, Mr Ryle?'

'Because it's my home, Inspector.'

'Okay. But why did you choose to make it your home?'

'I didn't *have* a choice. I was born here.'

McCadden raised his eyebrows as he turned. 'You were born in this house?'

'Born and reared, Inspector,' Ryle confirmed. 'And I wasn't always as noticeable as you might think. I played marbles and I chased in the woods like all the other boys. I was a *little* different, I suppose. My father died when I was eight.'

McCadden came back and sat on the armrest of the chair. 'But you haven't been permanently living here since childhood, have you?'

'No, of course not. I went to university in Cork. That was where I met Colm, my business partner.'

'And also your wife?'

'Yes, Miriam is also from Cork. When my mother died, five years ago, we came to live here.'

'Why?' McCadden asked bluntly again.

'Why? I don't know. I suppose I wanted to come back. And rather than have to sell the family home ... I'm an only child.'

McCadden glanced quickly around. The bookshelves here were stacked with works of history and philosophy. The walls carried a series of L. S. Lowry prints. Some of the furniture looked like the ancient bits and pieces the neighbours would've discarded two decades before and replaced with chipboard and melamine.

'Did you manage it?' he asked.

'What?'

'To come back. There's more involved than just a physical journey, isn't there?'

Ryle bowed his head again. 'Miriam is not entirely comfortable here, if that's what you mean,' he confessed quietly. 'As for myself, I ... I can't understand it sometimes. I think things have changed very much here.'

'In what sense?'

'I remember it as a very close community, but ... When I'm in the garden now, for instance, the two women on either side talk to each other as if I'm not there. I mean, it's not as if I don't know them. I grew up with them.'

They considered him a fool, McCadden thought. Ryle had achieved precisely what they all longed for. He'd escaped the limitations of poverty. And he was still living next door to them.

But McCadden said nothing.

'Miriam believes that we made a mistake,' Ryle went on sadly. 'She has hopes of a teaching job in Cork. So perhaps if that comes through...'

'When you were young,' McCadden put in then, 'did you go to the Christian Brothers' school? I believe it's the tradition here.'

'Oh, yes. Everyone went to the Christian Brothers. The boys, I mean.'

'How did you find the Brothers?'

'How did I find them? Do you mean while I was with them?'

'I heard they had a reputation for blunt teaching methods and physical cruelty.'

Ryle lifted his head, frowning a little at the turn the conversation had taken. 'You're not from Waterford, are you, Inspector?' he asked.

McCadden shook his head. 'No.'

'Where? Up north somewhere?'

'Somewhere,' McCadden conceded.

'Did you attend an all-boys school?'

'No. Co-educational.'

'Were you accomplished at sports?'

'I represented the school at a number of sports, yes. But can we get back to me asking the questions, Mr Ryle? I'm more comfortable with it.'

'No, you see, I was frail as a boy, Inspector,' Ryle said then. 'And I wasn't very good at sports. I remember a Brother Goodwin repeatedly demonstrating on me how violent fouls could be committed with a hurley stick. But I was also academically gifted, so I also remember other Brothers devoting hours of their free time to helping me individually. I suspect that everyone who was educated by the Brothers has a similar ambivalence.

The plain fact is, at a certain stage of our history, no one else was interested in educating working class boys.'

'Do you still keep in touch with the school?'

'I'm a member of the past pupils' committee. And I do my bit from time to time with career guidance.'

'So you'd know some of the current boys?'

'Vaguely.'

'Jason Whittle?'

Ryle tensed. It was obvious from the irritated expression on his face that he realized he had made a tactical mistake. He hadn't already asked why McCadden wanted to interview him. And he couldn't betray his anxieties by returning to it now.

He said, 'Jason is a neighbour's child. I know him to see him.'

He looked expectantly across at McCadden, waiting for the other to develop the topic. But McCadden made a sudden shift.

'The photographic equipment in the front room,' he said. 'Is it yours?'

Ryle was unsettled again. He frowned and moistened his lips. 'How do you mean?' he asked.

'Maybe it's your wife's, is it?'

'Oh, no. It's mine.'

'Are you a professional photographer?'

'No, no. It's an interest. I use it sometimes for computer graphics. But mostly it's an interest.'

'It's also an interest of Jason Whittle's.'

'Is it?'

'They have it as an extra-curricular activity in school.'

'I'm not sure. You see, I, ah . . .'

'Have you ever photographed Jason Whittle?'

'No! Yes!'

73

'Which?'

'I thought you meant . . . I did, actually, yes.'

'In what pose?'

'I'm sorry?'

'You know. Formal for the family sideboard. Casual for fun. What pose?'

'We didn't actually pose.'

'We?'

'Jason also used the cameras. You see, he has an interest in . . . As you already said . . . He was curious about photography.'

'When was he in the house?'

Ryle put his head in his hands and rubbed his eyes. He took three or four long breaths to steady himself. He said, 'There are certain limits to what language can do, Inspector. There are certain events, which . . . I mean, if they are dragged into public and defined, can only be made crude.'

McCadden nodded. 'Right,' he said.

'I'm not expressing myself very well.'

'No, I get your point. My line of questioning can make you seem defensive and evasive, and by implication guilty of concealing something.'

'Yes. Thank you, Inspector.'

'But can I be honest with you? I know Jason Whittle's father tried to assault you last Thursday night. You don't recognize me, but I was the one who rescued you.'

'Then I must thank—'

'Furthermore, most of your neighbours organized the destruction of your home to coincide with your return this morning. They also left an accusation on the wall downstairs. Putting two and two together, I'd say that your neighbours are convinced that the relationship between you and Jason is not what is generally accepted in our society. Wouldn't you? This is not my opinion. Just an interpretation.'

Ryle's hands were shaking. He interlocked the fingers in an effort to steady them. But they only trembled together instead of separately.

'I see,' he muttered.

'Look,' McCadden said gently. 'A couple of years ago I gave a small-time criminal a break by winking an eye. He'd fallen from grace again while trying to go straight and he had a son to bring up by himself. When it was later suspected, wrongly, that the boy was being sexually abused, some bright spark suggested that my leniency with the old man was in return for favours from his son.'

Ryle stared, clearly wondering if the strangely relevant story was true or not. 'Why are you telling me this?' he asked.

'If you haven't done anything,' McCadden explained, 'it will make you feel a little better. If you *have* something on your mind it will make you feel a little worse.'

Ryle drew a deep breath and gave a long sigh while releasing it. 'Jason,' he said then, 'is a very bright, very intelligent lad.'

'So I've heard,' McCadden confirmed.

'But his home . . . What can I say? It *retards* him.'

'So?'

'Well, this house, you see . . . It's another world for him. A better world. The books. The food. Even the quietness.'

'You don't have any kids of your own, do you?'

'No. Why do you ask?'

'All your material is for adults, including the books.'

'Jason is quite capable of handling that.'

'You have a VCR and a rack of cassettes downstairs. Most of the videos are passed for over-eighteens. At least one of them is officially banned in Ireland.'

'You're not suggesting I'm trying to corrupt the boy, are you?'

'Just illustrating a point. Does your wife know that the boy visits the house?'

Ryle looked away. 'No. I haven't told her.'

'Why do you think that is?'

'I'm afraid Miriam doesn't really like children. She finds the boys on the street particularly rough and unpleasant. And besides, it's not really wise to advertise such friendships in the current paranoid climate.'

'Don't you think that there's a danger your attitude might be taken for fear of openness?'

'No, not at all. No. When I was Jason's age, I had a close relationship with one of the Christian Brothers in the school. He was a mature, intelligent man. There was undoubtedly an emotional element to it. Romantic, if you like. Though not physical. But without it, I wouldn't have developed as I have. He opened up the possibilities of the world for me. This house is Jason's escape route. Things are far, far more complex than you can imagine, Inspector.'

'Right,' McCadden said. 'When was the last time you saw Jason?'

'He hasn't been around the last week.'

'That's not what I asked you.'

'I last saw him Thursday week eleven days ago.'

'And why do you reckon he hasn't come to visit since?'

'Fear. Consideration. Others have discovered his visits

and misread them. As you can see. And he doesn't want to compromise me further.'

'What happened the last time you saw each other?'

'In what way?'

'Every way, Mr Ryle. Where was your wife, for instance?'

'Miriam was in Cork. In fact, I'd just returned from dropping her to the train station. At seven. I worked at home until nine. At nine fifteen, while I was making coffee ... Is there something the matter, Inspector?'

McCadden shook his head. 'No, go on.'

But the surprise must have shown on his face, of course. It was the *precision* of Ryle's recall that intrigued him. Or the fullness of his invention, he thought. But either way, the man had so thoroughly rehearsed these details in his own mind that they came too smoothly to him.

'At nine fifteen,' Ryle said again, 'while I was making coffee, the doorbell rang. It was Jason. He was very drunk, I'm afraid. Quite dishevelled. And very distressed. He kept looking out the windows after coming in.'

'At what? Or who?'

'He wouldn't say. I tried to get him to tell me what had happened to him, but he was too upset. And too drunk, to be honest. I gave him coffee. He got sick in the kitchen downstairs, and then again in the bathroom up here. It sobered him a little. After that he fell asleep on this futon. When he woke it was almost eleven. He rang one of his friends ... Luke?'

'Luke Brady, yes.'

'He rang him to call here for him. Can a boy of thirteen leave his home at eleven at night?'

'It depends.'

'On the boy?'

'No, on the home. Did Luke call for him?'

'I don't know. Jason wouldn't wait in the house for him. He insisted on waiting outside. He seemed very tense and very uneasy by then. He wouldn't talk to me. When he left, it was as if his argument was with me.'

'And you haven't seen him since?'

'Not at all, no.'

McCadden glanced at his watch. It was almost two o'clock in the afternoon. 'Your wife is waiting for you to collect her from hospital, isn't she?'

Ryle nodded. 'Yes. But not for another hour.'

'You're going to have to explain the books and the broken door and the graffiti to her.'

'Yes.'

'And as I'm going to need to talk to you again and I can't guarantee calling when she's out, it might be better if you told her the truth.'

'Yes. Of course, yes.'

'What's the name of the woman next door, by the way? On your left.'

'Left? Mrs Long. Elizabeth Long.'

'Okay. I've arranged to meet an official from the Tenants' Association in there. I won't promise they're going to *like* you any more afterwards, but I can prevent a recurrence of the intimidation. In the meantime, you'd better consider whether or not you want to press charges and make a complaint.'

nine

A tense, elderly secretary led McCadden through stale-smelling corridors to the principal's office a little after ten the following morning.

Unexpectedly, the office door was closed against her. A reversible cardboard sign, now instructing callers to wait, hung from a white plastic hook. Clearly, although the message didn't spell it out, the man inside was moulding impressionable young minds.

The scene seemed to further fluster the already anxious secretary. Caught now between disturbing her boss and insulting a visitor, she even-handedly blamed both of them for her dilemma.

'There!' she complained. 'Now he's gone and seen someone! I told him you were coming. But then, you did get delayed a little in the traffic, didn't you? You couldn't manage to make it exactly on—'

'It's all right,' McCadden assured her. 'Not to worry.'

'He's always so punctual himself, you see. Which is a good and a bad thing, you know.'

'I don't mind waiting. I've got a little time.'

'Are you sure?'

'I'll soak in the atmosphere.'

McCadden sat on a hard plastic seat in the corridor

outside the office. Where hundreds of boys must have sat before him, he thought, and most of them preparing for their fate with all the enthusiasm of a visit to the dentist. Opposite him, another pupil was also waiting. A twelve- or thirteen-year-old lad with a pinched face and a stature so low that his scuffed sneakers swung free of the ground as he sat.

'What are you in for?' McCadden asked conversationally.

The boy grunted. 'Huh?'

'What did you do?'

The boy twitched and shrugged. 'I didn't do nothing. Butler did it.'

'That sounds familiar. What did Butler do?'

'Don't know.'

'Let me guess,' McCadden suggested. 'The two of you were smoking.'

'I don't smoke.'

McCadden sighed. 'You don't have to have those brown stains all over your fingers, you know,' he said. 'Not if you eat an orange every day.'

The boy scoffed cynically. 'Yeah, right.'

'The acid from the orange neutralizes the nicotine from the ... Don't you do any science?'

The office door opened before McCadden's disillusionment with teaching could deepen any further. A black-haired pupil with bitter resentment in his dark eyes was followed out by a tall, thin man who had to stoop to avoid the top of the door frame. The smoker opposite McCadden immediately jumped to his feet. And settled into a respectful slouch.

'Wait, Mullen!' the man snapped at him. 'Sit!'

The harshness shifted to a neutral briskness as he finished with the first boy. 'That's all, Butler. And don't forget. Five by a hundred for a week.' And then his manner quickened to warmth as he turned towards McCadden and advanced with his hand outstretched. 'I'm afraid my secretary double-booked an appointment. I'm terribly sorry to keep you waiting. I'm Colin Ruddell, the principal.'

'Carl McCadden.'

'Yes. Do come in, please. Would you like a cup of coffee, perhaps?'

McCadden had bizarre memories of school dinners, recollections that verged on the intensity of flashbacks. School coffee, he reckoned, was unlikely to be any less harrowing.

'No thanks,' he declined as they entered the office. 'I just had breakfast before I came out.'

'Good man,' Ruddell approved ironically. 'It's always nicer to have a late breakfast, I find. Not that I manage it myself much these days.'

McCadden didn't respond to the cut. The man exuded the bitter responsibility of command. How could he tell him that he'd come directly from home to avoid meeting the Chief Superintendent at the station after the desk sergeant had tipped him off about two possible leads? How could he confuse him with the revelation that he was playing truant?

Ruddell had walked across to close the window behind his desk and was gesturing outwards now with the same childish dissatisfaction.

'We're building a new hall at the moment,' he explained. 'A theatre. Or at least we were, until the workers went on strike a week ago. Now the silence from the site is more disruptive than the noises of construction ever were.'

'I saw the pickets as I was coming in.'

'The foundation of a good school is its worst pupils,' the principal muttered then.

McCadden frowned. 'Sorry?'

'Something one of the Brothers here said to me recently. The foundation of a good school is its worst pupils. I thought he'd made a mistake. He's rather old. It occurs to me now that it might have been a macabre joke. We were inspecting the construction work at the time. However . . . What can I do for you?'

As the principal turned from the window, eased himself into his deep swivel chair and carefully arranged his long legs under the desk, McCadden sat opposite him. The chair that had been placed there was particularly uncomfortable. But deliberately so, McCadden supposed. And the philosophy of the man who had chosen it was pretty widespread through society. *You're not in here to enjoy yourself, Mullen!* In his time, McCadden had heard that admonition in his own school, in the offices of superintendents and chief superintendents, in detention centres and prisons and police station interview rooms.

'To tell you the truth,' McCadden admitted, 'I was expecting someone else. I thought—'

'In what sense?' Ruddell interrupted with absurd touchiness. He didn't actually suggest that *someone smaller* was the answer. But he was clearly thinking it.

'This is a religious school, isn't it?' McCadden pointed out. 'Run by the Irish Christian Brothers. I was expecting a Christian Brother as principal.'

Ruddell laughed with relief. 'No, no,' he explained. 'Most Christian Brother schools are now staffed entirely by lay teachers. Catholic men and women, of course.'

'Of course, yes.'

'Imbued with the same ethics and dedication as the Brothers themselves.'

'Uh-huh.'

'But the order itself doesn't have the numbers any more, you know.' He leaned back and joined his hands over his stomach, now immensely comfortable with a subject he could enthuse about. 'A few years ago, there were almost one thousand five hundred Brothers in Ireland. Now there's only three hundred or thereabouts. There's only two thousand world-wide. The average age of the Christian Brothers today is sixty-three. The order had only one new seminarian last year.'

'Right,' McCadden sympathized. Statistics, he thought. The man's strength was with statistics. 'Although you get the impression, talking to people in the city, that they're still a very powerful influence, if not a continuing force.'

'Why wouldn't they be?' the principal demanded. 'The Christian Brothers were founded in this city. Up to a few years ago, they'd educated half its boys for almost two centuries. But here!' he interrupted himself. 'I might say the same about you!'

McCadden raised his eyebrows. 'Sorry?'

'I was expecting a uniformed guard. The secretary tells me you're an inspector.'

'Oh, right. Well, the fact is that your problem may have some wider implications. Bear with me if I don't go into them right at the moment. But I have to check them out.'

83

'Naturally, yes.'

'According to the station log, you reported that someone has been acting suspiciously outside your school gates the last few days. Is that right?'

'That's correct, yes.'

'Could you give me the details?'

'Yes. It's not always easy, you see, to spot anything untoward very quickly. There are so many people outside the gates at the end of a school day. So many cars collecting pupils. But late last week several pupils expressed concern to their own form teachers. A white car had been parked across the road outside. On Thursday. Again on—'

'Sorry. White car. What make?'

'I'm not at all sure, to be honest. Not my forte.'

'Are you saying that you saw it yourself?'

'Yes, I saw it myself. It was there again yesterday. This is why I notified the station. I had proof.'

'Did you take the registration number?'

'I tried. But the plates were covered in mud and no longer legible.'

'Very convenient.'

'Isn't it? The car drove away as I approached.'

'Anybody you recognized inside?'

'It certainly wasn't any of our parents, in any case. Strangers, I'm afraid. To myself, at least.'

'How many in the car?'

'There were two men.'

'Can you give me general descriptions?'

'The driver was a young man with long curly black hair. Very rough-looking. He was unshaven. He had a small, rounded face. The passenger in the front seat was a blind man. He had—'

'Blind man?' McCadden repeated.

The principal grimaced. 'Something of a prejudice, but I'm afraid they're always more frightening for children. It's the way they stare. We always read intent into the eyes, don't we, when they're only vacant. We always assume that they're hunting.'

'This blind man,' McCadden said again. 'He didn't have a black beard by any chance, did he?'

'He did, yes.'

'And burns, old burns, still visible on his face above the beard?'

The principal stared and leaned forward. 'Do you know him?'

I never go near the school, Ronnie Harris had insisted. *Not at all*. McCadden silently cursed himself. He knew now that he should've taken more careful note of the man's unsolicited protests. He'd remarked on the habit to himself. But in another context. How Harris had a genius for burying things and then standing guard over the grave.

He nodded unhappily. 'I know him, yes.'

'I've spent the entire morning,' the principal confessed, 'wondering why a blind man should be driven along to look at pupils coming from a school. And it was the blind man, you know. For the most part, the young driver had his face hidden. He wasn't searching. I only caught a glimpse of his features myself.'

'Yes, but the passenger window was wound fully down when you saw them yesterday, wasn't it?'

Ruddell frowned, thinking back. 'Yes,' he agreed then. 'It was, yes.'

'Even though it was a cold day.'

'Quite chilly, yes.'

'The blind man wasn't looking at your pupils, Mr Ruddell. He was *listening* to them. Searching for voices he would recognize. Do you know if he approached anyone?'

'Not that I'm aware of, no. I certainly haven't heard of any approach.'

'Would you do me a favour? Without making a crisis of it, have your teachers check if any boy was approached. Would it be possible to do that today?'

'Certainly, yes. We'll do everything we can.'

'What time do you finish at?'

'Officially, four o'clock. Some of the older boys may stay behind to study or play sports.'

'I'll be back before then to get the details. And also to keep an eye on things outside when you're closing. Do you remember a past pupil named Ronnie Harris, by the way?'

The principal shook his head. 'I don't think so, no. What year?'

'He's in his mid-thirties now. So, I suppose he would've attended here in the mid-seventies.'

'I came from Wexford eight years ago to take over as principal here. I don't go back that far. But we have Brother Hennessy back here again with us this year.'

'How do you mean?'

'I'm sorry?'

McCadden drew a circle in the air with his right forefinger. 'Back here again. What does it mean?'

'Oh! The Brothers travel from school to school within the country. They're not left permanently in one place. Brother Hennessy originally taught here in the seventies, I believe. He might remember.'

McCadden, thinking of Harris's violent outburst at

the mere mention of Christian Brothers, shook his head. 'No,' he said. 'It doesn't really matter.' He glanced at his watch, reminded of the second of the desk sergeant's tips. 'I have to meet someone else at the moment...'

'Of course, of course. Until later, then. What will we say? Three fifty? Good!'

ten

The woman was in her early sixties and lived alone in a small cottage on the opposite side of the woods. Her name was Peggy Whelan.

Twenty years earlier, before the city had stretched itself outwards, the cottage had been isolated in the heart of the country. Her husband had farmed the few acres around it and also worked part-time in a local tannery. She herself had cared for a profitable market garden. Now the countryside and the tannery and the husband and the garden were all dead. And Mrs Whelan was left only with her memories and her loneliness. And her fears.

'We had three children,' she explained. 'Two boys and a girl. But they're all away. The nearest lives in Dublin now. They come to visit and keep asking me to go and live with them. But I don't want to do that. In the end everyone has to have their own life, don't they? I always have, anyway. We had good neighbours all round us, too. But they're all gone as well now.'

When McCadden drove up the winding, pot-holed road to the cottage, he parked behind an old Mini Cooper that still seemed in working order. A young German Shepherd, dozing on the lawn, looked at him casually as he walked past and then went back to its sleep. He didn't have to knock twice on the front door. It was opened immediately by a slight, white-haired woman.

'You don't have problems around the cottage itself, do you, Mrs Whelan?' he observed after introducing himself. They were sitting in the cottage's bright front room, in front of a low turf fire. Again he'd been offered tea. Again he'd declined. 'Intruders,' he explained. 'Unwanted callers. That sort of thing.'

'Oh, no,' she told him. 'It's very quiet here.'

'That's what I thought,' he agreed.

'Do you know the area?'

'Not really, no. But your dog is very relaxed and you opened the door without hesitation.'

'Ah! You're very observant, Inspector.'

'Well ... But you were telling the guard who interviewed you about a blind man in the woods.'

'I was, yes.'

'And you described him as dark-haired, bearded, and very unkempt looking.'

'Yes.'

'You wouldn't mind going through the details again for me, would you?'

'Not at all.'

'When it began. What exactly happened.'

'This all started one day last week, you see. I'm almost certain it was Tuesday. I was taking Prince for a walk in the woods. There's a pathway down the road that leads through to the other side. On the way back, I came across the blind man.'

'Walking along the pathway?'

'No. In a clearing. It's one of those places the young

men and boys gather to drink. I've seen their litter afterwards.'

'Yes. What was the blind man doing?'

'This is the strange thing. He was on his hands and knees in the clearing, searching along the ground with his hands. I thought to myself, God the poor man has lost something, he's going to cut himself with all that broken glass and those open tin cans. I called over to him offering to help.' She drew a breath and looked slightly away in embarrassment. 'I'm afraid he was very abusive, Inspector,' she confided. 'I wouldn't like to repeat the names he called me.'

'There's no need to, Mrs Whelan.'

'He came towards me, shouting at me to move on. But Prince started growling at him and he stopped. He hadn't realized that the dog was with me.'

He couldn't have known at first that the woman was alone, either, McCadden thought. Which meant that Ronnie Harris had been very careless. And very desperate.

'Did you leave immediately?' he asked.

'Not because I was frightened. Not on that occasion. I thought he was sensitive. Some blind people are, I believe. They resent offers of help. So yes, I left him as he was. And mostly I forgot about it afterwards. But then, you see, I saw the same man there, in the same place, on Sunday morning. And of course, I hadn't Prince with me. I was walking to mass and I can't bring him into church with me. Although I must say I hate going out without him.'

'Is that your car outside the door, Mrs Whelan?'

'Yes . . .'

'Is it working?'

'Oh, it's regularly serviced, you know. And it's properly taxed and insured as well.'

McCadden smiled. 'I'm sure it is. I wasn't really asking about that. I was wondering why you don't drive to mass.'

She dipped her head in shame. 'I had a little accident, you see, some weeks ago. It wasn't even my own fault. But it's made me very nervous.'

'I'd go back to driving, if I was you, Mrs Whelan.'

She raised her head, slightly surprised by the suggestion itself and astonished that it had the support of a senior detective. 'Would you?'

'There's nothing wrong with your driving. And surely it couldn't make you as nervous as walking alone through the woods again.'

'Yes,' she realized. 'That's true, I suppose.'

'But you were saying,' McCadden prompted. 'Sunday morning.'

'Yes, Sunday morning. When I said that I saw the same man, I wasn't telling you everything. The blind man was there again, but now he had a younger man with him. It was the younger man who was doing the searching on Sunday. He had a heavy stick that he was beating down the bushes with. I pretended not to notice them and hurried on. I didn't come back home the same way. But it's a long journey around, and I was very late.'

'What did the other man look like?'

'He had long black hair, curled like a girl's. He hadn't a full beard, but he was unshaven.'

'Right,' McCadden said enthusiastically. 'That's very helpful, Mrs Whelan. I appreciate that. The situation is, these two characters have no interest at all in you. So you don't need to worry about them. And we'll make sure that they won't be in the woods again.'

'That's very kind of you, Inspector.'

'But I wonder if you'd do something else for me?'

'If I can.'

'Would you show me the clearing where they were? Is that possible? We could take your dog with us for the run.'

'I don't mind going back there. Of course I don't. Do you like dogs, Inspector?'

The walk, down the neglected road and then through the woods, was less than a mile and took them only ten minutes at a leisurely pace. Mrs Whelan talked about dogs and children on the way. McCadden couldn't comment on her kids, having never met them, but the German Shepherd they brought with them was exceptionally well-behaved. Friendly without being a nuisance. Lively without being frantic.

But the woman had other interests, and other concerns to think about. 'When they have so much more they can do these days, Inspector, I don't know why these boys do nothing but get into trouble. I remember my own children had nowhere near the same facilities . . .'

She drifted from complaint into reminiscence. But just as McCadden was beginning to enjoy the recollections, she suddenly interrupted herself again. 'Ah! Here it is!'

'This is it?'

'This is it, Inspector!'

The clearing, McCadden saw immediately, was one of those basic leisure centres for the alienated of the world. A meeting place for the lost. A space on the edge of life.

It was littered with revealing debris. Empty cider cans and plastic flagons. Broken beer bottles. Used condoms. And old syringes.

Some of the shrubs and branches at the back and edges were newly broken, where Harris and the other must have searched. But the effort had been wasted, McCadden was certain. Whatever Harris was looking for had probably been found and stolen by someone else within an hour of his loss.

McCadden sighed. 'We'll head back, Mrs Whelan,' he suggested. 'I've asked too much of you as it is.'

'Well, perhaps you could do something for me in return?'

'What's that?'

'I'd like to go back to the driving, you see. Like you said.'

'And so you should.'

'But would you mind driving behind me in the road a little? Just to give me back my confidence. You are going back into town, aren't you?'

'Yes . . .'

'And nobody's going to start bullying a Garda inspector, you see . . .'

McCadden was late for lunch as a consequence.

Rose Donnelly, still following the leads from the day before, hadn't returned to the station that morning and had left no messages. With nothing else scheduled until the schools closed at four and nothing to do while waiting for Donnelly except stay out of Cody's way, he walked across the road for something to eat in the Carnival Inn.

Ted Morris, the pub's owner, was arranging glasses behind the bar. As soon as he noticed McCadden's entrance, he abandoned the work. He quickly walked the length of the bar and leaned confidentially across the counter.

McCadden, about to order coffee and sandwiches, was silenced by a warning finger raised in front of his lips. He was beckoned closer. As he inclined his head, Morris whispered in his ear.

'Four-armed men raid new prosthetic store!'

McCadden drew back. He had no idea what the owner was talking about. The man ran a personal crusade against bad English. And possibly this was his latest find.

'Dreadful!' he lamented hopefully. And saw immediately that the guess was appropriate. 'Dreadful!' he repeated, more forcibly.

'What are you having, Carl?'

Frank Ryan and some other detectives were in a corner beyond the end of the bar. McCadden saluted them but didn't join the company. Instead, he sat alone in one of the gloomier booths.

He wanted to think while he was eating.

Ronnie Harris, he decided, was trying to recover something incriminating that he had dropped at what was probably the scene of a crime. But then, John Ryle was actually hiding something that was totally unacceptable to his wife . . .

A voice from his left almost immediately cut through his reflections.

'Well, hello there, Detective Inspector *Carl* McCadden!'

With a mug raised to his lips and his head stooping to drink, he looked upwards, through the steam that was rising from the hot coffee. Standing in the aisle outside the booth, now dressed in a chunky brown sweater and jeans and holding a nine- or ten-year-old girl by the hand, was the nurse from Accident & Emergency from the previous Thursday.

'Well . . .' he said. He wondered if he'd thought about her in the meantime. He couldn't remember now. The case had developed so quickly and taken so much of his attention. But was it ever otherwise? 'Nice to see you again.'

'This is my little sister, Sinead.'

'Hello, Sinead.'

'This is Detective Inspector Carl McCadden.'

'Right,' McCadden said. 'Now everyone knows me. And I know Sinead. But I don't have your own name yet.'

'It's Orla. Orla Stanley.'

'Aren't you a sergeant yet?' the girl asked imperiously.

'Well, inspector is higher, you see. You become an inspector after you've been a sergeant.'

'I think sergeant is better. I don't like inspector as much.'

'Right. Would you like to join me? Maybe I can change your mind.'

'Will we, Sinead?'

'I don't care.'

'See that man behind the bar over there?' McCadden said. 'Tell him what you want. Tell him it's for me.'

When the child was gone, her sister slipped into the seat opposite McCadden. McCadden gazed at her. Until he became conscious that he was doing it. And then aware that he was still holding the mug aloft.

He drank and asked, 'Why doesn't she like inspectors? Your sister.'

'Does it bother you?'

'No. But it interests me.'

'Why? Are you a child psychologist on top of everything else?'

'No, no. You see, it's possible that some Irish people are still not comfortable with the title. Because of our history. Her Majesty's Inspectors weren't exactly the people's champions when the country was ruled by England. Tax inspectors take out money. School inspectors our childhood.'

The nurse made a wry face. 'She's nine years old,' she said, 'but she's not *that* childish.'

'I suppose so.'

'Ireland's grown up now, you know.'

'We even have divorce, don't we?' McCadden said impetuously. He wondered why. Did he want to advertise his freedom?

But the nurse was patiently making her own point and not listening to him. 'Some things don't actually have a complex explanation, you see.'

'Is that so?'

'She prefers sergeants because my boyfriend was a sergeant and she liked him.'

'Ah! So what is he now? Your boyfriend.'

'Still a sergeant. *Was* my boyfriend, I meant.'

'Right.'

They watched the girl returning slowly to the booth with her order.

'Does she need a hand?' McCadden wondered.

'No, she wants to do things by herself.'

'I suppose—'

From behind McCadden, another voice anxiously interrupted him. 'Excuse me, sir.'

He turned. A uniformed guard was standing in the aisle, holding his cap in his hand. 'Yes?'

'The Chief Superintendent, sir. He wants to see you in his office.'

'Right. But if you couldn't actually find me . . .?'

The guard swallowed uncomfortably. 'I'm sorry, sir, but he said I wasn't to come back without you. He knows you're over here.'

'Shit!' McCadden lapsed.

But the nine-year-old didn't even blink.

McCadden looked upwards from her serious stare to the amused and challenging expression on her older sister's irresistible face.

'Sit down, guard!' he invited suddenly.

'I'm sorry, sir, but I—'

'Here, have a cup of coffee with us. Did they give you a time limit for finding me?'

'No, sir.'

'Then the two of us can return together in fifteen minutes and you'll have carried out your orders. You won't go back without me.'

eleven

A bald fat man was manicuring his fingernails in the Chief Superintendent's office when McCadden knocked and opened the door. Opposite him, Daniel Cody sat behind his desk and looked indulgently across at his guest's activity, as if trying to convince himself that he'd discovered a new spectator sport.

Obviously, the pair had been stuck with each other for quite some time now. Although they must have started on a warmer note, McCadden thought. Presumably, the fat man had vigorously made the point he'd come to peddle. The Chief Superintendent had undoubtedly promised action. They'd chatted pleasantly about the weather afterwards. And then, while waiting, they'd gone and nursed their irritation in silence.

Right now, they seemed to be on the point of blaming each other for their discomfort. Until McCadden's belated entrance finally rescued their relationship.

'Ah! At last, Inspector!' Cody greeted him sharply.

Gone was that casual familiarity he'd struggled to develop over the past year or so. This was to be a formal session, came the stern message. With chains of command and hierarchies in place and procedures properly adhered to.

Cody had glanced significantly at his watch as he spoke. And so McCadden lied diplomatically.

'I'd already left the Carnival Inn to follow up something. The man you sent had terrible trouble finding me.'

The Chief Superintendent's thin lips twitched with annoyance and nervousness. 'I see,' he said. And the two short syllables carried a heavy burden of scepticism. He gestured quickly towards the fat man. 'This is Mr Bill Toppin. Inspector McCadden. Mr Toppin will be a candidate in the forthcoming general election, Inspector. He has been quite considerate enough not to lodge an official complaint, as of yet, but he does strongly object to Garda harassment of his election workers.'

McCadden drew up a seat and shrugged, not knowing what the man was talking about. The fat man merely snapped his nail clippers to their folded position, put the instrument back in his pocket and then stared moodily at the dark surface of the desk. And in the silence, the Chief Superintendent was forced to keep running with the topic.

'The question is, Inspector,' he asked, 'did you or did you not instruct Detective Garda Donnelly to question active members of Mr Toppin's party?'

'Oh, that!' McCadden realized. 'That was some time ago. What's the problem?'

Toppin stirred in the chair that was too narrow for his bulk, making it creak very loudly. 'The problem,' he said, 'is the clear implication of some involvement in a criminal activity.'

'Whose involvement?' McCadden asked.

'At a sensitive time when such suggestions might be construed by people less understanding than myself as a blatant attempt to smear my reputation.'

'Are we talking about last Thursday week? Because if we are—'

'Especially, Inspector, when no crime was committed.'

'That remains to be seen, Mr Toppin.'

'I think if you take the trouble to talk to the parents, you'll find that it doesn't, Inspector.'

McCadden stared, and then suddenly sat back in his chair, feigning defeat and contrition. In reality, he was stunned. He turned the sentence over in his mind. *I think if you take the trouble to talk to the parents, you'll find that it doesn't, Inspector.*

Who was the man talking about? *What* was he talking about? Which parents had he interviewed or intimidated himself? What *crime* did he have in mind? Why hadn't he drawn on *Cody's* conviction that the whole affair was no more than a storm in a teacup?

McCadden could've asked, but he didn't want to betray his own ignorance. It was better, he decided, to leave the fat man comfortable for the moment. Leave him relaxed. And vulnerable. He wasn't going anywhere. He had an election campaign to run. He'd still be there when McCadden had sharper and more clearly defined questions to ask him.

'Let me check this out,' McCadden requested. 'I've been busy with other things, as the Chief Superintendent knows, and I haven't had a report on this yet. I wasn't aware of any problem. Can I come back to you?'

'Hopefully,' Toppin suggested, 'you may be able to return with an apology.'

'Right.'

McCadden whistled as he walked back through the corridors from the Chief Superintendent's office. Those who met him didn't bother greeting him. They recognized too clearly the symptoms of intense anger.

In the detectives' office, Rose Donnelly was sitting at her desk, typing a report with the fingers of one hand. The other arm was still resting in its sling.

'I've just been searching for you, sir,' she told him when he approached.

He stood in front of the desk, looking down on her.

'Rose,' he said, 'what would you think of an elderly man who makes a pleasurable career out of fondling and kissing babies and hugging small boys and girls?'

A Roman Catholic herself, she was permanently wary of his cynicism. 'Are we talking about the Pope, sir?'

'No, Rose, we're not.'

'Santa Claus?'

'Does the name Bill Toppin mean anything to you?'

'Yes, it does,' she admitted gloomily. 'Actually, that's what I wanted to discuss with you. Am I in trouble with the Chief Superintendent, sir?'

He seemed astonished by the thought. 'No, Rose, you're not in any trouble.'

'It's just that I got the impression from him—'

McCadden reached behind and pulled up a chair and sat. 'Forget about that,' he advised. 'Let's hear what you have to say about Toppin.'

'Not a lot. And still too much. For a start, on the Thursday night of the suspected assault on Jason Whittle, Toppin was the politician canvassing in the area.'

'So I gathered.'

'I contacted his election agent to get a list of the canvassers who were working with him that night. I did that yesterday. She seemed co-operative. In the meantime, I did some checking on the local party members myself. This morning, the election agent came back to me with some hokum about the information being sensitive and confidential and about the need to go through the party's head office with a formal request.'

'But you'd already talked to some people?'

'Yes, I had.'

'Have you met Toppin himself?'

'No.'

'Okay. Without going through the details of the interviews you did, just give me your assessment.'

'Well. When the three boys were chased by Ronnie Harris out of the woods and back into the estate, they ran into Toppin's group of canvassers. Harris backed off. The boys seemed to have made nuisances of themselves. In the confusion, something happened to young Hayden.'

'Like what, Rose?'

'Didn't you notice anything wrong with him when you saw him Saturday?'

'He had badly bruised or cracked ribs that were heavily strapped. He said he fell playing football. Are you suggesting that it happened with Toppin's canvassers?'

'Yes, sir.'

'No wonder he's edgy. Any witnesses, Rose?'

'Not any more.'

'Where did you hear it?'

'A young canvasser from the youth section of the party. She told me the story, then denied ever telling it to me, and had another story to replace it. What I do know is that Nicholas Hayden's mother accosted Toppin at his clinic the next morning, Friday. The local branch of the party was preparing for trouble. There was even a flicker of doubt about retaining Toppin as an election candidate. But then the whole thing just blew over. Nobody even remembers it existed now.'

'Have you spoken to the Haydens?'

'No, not yet.'

'You finish that,' McCadden said, tapping her report. 'But don't leave it out in the open. Then you can knock off. You want to get home early, don't you? You don't need to talk to Cody. I'll cover that. I'll bring you up to date in the morning. And good work, Rose.'

He glanced at his watch, calculating possibilities. It was two forty-five. He needed to be back at the Christian Brothers' school by four. The Haydens lived almost directly in front of the Whittles, along the third row of the estate, and if he wasn't delayed . . .

He decided to risk it.

But it was a mistake.

By the time he reached the estate, after being held up by the tailback from an accident in town, he was already eating into the minutes he needed to make it to the school. He thought then that the best option was to turn straight around and keep driving, and leave the visit until later.

But instead of being in school that afternoon, Nicholas Hayden was sitting on the front doorstep of his house, paring a short stick into a pointed weapon with a penknife. And McCadden couldn't resist a quick enquiry.

He parked and walked quickly up the pathway towards the house. The boy was so absorbed that he didn't notice his arrival.

'Out sick today, Nicholas?' McCadden wondered.

Simultaneously, as if both had been addressed and questioned, the boy looked up and his father appeared behind him in the hallway.

In his youth, Tom Hayden had done a little time for housebreaking and car theft and he still carried resentful memories. Unemployed for the last ten years, he now put his wasted and unwanted energies into body building. And into cluttering the expanding muscles with colourful tattoos. Even though it was cold that afternoon, he was naked from the waist up.

'What do you want now?' he demanded. 'Don't think I don't know you, McCadden, and what you're up to. You were already harassing the boy on the street.'

'Just checking that everything is all right, Tom.'

'Why wouldn't everything be all right?'

'You'd be surprised.'

'Go on! Surprise me!'

'The man who assaulted your son, Tom. He'll be coming back for another bite. You know that, don't you?'

Hayden laughed. And unfortunately for McCadden, the only thing he seemed surprised by was the absurdity of the suggestion. 'Nobody assaulted him, McCadden. He told you himself. He fell when he was playing football.'

'Then what are you so worried about, Tom?'

'Me? I'm not worried? Who's worried? What am I worried about?'

'Come on. You're watching him like a mother hen. You're sitting in there, no more than your arm's reach away from him. And you're on the defensive all the time. You're touchy.'

'And you're seeing things, McCadden.'

'Is your wife in, Tom?'

'That's none of your fucking business.'

There was something there, McCadden knew. He couldn't see it in Hayden's hardened, impenetrable face. But he could see it in the nervous blue eyes of the boy who was sitting below him.

But then, there was something *everywhere* in this shapeless case. Everywhere you put your foot down, you stepped on something nasty that squelched back at you.

McCadden raised his arm to make another point. But his wristwatch, on which he'd set the alarm, sounded just then, warning him that it was already four o'clock.

He turned away from Hayden and the boy. 'I'll be back, Tom.'

He hurried towards the car. Anxiety fuelled his urgency. He tried to calm himself. It was only a nagging guilt, he suggested, since he was failing to keep a promise.

He left the estate and drove quickly towards the school. Up College Street. Up Manor Hill. The traffic was light. Nothing delayed him. The T-junction at the top of the hill was clear. He pulled out without having to stop.

It was five past four, he saw from the digital clock on the car's display. And the school was only a hundred metres around the corner.

But as soon as he turned that corner, he knew immediately that he was already too late.

twelve

On the footpath outside the school, a small, excited group had gathered. A few young men, striking workers from the picket line inside, had already detached themselves from the knot to run into the centre of the road, and were pointing frantically with their placards, away from McCadden's direction. Others, though, were being sucked rapidly in to swell the crowd. Most were kids from the school itself. Some were neighbours scurrying from the surrounding houses. A few were distracted passers-by.

McCadden accelerated across the short distance. His noisy tyres turned heads as he pulled up. Already frightened, people backed away from him when he left the car and ran forward. Only the braver and burlier of the men considered tackling him.

Waving his ID above his head, he shouted, 'I'm a Garda! I'm a Garda!'

A channel opened up for him. In the centre of the ring of spectators, crying quietly and with blood streaming from his damaged nose, Jason Whittle was slumped on the footpath. A white-haired Christian Brother, dressed in a black soutane that had pale chalk dust spread across its front, stood over him protectively. But kneeling by his side, and gently lifting the boy from the concrete to his feet, was George Ducy, McCadden saw, the teacher who had been visiting Miriam Ryle in hospital the previous Saturday.

Jason himself was the first to recognize McCadden. By then he was standing up, cleaning his face with the tissues someone had given him and trying to stop the flow of blood from his nose.

'They got him!' he cried out. 'They got him!'

'Who, Jason?'

'The blind fellow! Old Harris!'

'Who has he got, though?'

'Luke!'

'Luke?' McCadden repeated. 'Luke Brady?'

A small, middle-aged man in a business suit cut in with a description. 'I saw it. My name is Jeffs. John Jeffs. I'm a chartered accountant working in—'

'What did you see?' McCadden interrupted.

'I was walking along here. The boys were coming out of school. The driver from the car that was parked over there—'

'No, that's not right,' a woman broke in. 'It was further down. Over there.'

'He just got out and went for this little lad who was passing by.'

'I was on the picket inside. I was coming out. The little fella here tried to stop them.'

'They bundled the little lad into the back of the car and just drove off like—'

'No, they put him in front as well. Remember? The blind man was in front all the—'

'No, the blind man stood out and—'

McCadden impatiently raised his hands, gesturing for

107

attention. 'All right, all right,' he cried. 'Did anyone notice the make of the car?'

'It was a white Toyota Corolla,' George Ducy told him calmly. 'One of the older models. Possibly about ten years old.'

The others fell silent around him, intimidated by his clarity and his controlled delivery. The long years of sitting quietly in schoolrooms, listening to teachers, had made a permanent impression.

'Did you get the registration?' McCadden asked.

'No, it was obscured by dirt.'

'Could you describe the man who took the boy? Not the blind man. The other.'

'A small, stocky man. In his twenties. He had long, curling black hair. He was dressed in blue denim jeans and jacket.'

'Okay. Are you visiting here, Mr Ducy?'

'I'm sorry?'

'The school. Are you visiting?'

'No, no. I work here.'

'Here?'

'I'm the senior English teacher.'

'But I remember you saying...' McCadden broke off, alerted by a sense of quickening curiosity in the crowd and deciding that his misunderstanding wasn't important enough to pursue right now. He said, 'I need you to do something for me, Mr Ducy. Take the names of any witnesses here who have to leave before the uniformed guards arrive. Give the guards the name and address of the boy who was taken. I need Jason to come with me. I'll have someone contact his parents and let them know where he is.'

For some reason, Ducy seemed to have grown uneasy.

Almost distracted. As if something other than the immediate drama was now disturbing him.

But McCadden had no time to analyse the uncertainty in the other's eyes. 'Do you understand?' he asked impatiently.

'Yes. Yes, of course.'

'Good. You come with me, Jason.'

In the car, McCadden strapped the boy into the front passenger seat and called the station on the radio while pulling away, describing the incident and the suspect vehicle. He left the line open afterwards, wanting to control the operation if Harris's car was spotted by a patrol.

'Do you know where they've gone, Jason?' he asked.

The boy shook his head. 'I don't, naw.'

'Sure?'

'How would I know?'

'Okay.'

McCadden turned right, down Castle Street, and right again at the next T-junction, passing his own flat on Manor Street and heading towards the estate where the boys lived and then the woods beyond it. He checked for Harris's car as he went. But he had little hope of catching it still around the city.

'Look, Jason,' he said. 'If we're going to find Luke in time to help him, you're going to have to tell me the truth.'

He glanced across. The boy had a paper handkerchief to his nose and was staring moodily out the windscreen. His lips were pressed tightly together. Obviously, McCadden thought, the truth had few attractions for him. One of those virtues that had never brought him anything but trouble at home in the past.

'Right now,' McCadden struggled to explain, 'I'm only interested in rescuing Luke. That's what you want too, isn't it? I'm not trying to trap you or hurt anyone else. Do you understand?'

The boy shrugged. 'What do you want, anyway? I don't know where they've taken Luke.'

'We'll find that out. But first, I want you to tell me exactly what happened the Thursday night before last. Everything you can remember.'

McCadden stopped at the traffic lights at the end of College Street, having driven in a wide circle since leaving Hayden's house. A patrol car came from Bath Street on their left and crossed in front of them, slowing to check the lines of cars around the intersection.

Again the boy stayed sullenly silent. Again, as they drove through the lights and out the Cork Road, McCadden had to prompt.

'Your parents had an argument that night, didn't they?'

'As usual,' the boy growled.

It was delicate, McCadden realized. Reveal that you knew too much about the boy's condition and you risked demeaning him. Pretend that you knew too little and he could afford to clam up and obstruct.

'You left the house early in the evening and met up with Luke and Nicholas Hayden,' he risked. 'Where did you meet them?'

'They were just hanging around.'

'What did you do?'

'We just hung around.'

'Right. Down in the woods?'

'Yeah, that's right.'

'Where you met . . .'

McCadden broke off, puzzled by something. A question had occurred to him clearly for the first time. One that should've bothered him earlier. What exactly was Ronnie Harris doing alone in the woods at seven or so on a dark evening *before* the boys got there?

Jason interpreted the pause as another question. 'We only met the blind fella,' he said. 'Old Harris.'

'Right. When we get there, I want you to show me the exact spot. But then what happened?'

'We were fooling around. We nicked old Harris's stick.'

'And he gave you a chase.'

'Naw. We legged it, but he wouldn't give us a chase then. He shouted at us. But it was only when we went back again that he chased us.'

'Really? I hadn't heard that before. What did you do to him the second time?'

'Nothing any different.'

'Did you take anything?'

'I think Nicholas swiped a handkerchief or something.'

'Right. When you were running back to the estate, did you see Nicholas Hayden being hurt?'

'Naw. I don't know what happened him. I knew he got hurt, but I didn't see anything. He went home to get it fixed up.'

'Before you started messing with the people who were canvassing in the estate?'

'No, after. We all had to scatter anyway. One of the Brothers out of the school was at the estate and nearly saw us all.'

111

McCadden frowned. 'Wasn't that later?'
'Luke said it was only Mr Ryle, and not to bother with him.'
'Sorry?'
'Luke. He said it was only Mr Ryle. But it wasn't. It was really one of the Brothers.'
'I don't understand, Jason. Why would it be Mr Ryle?'
'Sometimes he dresses all in dark clothes. And he was in himself, anyway. In the Brothers. When he went to school there.'
'John Ryle? He joined the Irish Christian Brothers?'
'Yeah.'
'Are you sure?'
'Ask anybody around.'
'Right. But listen, Jason. Wasn't it later that you had to hide from the Christian Brother?'
'How do you mean?'
'Didn't you go to buy some cider afterwards?'
'Yeah, we did.'
'Where did you get the money, by the way?'
'What money?'
'To buy the cider, Jason. It's cheap booze, but it still costs money.'
'Oh, Nicholas nicked it when he went back home. Do you get it? Nicholas nicked it. Like the book that...'
'Have you read it?'
'Read what? What do you mean?'
'The Dickens novel.'
He had, of course. And McCadden knew where. But the boy was still extremely touchy about two things. His relationship with John Ryle. And the uncertain connection between reading and toughness.
McCadden pulled over to the side of the road. Ahead

of them was the main route to Cork where John Ryle and his wife had come back from and where Miriam Ryle still longed to return to. To the left were the woods. On the right, and slightly behind, was the housing estate where the boys lived.

Harris's white Toyota wasn't visible.

McCadden switched off the engine and reported his position over the radio.

'We'll go carefully, Jason,' he said then. 'Bring me to where you can point out the place where you first met Harris, then we'll stop. When you went off to drink the cider, by the way, did you return to the same spot?'

The boy shook his head as he unfastened the seat belt. 'Naw. We went another place. Further in. A lot of people use it, but it was empty then.'

'A sort of big clearing, off a pathway?'

'That's it, yeah.'

'I've seen it, okay.'

They squeezed through a broken section of the wire fencing separating the wood from the road. A rough footpath, beaten into the ground from constant use, immediately presented itself. The boy followed it. And McCadden followed the boy.

'Is it far, Jason?' he asked quietly.

'No, we're nearly there as it is.'

'I wanted to ask you something else.'

He went sullen again. 'What?'

'After you drank the cider and left the other boys . . .'

'I didn't—'

'No, you did leave them, Jason, I know that. What happened?'

'Don't know,' the boy mumbled.

'What?'

'I don't know.'

McCadden reached out to touch the boy's shoulder and turn him around. There was confusion and guilt and shame in Jason's eyes. But no concealment. And McCadden thought he was telling the truth.

'How do you mean, Jason?'

'I can't remember,' the boy said. 'That's the truth. It's happened before after I do it. You know, drink the cider. I can't remember anything that happened.'

'What's the first thing you *do* remember?'

The boy hunched his shoulders and dipped his head. 'I know I told you something else the last time.'

'That doesn't matter now, Jason.'

'I remember waking up in Mr Ryle's house, you see . . .'

McCadden desperately wanted to probe deeper. The opportunity might never come again to have the boy so open about it, so removed from the conflicting influences of the adults in his life and from the simple codes of his friends.

But ahead of them, from beyond a cluster of young fir trees, they heard a sudden cry of pain.

'That's Luke!' the boy shouted as he swivelled.

'Ssshh!' McCadden warned.

thirteen

Ronnie Harris and his long-haired accomplice. The pair of them were both stupid and dangerous, McCadden had already decided. To lurk visibly outside a school on three or four consecutive days and then to abduct a child in broad daylight was the work of idiots. Worse, it was the bungling of a well-known and recognizable idiot. They'd acted without intelligence, without anything but the most rudimentary planning, and probably without any clear objectives.

The trouble was, if they were surprised now, he knew that their response would be equally dense. And equally dangerous.

So McCadden hesitated, waiting for support before he moved and for someone to take the boy off his hands to safety.

But his caution made the boy himself impatient. 'Why don't you go and *do* something?' he cried.

It was more nerves than courage, though. More tension than enthusiasm for action. In fact, when they heard someone behind them on the pathway, the boy turned in panic, terrified of being trapped.

It was only a uniformed guard approaching. A middle-aged man with a heavy moustache who moved with exasperating slowness, delicately lifting the brambles away from snaring his spotless uniform.

'Are you alone?' McCadden asked despairingly.

'Only myself, sir,' the guard confirmed. 'So far, anyway. I was serving a summons out the road and heard the call over the radio. I saw your car outside.'

'What's your name?'

'Patrick Knox, sir. My father was the sergeant in Dungarvan.'

'Right. This is Jason Whittle here.'

'Hello, Jason.'

'I want you to take Jason back home and let his parents know that he was helping me and that I'll call in on them later.'

For all his striving for a street-wise image, the boy left eagerly, and with something almost like gratitude. He wasn't really suited to trouble, McCadden thought. If he couldn't hide from it, he fled. He broke from home when his parents fought and then quickly slipped away from the gang he'd run to. Alcohol gave him blackouts. His constant desire was escape . . .

Alone again, McCadden advanced carefully along the pathway. An uneasy sense of being watched gradually settled on him as he went. Not from the front, where he might've expected an ambush. But from behind. Twice he looked back, worrying that Jason might've slipped his minder or that the ponderous guard himself had returned for more precise instructions. But there was no one there.

Beyond the cluster of young fir trees, he came on the area Jason had described for him. That, too, was empty now. And in itself, it seemed a place of no particular significance. Except perhaps as a landmark or a point of reference, he thought, since another pathway, cutting through the woods at a different angle, crossed the one he was already on.

Standing at the intersection, McCadden stopped to listen. The wind was light that afternoon, but it still made noises through the trees. Above the rustling of the leaves, though, he could hear nothing but birds. The place was still. And peaceful. And apparently deserted.

At least, until the wailing of a siren suddenly ripped through the calmness and started things moving.

It was actually an ambulance, speeding in the Cork Road and heading towards the Regional Hospital. But Harris and his accomplice obviously mistook it for a police car closing in and decided to leave before they were discovered. Fifty or sixty yards ahead, they broke from cover with the boy. The stocky man with the long, flowing hair was in the centre. On his left he held Luke Brady by the collar of the boy's jacket, on his right he guided Harris with an arm under the blind man's hand. Unaware that they were watched, they moved quickly, without even glancing back. They were heading for their car, McCadden guessed, which must be parked on the other side of the wood, near Mrs Whelan's cottage.

He slipped back among the trees, hoping to follow without being spotted. Over his radio, he reported again on his position and on the possible location of the white Corolla.

But like many blind people, Harris's hearing was sharper than average. He stopped abruptly on the pathway, dragging the others back to him, and dug in his heels to argue with the stocky man.

The sounds of their dispute were carried on the wind to McCadden. From behind a broad tree trunk, he watched the man turn and search behind. He was convinced that he was well enough hidden to escape detection. And yet the others were immediately alerted and started running away.

He had no alternative, then, but to break from cover himself and give them chase.

He gained quickly, of course. Handicapped by a stumbling boy and a blind sidekick, the long-haired man could manage to move no faster than the pace of a brisk walk. Glancing over his shoulder, he realized instantly that he was going to be caught. Without warning then, he released Harris and swerved to his left, dragging the boy along with him into the woods.

Like a detached wheel from a crashed car, Harris bounced on by himself for a while longer. Then he too stopped. Already disorientated, he distracted himself more by twirling wildly. He lifted his head and called forlornly, 'Cooney? Where are you, Cooney? Cooney?'

More careless idiocy, McCadden thought.

He didn't delay. He left Harris to be picked up by the uniformed guards. And he swung left himself, after Cooney and the boy.

He saw them weaving through the trees, less than twenty yards in front. Even though his own attention was now divided between watching them and dodging obstacles, he gained again. Cooney, still retarded by his hostage, was moving slower than him.

And then, for no apparent reason, just as he was confident of reaching them, he suddenly lost sight of them. Darting to the right, past a fallen tree, they dipped behind a heavy growth of blackberry bushes. And they never emerged again.

McCadden ran on. Beyond the tree and the bushes

was a small, circular clearing. But it was empty. He walked across and stood in its centre, over the ashes and the charred wood from an open fire that had been lit there recently. Hedges encircled him. And he knew that Cooney, ducking below them to stay out of sight, could've dragged the boy in any direction he liked.

On the point of using his radio again, McCadden hesitated, imagining he heard a sound. He held his breath to listen. And caught the sound again. A low moaning. From the bushes to his right. The pitch of the voice telling him that it was the boy and that the boy was hurt.

But turning immediately to investigate it was a mistake, he discovered. It left him exposed to attack from behind.

But even as he was advising himself of the danger, he heard Cooney charging from his hiding place on the opposite side.

Half-swivelling, he simultaneously ducked and swerved. And he was lucky. Something swished past the left side of his face, missing his head by inches, and broke painfully across his shoulder. It was a rotting branch, he saw as he recovered. Half of which was still in Cooney's hands.

Cooney jabbed at McCadden's face with the jagged weapon. McCadden swerved again. Off balance from the lunge, Cooney tottered a little forward. With his left hand McCadden caught the branch and tugged it. He swung his right fist into Cooney's advancing face. The contact broke something. Not in his own hand. In the nose or jaw that met it. He heard the crack of fractured bone. The other's grip loosened on the branch and the wood fell to the ground, rolling behind McCadden. He felt blood splattering his jacket and saw the glazed, astonished look in Cooney's eyes that he'd seen so often in the boxing ring, when one of the fighters had taken too much punishment.

But they were now struggling outside the area that the open fire had dried. The ground underneath was wet and muddy. The backward tug and forward punch had unsettled McCadden. He was balancing on his heels. When his shoes slipped on the greasy mud, he went down heavily. He instinctively reached out to save himself. But all he managed to grab was Cooney's denim jacket. And all he achieved was to drag the other down on top of him.

He fell awkwardly. And unluckily. The back of his head cracked against the fallen branch and Cooney's forehead butted into his unprotected face. For a few moments, he was aware only that he was losing consciousness. He had a helpless glimpse of Cooney recovering before him. Without understanding how they got there, he saw that the branch was again in Cooney's right hand and that his left held a large hunting knife. The knife was quickly put away. But the branch was raised by both hands above the man's dishevelled hair and was about to come down across McCadden's face.

McCadden blacked out . . .

He couldn't have been out for very long, he decided afterwards. And he couldn't possibly have taken the blow that Cooney intended. When he woke, his shoulder was a little sore from the first knock and the back of his head and his right cheek ached a bit from the fall and collision. But that was all the damage he'd taken.

He raised himself on his elbow, his vision still blurred from dizziness and from the moisture in his eyes. Some distance away, in one of the narrow gaps between the bushes, he thought he saw Cooney standing alone, looking back and waving at him cheerfully. But then, as the absurdity of it occurred to him, the image shifted crazily to flashback and merged with a clerical figure in a black soutane who had white chalk dust spread all over his habit.

McCadden rubbed his eyes to dry them. He focused again. And saw then that the gap was actually empty, except for a tree's shadow falling into it.

He got unsteadily to his feet. Without hope, he went across to the bush from where the boy had been moaning. Someone had lain there, he saw. The grass and the brambles were beaten down. And some fresh blood still dripped from the blades of grass.

He was gone now, of course.

But where?

Even as he was stooping to examine the scene more closely, the answer was brought to him. From away in the distance, over towards Mrs Whelan's cottage, he heard the German Shepherd barking furiously and then the shouts of men calling on others to stop.

He thought at first that Mrs Whelan herself might be in danger and after finding the pathway again and running the length of it, he went immediately to the cottage. But there was no one there. The dog stood tensed in front of the house, barking aggressively. And Mrs Whelan's Mini was neatly parked in its usual spot.

McCadden stopped to recover. Bent over, with his hands on his knees, he drew short breaths that tore sharply at his chest. He felt light-headed. From the fight and the run. But he still managed to search around.

It was beyond the cottage, he saw, two hundred yards

or so down the narrow road and on the crown of a bend, that the white Toyota Corolla had been pulled in tight against the ditch. And that was where the action was.

Although not exactly at the car itself. As McCadden discovered while walking down, the bend concealed another cottage. A derelict one. Once inhabited by Mrs Whelan's neighbours, he presumed. And probably once as sparkling as her own home. Now its roof had rotted and sagged. There were gaping holes where the slates had caved in. Weeds flourished in the open doorway and the broken windows. And a wild creeper clung to the chipped and filthied dash on the exterior walls.

A uniformed sergeant and three guards stood uncertainly outside it. All were breathing heavily. And obviously at the end of a failed chase.

'They're after holing themselves up in there, sir,' the sergeant reported. 'We nearly had them. But they saw us before we were on to them.'

'How many?'

'Two men and the boy. We would've followed them in, but they were threatening to do harm to the boy.'

'Any guns?'

'Not that we saw, no. I think if they had, they might've used them to get to the car and away. One of them had a knife, all right.'

'Have you talked to them?'

'Apart from shouting at them to stop, no, we haven't.'

McCadden nodded. 'Right,' he said. 'Take the men back. Well out of range. I'll see if I can get anything out of them before it gets out of hand.'

From the road, he walked across the waste ground that must've once been someone's front garden. There was no lawn now. No footpath was visible any more. And there wasn't even a front door it could lead to.

He stood outside the darkened hole of the doorway and called in. 'Ronnie? Are you in there, Ronnie? This is Inspector McCadden.'

'Fuck off, McCadden!' his greeting was returned.

'Right,' he said. 'Can we talk a little, Ronnie?'

'I'll talk, you fucking listen. Are you listening?'

'I'm listening.'

'I want all the guards gone out of here. We're taking the boy out. I'm not telling you when. But we're taking him out. And when we do, if we see any of you shower around he's going to get it. There and then. With this knife. No fucking messing, boy.'

'Right,' McCadden accepted. 'Is the boy okay at the moment?'

'There's nothing wrong with him.'

'Let me talk to him, then. Can you hear me, Luke?'

'Don't be trying any of your funny business now, McCadden.'

'Can you hear me, Luke?'

The boy's voice was breaking with fear when he was allowed to call back. 'I can hear you.'

'Are you all right?'

'I'm okay, yeah.'

'That's enough now, McCadden,' Harris came back in. 'Are you listening? This is what we want and you'd better not try anything else. Get all the guards out of there . . .'

fourteen

A little after six o'clock, when the light was failing, Chief Superintendent Cody finally rode in with reinforcements and brought with him what he described stiffly to McCadden as a trained hostage negotiator from the adjacent district.

McCadden was reluctant to leave. Not because he was making progress. Ronnie Harris's demands had reeled drunkenly from the comical to the worrying, from helicopters and lottery jackpots to basic medical supplies. There was no consistency to the requests, no logic in the pattern, and little hope of progress.

But McCadden felt responsible for the situation. If he'd reached the school on time, he reminded himself, as he'd promised the principal, the snatch simply wouldn't have happened. If he'd organized cover when he'd anticipated being delayed at the Haydens' home...

But for the same reasons, of course, he wasn't in the strongest position to resist Cody's order to stand down.

'If it breaks, I'll need to talk to them first,' he still insisted.

'I don't think that will be either desirable or necessary,' Cody told him coldly.

McCadden shrugged with irritation. 'All three have some involvement with Jason Whittle and some connection with whatever happened to Jason.'

'That is pure speculation.'

'It's why they've ended up in there.'

'You haven't convinced me of that.'

'I haven't convinced anyone of that! I wasn't given the resources to do it!'

'Inspector—'

'Now I've got half the force out here with me, along with a doe-eyed hostage negotiator!'

Cody drew a long, painfully controlled breath. He didn't admit to an error of judgement in the case. It wasn't his style. Instead, without setting anything awkward on the record, he hinted at a possible trade-off. 'Have you come back to Mr Toppin yet, Inspector?'

'No. I've been too involved with this.'

'He is extremely anxious to clear the matter up quickly.'

'So am I.'

'We all are, Inspector.'

'Right. This is why I'm so eager to talk first to the three inside. *Then* I'll have clarification for Mr Toppin.'

'Quite. I'll see that you're kept informed, then. In the meantime, please report to the hospital. I believe you were injured in the struggle.'

'Right.'

McCadden got nowhere near Accident & Emergency that evening, though. He thought about going. He even wondered if he'd have the luck to catch Orla Stanley on duty again. But he knew that if he checked in they'd hold him for observation overnight. And he couldn't afford the time and the distance from the case. Not with

Cody still searching desperately for valid excuses to exclude him.

Instead, he walked back down to Mrs Whelan's cottage to apologize to the woman. Another promise that he'd faltered on, he lamented. Harris and Cooney were supposed to be cleared from the woods. And they'd just moved in as her next door neighbours.

Mrs Whelan was sensible about it, though. And she seemed too excited by her return to driving to spoil her pleasure with worry.

From there, McCadden strolled back through the woods, stopping once at the larger clearing, where a cider party was getting under way around a blazing fire, and again at the intersection of the pathways, where the boys had originally taunted Ronnie Harris.

What was a blind man doing alone at this spot, he wondered. A hundred yards from the main road. A lengthy walk from his own house. In darkness. Over treacherous ground. Had there been someone else with him? Someone the boys hadn't seen? Someone they'd recognize and who'd been forced to stay out of sight?

McCadden's car, parked on the side of the main road the last two hours or so, was still unlocked. And luckily, still there. He turned it round and drove back the short distance to Jason Whittle's home.

As he pulled in, he noticed that there was a light on in the front room of John Ryle's house a little down the street and that their front door had already been repaired.

Except for a few subdued kids playing skipping, the street, he thought, was unusually deserted. And what hung around the place, it seemed to him, was an atmosphere of awkward shame. With typical haste, people were now convinced that it was Ronnie Harris who was threatening all their children. And as for their abandoned certainties about John Ryle, the previous bogey man ... Well, they were desperately trying to forget all that.

Jason Whittle wasn't at home when McCadden rang their doorbell. His father wasn't at home. And neither was his mother. One of Jason's younger brothers, a nine-year-old, was simultaneously watching a horror video and minding the house. He didn't know where Jason was. In fact, he didn't really know where anyone was. All he could tell McCadden was that their mother had been there when Jason was safely delivered by the uniformed guard.

McCadden felt a little depressed as he walked back to his car and started driving home. Part of it was the aftershock of the incident and the injury. Part was despair at the carelessness with which people handled their own children.

His flat, on the top floor of an old Victorian town house in Manor Street, was cold from being empty all day. He lit the open fire that he'd set before leaving that morning. As he worked, it occurred to him that he hadn't eaten since his light lunch at the Carnival Inn. But he didn't really want a full meal. When the fire had taken, he sat in front of it with a pot of fresh coffee and a couple of rolls that were left over from breakfast.

Looking for something to read, he reached almost instinctively for Philip Larkin and Catullus. The bleak and the acid.

But what else could he enjoy in the circumstances, he decided.

His mind drifted over the question. He thought of

Orla Stanley and of their agreement to meet again the next evening. He thought of the odd truth that he wasn't actually looking forward to that meeting, despite liking the nurse very much, and then of the impossibility of carefree sentiment while investigating a case of child sex abuse.

He became aware of feeling cold again, despite the roaring fire and the hot coffee. He shivered a little. He poured another coffee, but found the taste had died on his palate. Maybe he should've gone to the hospital, he regretted gloomily. Maybe he was actually concussed.

The idea suddenly frightened him. The feeling of helplessness. The prospect of brain damage. And the thought that no one would even know.

He wished he had someone to talk to. He wished there was someone to laugh at him in his life, someone to convince him that there was nothing wrong with him.

His physical tiredness and the warmth of the fire pulled him towards unconsciousness while he worried. His nerves, agitated by the coffee and the fear, warned him against succumbing. In the uncertain state between, as he lurched in and out of sleep, he had one of those brief and vivid dreams in which he was both helpless spectator and helpless participant. Its theme was his own mortality. But its style was bizarre. Violently protesting that he wasn't religious, he watched a grim cleric slowly advancing towards his death bed . . .

It was suspicion that woke him and doubt that finally rescued him from hypochondria. And once he was alert again, with only the *memory* of intense fear from the dream still clinging to him, it was his own puzzlement that convinced him he was normal. Bewilderment, after all, was no more and no less than his usual condition.

He stood up. He placed his coffee mug beside the pot by the fireplace. Some of the coffee from the last serving had spilled on the floorboards, he noticed. He mopped it up with tissue. He threw the wet paper on the open fire and put the fireguard in place.

Walking across to the coat rack, he pulled on his black leather jacket, searching its pockets for his car keys as he zipped it up. And only then, glimpsing his wristwatch underneath his sleeve, did he finally think about checking the time, when it occurred to him that he might've slept much longer than it seemed.

But it was only a little after eight, he saw. And he'd been home for less than an hour.

Even so, the temperature had already dropped outside. As he went downstairs and into the street and walked to his car, he hunched against the cold and remembered the two men and the boy in that exposed and derelict cottage out the road.

He turned right up College Street and Manor Hill, and right again along the length of Barrack Street, following the same route to the Christian Brothers' school as he'd done four hours earlier. The school was closed now, of course, although some of its buildings were still in use. There was a parents' meeting in the hall. And a few of the classrooms had their lights on for other activities.

But McCadden wasn't interested in the school itself. Not now. He drove beyond it and parked, and then walked around the chapel where the coffin of the order's founder, Edmund Rice, lay in the mausoleum, until he reached the living quarters of the Brothers themselves.

Over to his right, just visible on the edges of the light that was spilling through the windows of the school hall, he could see the shadows of the wire fence and the closed gate at the entrance to the construction site for the new theatre. There were no pickets on duty at that hour, of course. No workers marching silently up and down in the darkness. But some of their placards had been left, neatly stacked against the wire fence, waiting to be picked up and carried again first thing in the morning.

A small, white-haired Brother, dressed in the order's black soutane, opened the heavy oak door when McCadden rang.

'Brother Stevens,' he introduced himself after McCadden's explanations. 'Won't you come in, Inspector?'

They went to a compact sitting room to the left off the wood-panelled hallway, where two other Brothers were reading by the open fire. A tall, curly-haired man with a heavy book on his lap was introduced as Brother Hennessy. He smiled agreeably, wondered mischievously if McCadden had an interest in early Greek philosophy and closed his book before McCadden could respond. The third, a Brother Traynor, stayed morosely behind his newspaper until a second summons flushed him out. There was a time, McCadden reckoned, when this man had been a strong and ruddy-faced country lad. Now, in his mid-sixties, his face was mottled and puffed and his big frame was only a burden to him.

Stevens settled himself on the couch opposite the fireplace and invited McCadden to join him. 'Will you have a drink, Inspector?'

'Well,' McCadden accepted, 'as it's more a social than an official call and I'm no longer on duty ... Would you have a whiskey?'

'We would, indeed.'

McCadden settled himself on the couch, feeling a strange uneasiness in this all-male company. A pretender, he decided. That's what he was. With his easy jests and his sociable whiskey.

Stevens poured at a cabinet in the corner. Traynor, McCadden noticed, watched him hungrily. As Stevens walked back, his gleaming black shoes left greyish, uneven stones or pebbles on the carpet. He stooped to pick them up and tossed them on to the fire before continuing.

'I only bought them this morning,' he complained, indicating the shoes.

McCadden nodded his sympathy. 'How many Brothers are here altogether, by the way?' he asked.

'Ah,' Stevens said wistfully. 'There was a time, you know, and not so long ago, when more than thirty of us lived in the community here.'

'Right,' McCadden said. He took the offered whiskey, drank a little and put the glass on the low table in front of him. 'But how many are here now?'

Stevens gestured sadly as he sat. 'Only ourselves these days, I'm afraid.'

'Just the three of you?'

'That's right.'

'Okay. Which one of you did I see outside the school this afternoon?'

'That'll be me,' Traynor said. He still had a heavy rural accent and clogged his vowels when he spoke. 'And if I'd been a few minutes earlier I could've stopped the whole thing.'

'What did you do afterwards?'

'What could I do? I went back into the school.'

'Did you leave again?'

'Not after that, no.'

'Did any of you leave at any stage after four o'clock today?'

'I was in Stradbally most of the day, Inspector,' Stevens explained. 'Do you know it? It's about twenty miles up the coast. I've just got back.'

The other two shook their heads. Hennessy put away his book and Traynor finally folded his paper, both apparently mystified by the line of questioning.

'You must be a terrifying conversationalist when you *are* on duty, Inspector,' Hennessy observed.

McCadden smiled. 'I've been so long at it, the line between work and conversation is blurred now, anyway. Do any of you teach a lad named Jason Whittle, incidentally?'

Hennessy sighed. 'None of us teach at all now. We're too old. Past retirement age.'

'But you know Jason Whittle?'

'Of course, yes.'

McCadden drank a little more of his whiskey. It was very smooth and particularly mellow. And obviously reserved for visitors. 'Could you think back,' he suggested, 'to last Thursday week. Early in the evening. Okay? Do any of you remember seeing Jason that evening?'

'Where would we see him, Inspector?' Traynor wondered.

'That's what I'm asking you.'

'He wasn't back in school for something, was he?' Stevens asked.

McCadden shook his head. 'No.'

'We're hardly ever out, you see. Maybe we'd go to a

debate or some other function in another school. Otherwise we wouldn't be out. Not in the evenings, anyway.'

'Luke Brady and Nicholas Hayden were with him,' McCadden prompted. 'The three boys were together. No? There was a large group of party activists canvassing for Bill Toppin in the estate where Jason lives. Do you remember that? The boys bought cider and went to the woods to drink it.'

'They're only thirteen, Inspector,' Traynor pointed out. 'Where would they be able to buy cider?'

'I'd like to know. Do you?'

He looked around the faces staring back at him. Stevens's was small and rounded. Traynor's loose and flabby. Hennessy's severe. But for all the differences in texture, they shared the same expression. Puzzlement.

'You don't remember?' McCadden tried forlornly again.

'I think we would, Inspector,' Hennessy pointed out, 'if any of us had actually seen any of the events you describe.'

'Right,' McCadden accepted. 'But it leaves me with a problem. All three of the boys saw a Christian Brother at some stage that Thursday night. Have you any ideas to help me out? Was there a Brother visiting you from another community that night, for instance?'

'No. We've had no visitors recently.'

'Some other type of cleric, perhaps?'

'There are priests, obviously, and Brothers from the De La Salle Order in the city. But no Christian Brother boy would be guilty of confusing us with anyone else.'

McCadden shrugged and finished his whiskey. 'John Ryle,' he said then. 'Do you know Mr Ryle?'

'He's a member of our past pupils' committee.'

'Did any of you know him when he joined your order as a teenager in the, ah ... seventies, wouldn't it be?'

Hennessy nodded. 'I did, yes.'

'Would you have a photographic record of his time as a Brother?'

'He was never ordained, Inspector. He left when he discovered that his vocation was elsewhere.'

'I mean, a photograph from the period, showing him in the black soutane and white collar.'

'Of course, yes. But why ...?'

fifteen

At six o'clock the following morning, when he could least handle another shift in the case, the telephone rang in McCadden's bedroom.

He'd climbed the stairs to the open loft at eleven the night before, after coming back home from the Christian Brothers. An early night, he'd settled for. Rest. Let the mind refresh itself. But he hadn't actually slept for a long time afterwards. Isolated from the action, he felt restless and frustrated. Unable to understand either what was happening now or its origins in the past, he kept himself awake with theories and with elaborate constructions. All of them were plausible. But none had better claims than any of the others.

When the telephone rang at six, he was less than four hours into an exhausted sleep.

At first, his mind didn't want to do anything at all with the noise, except accommodate it in a dream. But the sound was too persistent. The dream itself had to mark time just to keep making sense of the din. And it was the lack of movement in his brain that finally woke him.

He reached out, and found that he was lying so close to the edge he didn't even have to change position to lift the receiver from the table beside the bed. 'Hello?'

Frank Ryan was on a mobile phone. His voice was recognizable. But his words were muffled and indistinct.

McCadden said blearily. 'Frank? Frank? Are you eating breakfast, Frank? I can't hear you.'

For a few seconds afterwards, there was nothing but crackling on the line.

'Is that better?' Ryan was heard then. 'Hello, is—'

'Yeah, I can hear you now.'

'These fucking things,' Ryan complained. 'I think there was a cow standing between us, deflecting the signal.'

McCadden stared at the blurred display on the digital clock. 'It's six in the morning, Frank.'

'Yeah, I know that, Carl.'

'Where are you?' But the cow supplied the answer. 'Are you at the siege? Has it broken?'

'Like hell it has. That's why you're back on stage, Carl. The Chief Superintendent wants you out here. Now.'

'Couldn't it wait another couple of hours?'

'No. It's not really him, actually. It's Ronnie Harris, insisting on seeing you . . .'

Although the flat itself was still warm from the fire he'd kept going through the night, the morning outside was bitterly cold. There was no wind, but a damp, thick mist hung heavily on the air. Looking out the loft window, McCadden could see that the orange street lamps were almost completely shrouded and that a thin layer of frost had formed on the grey slates of the roofs opposite.

He dressed in his heaviest jeans and sweater and pulled on a ski cap and ski jacket after drinking a couple of coffees downstairs. The streets were almost deserted when he stepped outside. His footsteps echoed in the quietness as he walked along the pathway. And when he started the car, its coughing sounded harsh and disruptive.

Visibility was poor and he still wasn't fully alert, so he drove slowly down Manor Street and out the Cork Road. On the narrow, pot-holed road, just beyond Mrs Whelan's cottage, a uniformed guard directed him nervously to a space between the parked squad cars.

Even though it was cold and early, there was quite a crowd behind the cordon that had been thrown around, the derelict cottage. The story had broken on the national news the night before, and along with the merely curious, a local camera crew from the television station was now in position. The conditions were too poor for filming, of course. The crew were standing around, adding to the cloud cover by smoking heavily, and chatting to the equally bored reporters from the newspapers.

But it was a local hack, Toady Wade, with his insider's knowledge, who was the only one to understand the possibilities in McCadden's arrival.

Wade was a freelance, and very successful at his job. His selling point was sensational sex. But like a lot of guys who were preoccupied with the thing, McCadden thought, he never seemed to be getting very much of it himself.

'Morning, Inspector,' he breathed after sidling across to McCadden's car.

McCadden nodded as he stepped out. 'Fancy meeting you here, Toady,' he joked. 'If the other guys see you talking to me, they'll think I'm important.'

'I won't take notes,' Wade revealed. 'I just wanted to get your opinion, Inspector.'

'Don't have any.'

'Do you think we might be dealing with a ring here?'

'What kind of ring, Toady?'

'A paedophile ring. The boys are not the first to disappear in Ireland are they?'

McCadden shook his head. 'I don't know, Toady. Like everyone else, I usually rely on the newspapers for my facts. Although when I open tomorrow's edition and read the headline *Gardai Unsure about Origins of Paedophile Ring*, I'm going to be just as surprised as you'll be, won't I?'

Beyond the cordon, a large white caravan had been parked on a clearing opposite the ruined cottage. This was now the control centre of the operation. When McCadden climbed its two narrow steps and opened the door, the warmth and smell of bodies packed tightly together in a small space came strongly to him from inside.

The Chief Superintendent, he saw, sat alone at his command desk poring over reports that he must've already studied in detail. At the back of the caravan, among a group of other detectives, Frank Ryan was fiddling with what was probably his mobile phone, although it looked more like a fragile toy in his massive hands. On a couch in the centre, Luke Brady's mother and father, wrapped in separate duvets, were sleeping against each other in sitting positions.

McCadden, still dull and reluctant, had expected all this. In fact, he hardly even registered the details.

So what woke him up was something else.

Stretched along another couch, opposite the Bradys, with his Nike trainers sticking out from under the bottom of the blue duvet and his white plaster cast jutting from the top, was the sleeping figure of Joey Whittle.

McCadden managed only the opening to his astonishment. 'What—?'

'Sit down,' the Chief Superintendent said to him simultaneously.

It was actually an invitation, but delivered so curtly that it came across as an ill-tempered order.

Cody looked drawn and haggard. The colour had washed so completely from his face that only the difference in textures betrayed the line between his white hair and his pallid skin. He must have stayed at the scene all night, McCadden decided, driven by that sense of personal responsibility for the job that he carried about with him. It was the only passion the two men shared. And the only real bond in their working relationship.

'I'll bring you up to date,' the Chief Superintendent said.

'Has something happened?'

'No. There's been no progress since last night. No movement at all, in fact. I meant . . .'

'Where's the hostage negotiator?' McCadden wondered.

Cody gestured vaguely, without a lot of respect or conviction, at a bedroom compartment behind him. 'Resting.'

'Did he get very far with them?'

'They were given food and blankets and sleeping bags yesterday evening. Further food was delivered at intervals. Their demands diminished through the night. Now they have none. Apart from seeing you.'

'Who asked for me?'

'Harris himself.'

'Do we have anything further on the other man, Cooney?'

'No, nothing as yet. And their car was stolen in Wexford last week. But the point I was about to make is this, that they haven't created the situation for any ulterior purpose. It's accidental. There's nothing we can offer them. The only outcome is their arrest . . .'

McCadden, already knowing all this, became impatient. 'What's Joey doing here, by the way?'

'Joey?'

'Whittle. The man in the plaster cast who's sleeping on the couch.'

'He's here because of the boy, of course. Why else?'

'Right,' McCadden said softly. But it was an expression of doubt rather than acceptance. He couldn't yet understand the connections. And he wasn't given time to develop them.

'I want you to respond to this request of Harris's,' Cody was instructing. 'Without endangering yourself. I don't want an additional hostage. There's enough as it is. And without radically altering the current situation. Merely exploratory.'

'Okay. Have we got a plan of the interior of the cottage?'

'You won't need to enter. Stand at the door, where the negotiator talked from.'

'I'd still like an idea of what's inside.'

Cody sighed and turned to look down towards the end of the caravan. 'Sergeant!' he called.

Luke Brady's mother stirred and moaned in her sleep at the summons, but she didn't wake. Beyond her, Frank

Ryan took a manila folder from a table and brought it with him as he came gently up.

'The interior of the cottage,' Cody told him.

As McCadden accepted the photocopied sheet Ryan drew from the folder, he asked, 'Is this from the negotiator?'

Ryan shook his head. 'He never got inside. These are the original architectural drawings.'

The cottage had four rooms, according to the sketch. The front door opened directly on to the main room. Two doors on the left presumably led to bedrooms. A door at the rear to a small scullery or kitchen.

'The two rooms at the back are not in play,' Ryan explained. 'The roof's caved in back there and there's no cover. The last we knew, they were all in this first bedroom here on the left.'

'Have they slept?'

'Harris has, we think. Cooney not. Unfortunately for him, he's the only good pair of eyes between them. They had no reason to keep the boy himself awake.'

'What's their condition?'

'Cooney is desperate. And probably resentful. He knows he has only another twelve hours or so before he's out on his feet.'

'Is there tension between them?'

'Considerable, we think, yeah.'

'So does this sound like a last play to you?'

Ryan nodded. 'That's exactly what I think it is, Carl.'

'Okay,' McCadden said, 'we'll give it a try, anyway. How do you let them know that I'm coming? I don't want to get them too excited.'

Cody indicated the telephone on his desk. 'You can tell them yourself. That's a direct line into the cottage.'

When McCadden lifted the receiver, it was answered immediately on the other side.

'What is it?' a voice growled at him.

'Ronnie? This is Inspector McCadden.'

'About fucking time!' Harris greeted him ungraciously.

'You wanted to talk to me.'

'Yeah.'

'What about?'

'I'll tell you that when you get in. Just yourself. No funny business. And hurry it up. You hear me?'

'Have you got lights set up, Frank?' McCadden asked as he replaced the receiver.

'Enough to play a soccer match under.'

'Keep a good, strong searchlight on me while I'm out there. Tell him to track me wherever I go, regardless of what I do.'

'You have it, Carl.'

sixteen

The mist had thinned a little by the time McCadden stepped back outside the caravan. The grass, still stiff with frost, crunched under his feet as he walked across the clearing. Like an uncertain child, he stopped at the edge of the narrow road, waiting for the searchlight to come on and pick him out. Then he crossed, dodging the iced pools in the pot-holes on the surface.

As he approached the cottage through the waste ground where a garden must've flourished once, he called out loudly, 'It's McCadden, Ronnie!'

He stopped at the gaping front entrance to the house. Two steps led up to the threshold. He climbed them and stopped again in the doorway. He wondered where the long-haired Cooney was watching him from. And he wanted to force him to reveal his position by calling instructions.

But instead, it was Harris who demanded, 'Where are you, McCadden?'

The voice had come from the main room, and over to McCadden's right.

'I'm in the front doorway, Ronnie.'

'Come in, will you, for fuck sake!'

'What do you want me for, Ronnie?'

'What do I want you for? That's a laugh! You're the one that got us into this mess. So you can fucking get us back out again.'

'How am I going to do that?'

'I'm going to do a deal with you, that's how.'

'I can't do deals, Ronnie. I don't have the authority.'

'Well, you'll have to go and get it.'

'Why don't you talk to the Chief Superintendent?'

'Because you're the only one's going to understand what I'll be giving you. The rest of them wouldn't have any . . . Where are you, McCadden?'

'Still in the doorway, Ronnie.'

'Would you come fucking in! I'm getting tired of this.'

'Tell me what you're offering to trade first,' McCadden said.

But he moved as he spoke. Just a couple of paces. Silently. Warily. And as he went, the light from behind followed him, spilling in narrow shafts around his body. Enough to dimly illuminate the cottage.

On the left, in front of him, the still intact door to the first bedroom was wide open. He could see nothing beyond it. On his right, in a far corner of the room, he could just make out the shadows of Ronnie Harris and Luke Brady. Both were fattened by the sleeping bags and blankets they were wrapped in, but it was still clear that the blind man was holding the boy in front of him, with his left arm around the kid's neck in a headlock. McCadden couldn't distinguish the expressions on their faces or whether the blind man also had a weapon. But he did establish that the room was otherwise deserted.

'I'll tell you what I'm offering, McCadden,' Harris was saying. 'You wanted to know what went on out in the woods here the Thursday before last. Well, I can tell you. So you see, I'll be...' He stopped, alerted by something. And then he shouted angrily, 'Have they got lights on you, McCadden? Are they shining lights on you?'

'I can't see where I'm going otherwise, Ronnie,' McCadden pointed out.

'I can't fucking see at all!' Harris screamed. 'Have you forgotten that?'

'Of course I haven't.'

'Get rid of the fucking lights, McCadden! Do you hear me?'

'Okay, Ronnie. Okay.'

The long-haired accomplice was hiding in the bedroom on the left, McCadden thought. If anyone passed the doorway, they'd be attacked by him from behind. And the only one foolish enough to pass, in darkness, would be McCadden himself, lured on by the promise of information. Or so they'd calculated.

They needed another hostage, he guessed. They had a plan. And they needed another body to carry it through. Harris himself was trapped. Unable to see, he couldn't afford to move from the cottage and couldn't afford to trust any guarantees of a safe passage. But what he could do was buy some time for the other by staying where he was with the boy. With one captive as a shield for himself and another as a stalling device in the cottage, Cooney had a chance of escaping.

'McCadden?' Harris was shouting again. 'Where are you, McCadden?'

'I haven't moved, Ronnie.'

'Well, you fucking should've! I told you! Get rid of the lights! Either that or the kid here is going to suffer for it. Do you hear me?'

The boy squealed suddenly, either from pain or fear.

'Okay, calm down, Ronnie,' McCadden pleaded. 'My fault. I wasn't to know. I'm going back out, Ronnie. Okay?'

'No, it's not okay!'

'I'm walking across to tell them to kill the lights.'

'No, no! Just signal to them!'

'I don't want to do that, Ronnie. They might get the wrong idea and storm the place. You know what I mean? Then we'd all be sorry. Signals are dodgy. So is shouting in this weather. I'll be back in a minute. Okay?'

'Well, make it fucking quick, McCadden! For the kid's sake.'

McCadden got out before Harris remembered that there was a telephone sitting beside him. He walked briskly back, shielding his eyes from the glare of the searchlight that kept faithfully on him all the way. Beyond it, on the grass outside the caravan, he explained his reading of the situation to Cody and Ryan.

'Have we got infra-red binoculars?' he asked then.

'In the caravan,' Ryan told him. 'Why?'

'I think you need to train the searchlight on the door, lock it in that position and then extinguish it. You watch me through the binoculars in the darkness. When Cooney comes from the bedroom, switch the lights back on. Get some people ready to move on that signal. They'll have to come from the back around the right-hand side. He's watching through that window on the left. I'll take Harris and look after the kid when it happens, because I'll be closest to them. What do you think?'

Cody was too *tired* to think. And yet he was also

suspicious of caution. He was eager to end the siege. And yet he was wary of heavy-handedness. Above all, he was painfully conscious of recent lapses and of how little time he had to reach the right decision now.

'Isn't there a high element of risk involved, Inspector?' he wondered.

'Someone might get hurt,' McCadden admitted. 'But it won't be the kid. I can guarantee that.'

'I don't get it,' Frank Ryan admitted suddenly. He'd gone to fetch the binoculars and had been standing there, frowning, since he'd come back. 'Why would they need another—?'

'And what if Cooney doesn't actually attack?' Cody interrupted impatiently.

'Then I only talk to Harris,' McCadden promised. 'As we intended.'

Cody nodded wearily. 'All right, then. But be careful,' he advised. 'Be *conservative*.'

'No problem.'

Again McCadden walked across the crisp grass to the edge of the roadway after the lights were switched off. He called over. 'I'm coming back now, Ronnie. All the lights are out. Okay?'

He kept talking as he went, reporting on his progress. Past the road. Through the rutted garden. 'Almost there, Ronnie,' he cried. He reached the threshold again. He paused a moment. He said, 'I'm coming in now, Ronnie.' Over on his right, around the corner of the cottage, he saw the first of the men that Ryan had picked, signalling their readiness.

Knowing that Cooney was watching him, he couldn't afford to acknowledge the sign. But he did fall silent as

147

he stepped inside. Trying to disguise his position as much as possible. Trying to make himself a more difficult target.

But Harris, either anxiously or cleverly, forced him to talk once more. 'Where are you, McCadden?'

'Just inside now, Ronnie.'

'I have to keep hearing you, you see. Otherwise you might be sneaking up on me.'

'Right. It's just that it's slow going, Ronnie ... in the darkness ... with all this rubble ...'

He talked in bursts, deliberately breaking up the phrases so that he could listen frequently. The thought crossed his mind that he could simply ignore Harris and surprise Cooney instead. He knew where the other was. The advantage was with himself ...

But it was too dangerous to risk it. And too confusing for the others waiting on his movements.

He walked on. And he talked.

'I'm almost right there, Ronnie ... if I'm guessing right ...'

And from behind him, in one of the gaps between his words, he finally heard the slight creak of a moving shoe or sneaker. For an instant he was conscious of being both cold and vulnerable. As if he was naked before an enemy. For an instant he was uncomfortably aware of total reliance on someone else.

But in that same instant, the searchlights flashed on.

In the sudden glare, he sprang forward. First to escape the lunge from Cooney behind him. And then to dive towards Harris once he'd located the blind man and the boy.

As he landed, he heard the shouts of the others pouring through from the front and back doors. 'Armed

Garda! Drop your weapons!' His only fear, suddenly suggested by the cry, was that Harris might be holding a knife on the boy beneath the covers.

But the blind man was too surprised and too disorientated. With no idea what was happening, he instinctively tightened his grip on the boy's neck. McCadden chopped him hard on the biceps, deadening the muscles. The grip loosened. Rolling away from him again, McCadden grabbed the boy and carried him with him. And Harris barely had time to howl with pain before the other detectives were swarming all over him.

In the light from their torches, McCadden saw that Cooney was now spread-eagled on the ground and about to be cuffed. A knife had been knocked from his hands to the floor and lay among the rubble from the ruins.

'Are you all right, Luke?' he asked.

The boy was shivering violently. 'Yeah. Yeah.'

'Did either of them hurt you?'

'No, it was okay. Okay.'

McCadden stood up. And as he did, he found that the boy had his arms around his neck and was hugging him fiercely. It wasn't affection, he knew. And it wasn't even gratitude. It was something more basic than either. It was fear. And the need for protection.

He picked his way through the rubble on the floor, between the captors and the captives, and carried the boy outside. With the lights and the crowd and the clinging child, he felt faintly embarrassed. But the scene didn't last. Within seconds, Luke Brady's parents were running from the caravan to reclaim their burden.

Behind them, moving awkwardly across the ground as he tried to hurry, with the plaster cast held to the side like a broken wing, came Joey Whittle. There was fear and anxiety on his unshaven face. The expression in his eyes, expectant and hopeful at first, suddenly shifted to despair as he advanced.

But he wasn't looking at the boy McCadden was now handing over to Mrs Brady. He wasn't even looking at McCadden himself. He was staring beyond McCadden, towards the derelict cottage.

And so were the others, McCadden noticed now. Cody. And Ryan. And the uniforms surrounding them. They were all looking eagerly towards the cottage. As if the drama wasn't actually over. As if something else was about to happen.

And yet Harris and Cooney had already been handcuffed and led away to the squad cars . . .

Reluctantly, sensing a problem he had missed, McCadden also turned. Two young detectives were coming from the doorway of the cottage. Their arms were spread wide, indicating that their search had been fruitless.

Someone moved quickly past McCadden then. It was Whittle, he saw. A yard or two in front of him, the man pulled up as he read the signals from the two detectives. For a few moments, his whole body was as rigid as the cast on his arm. And then he swivelled, his face contorted with anger and with pain.

'Where is he, McCadden?' he demanded. 'Where the fuck is he?'

And only then did it click for McCadden. The little things that had earlier nudged his curiosity without detaining him. They now came together to explain each other. Toady Wade's suggestive claim. *The boys are not the first to disappear in Ireland* ... The Chief Superintendent accounting for Whittle's presence at the siege. *He's here because of the boy, of course* ... Frank Ryan not understanding why the abductors needed another hostage.

'Frank!' McCadden called desperately. 'Frank!'

But Ryan and Cody were already at his side.

'Where's the other one, Carl?' Ryan was asking.

'*What* other one?'

'Jason Whittle.'

McCadden shook his head. 'Jason Whittle was never in there, Frank. He was brought home by one of the uniforms about five o'clock yesterday afternoon. He was returned to his mother. I checked that myself when I knocked off last night. Where did everyone get the idea that Jason Whittle was inside?'

'His father, Inspector,' Cody put in. He raised his head to watch Joey Whittle insisting on re-entering the ruined and empty cottage with the two young detectives. 'His father arrived some time after you left last night. There was some confusion.'

'Quite obviously.'

'But the thing is, you see,' Ryan spluttered, 'Jason Whittle *is* actually missing.'

'Missing?' McCadden repeated. 'How missing?'

'He's disappeared, Carl,' Ryan explained. 'He's been gone from home all night. We know that because we have someone down there with the mother and the rest of the kids and she would've obviously reported if the boy returned. That's why we were sure he was here.'

'Mr Whittle was adamant that you yourself were the source of this information,' Cody explained.

151

McCadden shook his head again. 'Me?' But he was too despondent to really feel indignant. 'It wasn't me,' he said. 'And it wasn't Ronnie Harris. I mean, whoever is responsible for Jason Whittle's disappearance, it wasn't Ronnie Harris.'

seventeen

On a light breeze, the smell of grilled bacon travelled up to them from Mrs Whelan's cottage as McCadden and the Chief Superintendent finally returned to the caravan to talk.

It was already ten o'clock. By then, Luke Brady had been taken to hospital with his parents. Harris and Cooney had been brought to the station for preliminary interrogation. A couple of detectives had accompanied Joey Whittle home to redirect the search for Jason. And Frank Ryan was tidying up outside, preserving the scene and operating as chief steward for the dispersing crowds.

But for all the activity and all the progress, the Chief Superintendent's anxiety, lifted for an instant by the rescue, had now deepened even further. The dashed promise of a resolution had only sunk him lower, reminding him again how his own complacency had contributed to the crisis. As he climbed the steps to the empty caravan and slumped behind the desk he'd been using, he seemed already drained of energy.

'Whatever views we held before,' he said wearily, 'I think we now have to face a rather brutal fact. We may well be dealing with a violent, manipulative father here.'

McCadden tactfully ignored the inclusion of himself in both the original errors and the current revision.

He thought about the suggestion. Joey Whittle's accusation of John Ryle and his theatricals at the siege could be elaborate diversions, he accepted. It wasn't unknown for parents to spend weeks searching for missing kids they themselves had murdered. And Whittle didn't like the boy. In fact, he resented him. With a few decent breaks, Jason would get an education and rise far above his old man.

'It's possible, I suppose,' he conceded.

'But you don't think so.'

'I've never *felt* that Joey's violence was directed against Jason.'

'Even when he's drunk?'

'He neglects the boy. It makes him feel guilty.'

'And guilt has to be exorcised or obliterated. Somehow or other.'

'But he doesn't hit the *boy*. He hits *Ryle*. Or *Harris*. The way I see it, hitting someone else is more compensation for his own neglect than anything else.'

'No doubt,' Cody muttered without enthusiasm. 'Nevertheless, until it is proven otherwise, the father must be considered a primary suspect in his son's disappearance. Furthermore—'

They felt a vibration under their feet along the floor of the caravan and at the same time heard a noise from the compartment behind Cody. McCadden frowned. Cody, living more on the edge of his nerves, immediately jerked upright. They looked at each other, baffled.

A few seconds later, the sliding door of the bedroom behind the desk was slipped open on its runners and a sleepy, crumpled young man made an appearance, yawning heavily and stretching widely inside his creased clothes. It was the hostage negotiator, whose well-deserved rest everyone else had forgotten about. Clearing his gluey eyes, he looked in amazement at the almost deserted command centre.

'Eh?' he exclaimed. 'Where is everyone? What's going on? What's happened?'

McCadden cushioned the shock for him. 'You softened them up,' he said.

'What do you mean? Who? What?'

'But it was on a slow fuse,' McCadden expanded. 'They missed you so much they weakened when you went asleep.'

Cody, wary of irony even when he was healthy enough to cope with it, suddenly got up and suggested fresh air again. They left the baffled negotiator behind, but only made it to the bottom of the caravan's two steps before stopping again in the clearing outside.

The morning was bright and fine. The mist had completely cleared. The frost had melted from the grass, but the moisture had made it muddy underfoot from all the heavy traffic. A couple of uniformed guards were patrolling outside the derelict cottage in front of yellow crime-scene tape. The crowds, and the media people, had gone.

Cody took a deep breath and massaged his tired eyes. 'I don't know whether I asked you this already,' he said stiffly. 'But did you get a chance to talk again to Mr Toppin?'

McCadden shook his head. 'Not yet, no.'

Another time, the insistence would've provoked an irritated response. But he decided to make allowances for the circumstances.

It was Cody's most basic failure, he thought, that he was too *naively* an old-fashioned man. He simultaneously respected and undervalued women. He was a father with little experience of caring for the smaller needs of his children. And he admired the power of politicians. His deference had nothing to do with party favouritism. It reached across the political divides. It was just that, in his solid old-fashioned view, the office enhanced the individual.

'You'd better go and take charge of the investigation into the boy's disappearance,' Cody was saying now. 'But I'm sure the thing has shifted so rapidly that Mr Toppin will be satisfactorily out of the picture from here on...'

Kakistocracy, McCadden remembered as he drove back towards the city. It meant government by the worst. And while he was amusing himself, if a little perversely, *prolicide* and *filicide* were the terms for killing one's own child. The last two Cody had near enough suggested tagging on to Joey Whittle. With a decent question mark after each, of course.

Within a few minutes of reaching Whittle's house, though, McCadden had discounted the charge.

He was lucky with his timing. Driving through the estate, he passed Corina Whittle on her way home. She'd obviously been shopping. A plastic bag full of groceries was hanging from each handle of the buggy she was pushing. Three of her children were with her. A five-year-old twin clung to each side of her thin denim jacket and a bawling infant squirmed in the buggy itself.

It was hard to imagine her looking any worse than she usually did. But she did. She looked *far* worse. She walked as if in a trance, as if guided by some careless external control. When McCadden stopped to offer her a lift, she drifted straight past his greeting, without hearing him or seeing him. The loose wheels of her buggy rattled over the uneven footpath as she turned a nearby corner and was gone from his sight.

McCadden drove on, taking the longer route around to the house to avoid overtaking her again. In the distance, towards the end of the street, he could see one of the young detectives on his rounds, gathering information as he called from door to door.

As with every crisis in the estate, the surrounding neighbours had been brought to their front doorsteps and gardens to talk about the tragedy. One of them, a heavy, middle-aged woman, stared warily at McCadden as he parked the car and went to ring the Whittles' bell.

There was no answer. But as he turned away, Corina Whittle appeared again on the street, passing the young detective and advancing on the house. She still didn't see McCadden on her doorstep. And he had to call out to alert her before she actually bumped into him.

'Mrs Whittle?'

She started and stared upwards at him from the bottom of the pathway.

'It's Inspector McCadden, Mrs Whittle.'

'Have you found him?' she asked, instantly hopeful. 'Have you found him?'

'No, not yet, I'm afraid. Where's Joey, Mrs Whittle?'

Her thin mouth twisted with hate. 'Him! Where would he be? Drinking somewhere! It won't make no difference to him.'

'Could I step in?'

Inside, the bawling infant was left strapped in the buggy in the hallway, with only a packet of defrosting chips to play with. The twins, still clinging to their mother's jacket, were dragged with her to the front room, where they abandoned her to turn up the volume on the television that the two finches were already watching. Corina folded herself into the battered couch and lit a cigarette.

'You were here yesterday evening when the guard brought Jason home, weren't you?' McCadden asked.

She nodded defensively and sucked on her cigarette. 'What about it?'

'What happened after that?'

'He went out again.'

'Did he not have anything to eat?'

'The dinner was there for him. I can't force it down his throat, can I?'

'Did you see him for the rest of the evening at any time?'

'There are other ones to look after, aren't there? Younger ones. I have only two eyes in me head.'

'When did you suspect that he was missing?'

'Some of the others from the street came to call for him. Friends of his. They said he wasn't out and they couldn't find him then. When they came back after trying everywhere again, that's when I knew.'

'Why did your husband think that Jason had been taken along with Luke Brady?'

She turned her head away. And there was a set look of determined bitterness on her sharp features.

'Did you tell him?' McCadden asked.

Again she didn't answer. So that he knew she had.

Joey Whittle's long vigil at the siege was no charade to cover his own guilt, McCadden realized. It was a private hell that his own wife had created for him. She'd coldly set him up. Knowing that he'd immediately hurry out there, she'd told him a terrible, plausible lie. Using what was left of his parental instincts as the blade and manipulating what little good remained in him, she filleted and gutted him. And all the time, she'd anticipated with pleasure both the agony of his wait and the utter desolation of his discovery that the agony had been wasted.

In their private war, McCadden accepted, everything could be drawn on as a weapon. But a hatred that abused the disappearance of your own child to score another wound was surely too deeply poisoned.

He felt a little sick as he left the house afterwards. And his conversation with the young detective questioning in the area did nothing to improve his condition.

'No one saw him, sir,' the detective reported. 'So far, anyway. Not one single person saw him last evening.'

'No one noticed him,' McCadden corrected dully. 'They might've seen him, but they didn't notice him. No more than they would on any other evening. It probably means that nothing unusual happened on the estate itself. Either that, or he deliberately slipped away to avoid being seen.'

eighteen

It was two o clock in the afternoon before McCadden was finally allowed to talk to Luke Brady. By then, he already knew that neither Harris nor Cooney had seriously harmed the boy. Apart from a few minor bruises, there were no external injuries. And whatever their reasons for the abduction, it had nothing to do with sexual abuse.

So far, it seemed the pair were holding out under interrogation. They were stubbornly revealing nothing about their motives and admitting to little but the blindingly obvious.

Of course, since they had no involvement in the Jason Whittle enquiry, the detectives questioning them had no real incentive to keep probing aggressively. And McCadden, wanting to interview Luke Brady first, before the boy learned of Jason's disappearance, had put off his own turn until later.

The trouble was, finding a location for the conversation with the boy.

Along with other youngsters in their early teens, Luke had been placed in the children's ward. According to the doctor, the company and the environment were supposed to help restore his sense of normality.

McCadden suspected the usual shortage of bed space. Not the doctor's fault, of course. So he said nothing. He was about to settle for a screen around the bed, when the ward was ingeniously emptied by the matron, who organized a showing of the latest movie release in the video room and then breezed past the humbled doctor at the head of the charge, like an overweight Peter Pan.

Both the boy's parents were also at the bedside.

Luke's father, who worked in a local machinery plant, was a short, muscular man, always ready to take offence, and always on the defensive. His mother was a very concerned, but very baffled, middle-aged woman.

Both obviously tried their best for their kids. But they were crippled by fatalism, by a sense of helplessness that was encapsulated and excused by the few stock phrases they kept sprinkling the conversation with. *Sure, what can you do with them these days? I'm blue in the face talking to him. He's only a lad, when it comes down to it. They won't listen to you any more.*

The parents sat on hard plastic chairs on one side of the bed. McCadden, who sat on the other, had the strange sensation of being at a dinner table, with the boy himself as the only course.

'When are they going to let you out of here, Luke?' he opened.

The mother was in immediately, interpreting the question and supplying the answer. It was how she fooled herself, McCadden thought. By talking. It was how she convinced herself that she still had some knowledge of and influence over the boy's life.

'They're doing a few more tests on him,' she said.

'Right.'

'Small things. That's all.'

'I'm sure it's nothing, but—'

'Then he's allowed home.'

'Anyway, Luke, you did well,' McCadden praised then. 'You handled it very well.'

But again the mother cut in before anyone else. 'He's only a little lad you know, and he's . . .'

Unable to find a direct line to the boy, McCadden already felt frustrated. He smiled grimly. And plotted. What he needed to do, of course, was to establish a separate communication under the public one.

He laughed and said directly to the mother, 'Who would've thought that going to school could be so dangerous. He might've been safer mitching.'

The woman looked at him uncertainly. She opened her mouth to respond. But since she had to think about it, she said nothing immediately.

The real meaning of McCadden's joke was felt only by the boy. And the suggested trade-off was obviously understood. McCadden would say nothing about the boy's activities. If the boy talked privately to him.

Some agreed signals, which would've infuriated the father if only they weren't invisible to him, must've passed then between Luke and his mother. And for all her intrusiveness, of course, the woman was mere putty in her son's hands.

'Come on, Willie,' she suggested suddenly. 'We'll go out and get ourselves a cup of tea, will we?'

The man started at this strange idea. 'What?'

'I'm parched,' she tried to persuade him.

The husband bristled. 'And what? Leave Luke here all by himself, is it?'

'He'll be all right. Won't you, Luke?'

'I will, yeah.'

'What's your man there going to be saying to the boy? Tell me that! I never had guards around the house in me life and I'm not going to start it now!'

'He's only trying to help, Willie.'

'It don't matter a damn what he's trying to do.'

'The boy's tired, Willie. He's too many people at him at the one time. Let him have a bit of peace, for God's sake...'

'If you think I'm leaving here, you have another thought coming...'

Five minutes later, as he watched his parents still arguing while they left the ward, the boy sat up in bed and grumbled morosely to McCadden. 'He'll be back again in a few minutes anyway. He's always like that.'

'Right,' McCadden accepted. He looked through the gap the father had suspiciously left in the drawn screen and saw that they were finally alone. 'Then we'd better get to the point. You came in to see me on Monday and I appreciated what you passed on to me then. It was very valuable. But I have this feeling that you're not telling me everything you know about that Thursday night.'

'I am. I told you everything.'

'Let me put it like this, Luke. The two characters who kidnapped you are going to be charged and then released on bail. You know what that means, don't you? They'll be free until they come to trial. They're going to come looking for you again.'

The boy shook his head. 'Not for me, they won't.'

'Unless you tell me exactly what they wanted from you.'

'They won't be looking for me.'

'No?' Alerted by the boy's unusual certainty, McCadden worked through the possible explanations in his mind. 'Why not?'

'They thought I was after taking something on them.'

'That Thursday night? You took Harris's cane.'

'Not the cane. Something else.'

'What?'

'I don't know, do I? *I* didn't take it.'

And from the slight emphasis on the final *I*, McCadden understood. He said quietly, 'But one of the others did. Right? Did you tell them the names of the other two lads?'

The boy grew uneasy then, twisting the sheets around his restless fingers. 'I had to, didn't I? It wasn't just ratting. They had a knife and I . . .'

'I'm not blaming you, Luke,' McCadden assured him. 'You were right. But it wouldn't be right now to leave your friends in danger from Harris, would it?'

'It's not only Harris they're scared of.'

'How do you mean?'

'Look, I promised Nicholas I wouldn't say anything. I can't break a promise, can I?'

The old code, McCadden lamented. He said, 'You told me about John Ryle when you thought Jason was in danger. This is no different. What about Nicholas?'

'I don't know. He got battered, didn't he?'

'Battered? How?'

'How do you ever get battered? Some fella three times as big as you. Some adult.'

'I thought Nicholas fell while running away.'

'He didn't fall.'

'Who hit him?'

'I don't know. A big bald fella on the estate.'

'Living on the estate?'

'Naw.'

'The one with the group that was handing out the leaflets that night?'

'That's him, yeah.'

'Give me the details, Luke.'

'When we were running away from Harris—'

'No, hang on.'

'You said give you the details.'

'No, hang on. Something just struck me. You stole Harris's cane. He didn't chase you. You went back. Why did you go back?'

'It was just a dare, you know.'

'Who made the dare?'

'Nicholas did.'

'Right. But Harris chased you the *second* time. Who was in the lead when you were running back the second time?'

'How do you mean?'

'This is just a guess. Right? But one of you must've sprinted ahead, faster than the other two.'

The boy raised his eyebrows in surprise. 'Yeah, it was Nicholas. He legged it. He was gone.'

'And you hung back, taunting Harris with names and leading him in the wrong direction.'

'Nicholas asked me to.'

'That's how Harris caught up with you, by the way,' McCadden pointed out. 'He recognized your voice.'

And that's why the blind man had crossed a main road that night, over to the estate, he thought. A foolish adventure that had previously puzzled McCadden. Luke Brady had been just a little away from Harris, leading him on.

The boy was getting excited about it again now, worrying that he was talking himself back into trouble. 'Nicholas said his leg was hurting him. He said he was going to get caught. That's only why I did it.'

'Nicholas was sprinting ahead, Luke. There was nothing wrong with his leg.'

'But he *said* there was.'

'It doesn't matter. It's not important. Where was Jason? With you or with Nicholas?'

'Jason wouldn't be fast enough to keep up with Nicholas. No way. And he was too scared to stay with me.'

'Right. So what was happening when you caught up with them again?'

'It was back in the estate. The big bald fella had him. Nicholas was after knocking over some woman or something. He didn't mean to. He just bumped into her. He said the big fella hit him because of it. Real bad. He was crying. He had to go home.'

'And when he came back out, you all went off to buy the cider?'

'Yeah.'

So basically, McCadden thought, there were three separate experiences and three separate accounts. They hadn't existed as a group for that vital period. Hayden was in the clear ahead. Luke Brady was behind with the blind man. Jason was somewhere in between and not really aware of either.

Through the gap in the screen, he watched the boy's parents returning to the ward as he was thinking. The stocky father strained like a bow-legged bull terrier on a leash. The mother still detained him, although with nothing stronger than a hand on his arm.

'Did you tell all this to Ronnie Harris, Luke?' McCadden asked quickly.

The boy nodded, his eyes shifting anxiously between his parents and McCadden, wondering if he'd done enough to escape betrayal. 'I had to, yeah. He had the knife.'

'Did you tell him before or after he brought you to the woods?'

'After he found out that I didn't know what he was looking for and that I hadn't taken it anyway. After we got to the woods.'

'Are you all right there, Luke?' the boy's father demanded suddenly from the end of the bed.

McCadden rose. 'He's fine,' he said warmly. He patted the boy's arm, shook the father's hand, and then the mother's. 'That's a very brave lad you have there. And very helpful. You'll probably have someone else along to take a signed statement. It's just a formality . . .'

nineteen

Bill Toppin didn't actually live in Waterford city, McCadden discovered. The family home was about ten miles to the west of the city, up a narrow lane that slipped quietly off the main road to Dungarvan and Cork.

He was settled in the middle of rich agricultural country, then, but not a farmer himself. He was the owner of a major bottling plant back in Waterford, but still not a city dweller. Toppin's domain, McCadden thought unkindly, was almost as broad as his girth. And since both the urban and rural areas were parts of the same constituency for the forthcoming general election, the balance in his life seemed to be finely calculated.

The house itself expressed the same desperate search for inclusiveness. The original farmhouse of rough grey stone and sunken windows was still standing, but the extensions on either side were out of character. They were modern, and featureless, and coloured a pale cream. To McCadden, pulling in to park in the front driveway, the whole thing, the sombre centre and sparkling flaps, looked like a dappled seagull with pure white wings.

Stepping out and glancing along the length of the

spread, he wondered which of the four front doors he should try first. But from the other side of the rise that the house was built on, before he could make up his mind, he heard the noises of children arguing. He walked to the crest of the slope and saw two young boys in the play area below him.

They were obviously brothers. And just as obviously, they were also sons of Bill Toppin. Both were overweight and were already afflicted with their father's heavy jowls and multiple chins. Both wore thick-rimmed glasses and had bleached, almost colourless hair.

They weren't playing together. In fact, McCadden decided, they weren't actually playing at all. The older, about twelve years old, was hammering a tennis ball into the soft ground with the edge of a hurley stick. The other lad, three or four years younger, was digging a grave with a cricket stump.

'Hi, how are you!' McCadden called down.

Both looked up, scowled and went indifferently back to their separate entertainments.

'Is your father in?' McCadden wondered.

From behind, a woman's voice summoned him anxiously. 'Hello there! I say! Hello there!'

He turned. A small, slim blonde woman was hurrying from the oldest section of the house, waving a green and white tea towel at him.

'Can I help you?' she offered. 'You seem to have gone astray.'

'I'm Detective Inspector McCadden, from Waterford. I called to see your husband.'

'Oh, I see. Yes.'

'I rang his workplace in Waterford. They said he was at home.'

She glanced at the little gold watch on her slender wrist. 'Did you organize an appointment?'

'We have a long-standing arrangement.'

'My husband is holding a clinic at the moment, you see. Not a medical clinic, now, but—'

'I know. He's a politician.'

'Always on Wednesday afternoons here, between four and six. His clinic. Mondays and Saturdays in the city. Thursdays in...'

The woman was in her mid-thirties, McCadden calculated. The older of the truculent kids was barely into his teens. Maybe excess weight and premature baldness had given him the wrong impression of Toppin's age.

'There doesn't seem to be anyone else around at the moment,' he interrupted. 'Perhaps he's free.'

'Oh, that's where you'd be mistaken now.'

'Is that right?'

'There's another entrance, you see, from ... You'd better follow me.'

They went through the house, into the rear garden, at the bottom of which was a small, flat-roofed building where Toppin held his clinics. As she opened the door to the waiting room, his wife saluted all the constituents by name.

'Hello, Mary. Nice to see you again, Tom. How's Frankie, Bridie?'

They were all local people, McCadden saw. All farmers. No doubt they broke into their overworked lives to steal a few hours to come here because they wanted references that might help sons and daughters get a job, because they needed planning permission for a barn, because they didn't understand how to go about getting the medical card they were entitled to...

It was what they voted other people in for. It was what their elected representatives did for them.

Most Irish politicians, McCadden knew, managed to get through careers of fifteen or twenty years without once coming up against the challenge of political thought. The had party machines to do that sort of thing for them. Some complained about the limitations. Few did anything to change it.

Toppin seemed to be one of the majority who actually thrived on the trivia. When he came from the consulting room, with his left arm benevolently around one satisfied constituent and his right warmly extended to the next, he looked like a jolly magician capable of pulling a separate rabbit from a bottomless hat for every child in the audience.

His wife's approach and whispered explanations toned the colour down a bit, though, and by the time he shook McCadden's hand he was almost bland.

'I hope we can be brief, Inspector,' he said curtly. 'Would you like to step in? I'll just explain to my constituents...'

McCadden wandered in through the open door, into the small office beyond.

The first thing he noticed was a large poster on the wall behind the desk. It showed a powerful arm throwing a straight jab with a red boxing glove and had the slogan blazoned in the same garish colour: LEADING IN THE FIGHT AGAINST CRIME. It was going to be one of the major issues in the election campaign. Not the realities of crime and the realities of punishment, McCadden thought sadly. But only what politicians promised to do about it all.

There were other posters from different campaigns

around the walls, even if the ones of Mr Toppin's party announcing previous blitzes on the criminal fraternity seemed to be missing. The empty spaces were agreeably filled, though, with photographs of the man's broad range of interests and involvements.

McCadden had wandered through the exhibition and was back again at the boxing poster when Toppin himself returned to the office.

'Glad to see we're on the same side,' McCadden remarked.

'You may be gladder still when we're returned to office,' Toppin promised. 'We'll be giving the Gardai far greater powers, and far less leeway for turning a blind eye to the minor offences that plague our society and that develop into major offences. The policy is known as zero tolerance. I'm sure you're familiar with it.'

'I've heard of it.'

'The public are sick and tired of young thugs ruling our streets, Inspector. We intend making the streets safe again for the ordinary citizen.'

As Toppin sat down, McCadden ambled back to one of the photographs hanging on the wall. It was a formal shot of a school group, a class of thirteen- or fourteen-year-old boys with two lay teachers and half a dozen Christian Brothers. The pubescent Toppin, the plump template from which the adult had expanded, was taking up so much unallocated space in the centre of the second row that he was nudging the boys at either end of the line more or less out of the frame.

Since he recognized the location, McCadden asked, 'Did you attend the Christian Brothers' school in Waterford, Mr Toppin?'

'Yes, I did.'

'Pleasant memories?'

'I held my own there.'

'I'm sure you did.' McCadden tapped the glass at the figure of a small, curly-haired youngster who was dressed in the habit of the order and standing on the extreme right in the back row. 'Is that John Ryle there?'

'He was a few years ahead of our class. I believe he left the order shortly afterwards.'

'Did you know a boy called Ronnie Harris, by the way? Judging by the dates, he may be a contemporary.'

'I think you'll find him sneering somewhere in the top left-hand corner.'

McCadden found the younger Harris. And found the description accurate.

'It's funny,' he said, 'how the future prospects of every boy already seem to be etched on his face.'

'The Jesuits used to boast that they could take the boy and give you back the man,' Toppin answered. 'The Christian Brothers were far more realistic, Inspector. And got less credit for it. They never promoted a belief in alchemy. They always knew that it was really a question of keeping the hopeless cases in check with stern discipline so that the brighter could advance.'

'Do you agree with them?'

'I haven't yet seen the young thug who was improved by sympathy, Inspector.' Toppin made a play of studying the enormous Rolex watch on his wrist. He said crisply, 'Now. Is there a point to all these questions?'

McCadden innocently raised his eyebrows. 'Hm? I thought we were just chatting.'

'I hope you haven't travelled all this distance to offer nothing more significant than chat, Inspector. And I do have constituents waiting.'

'Right,' McCadden accepted. 'Just clear up one small thing for me, though, if you wouldn't mind. On this zero tolerance policy.'

'What is it?'

'A bunch of kids. Right? They're twelve or thirteen years old. They're messing around on a housing estate. Disturbing people. Damaging property. What are you suggesting? Put them in institutions?'

'Of course. It will deter them for the future.'

'Even if it did . . . We don't have the prison spaces.'

'My party will be implementing three thousand new prison spaces when we're returned as the next government.'

'But that's the criticism, isn't it? All this is aspirational. It hasn't been costed.'

'I think if you take the trouble to read our policy document—'

'What about an adult who beats up one of the kids?'

'I beg your pardon?'

'An adult. He's tired of all the hassle. He's under pressure himself. He suddenly snaps, grabs one of the kids and beats him so badly that the child is hospitalized.'

'What are you suggesting, Inspector?'

'I'm asking a question. I mean, are we talking about zero tolerance for everybody, or zero tolerance for deprived kids and a kind of three-quarters tolerance for privileged adults?'

'I don't think you quite appreciate where you are drifting, Inspector.'

'Possibly not. You want to blow me back on course?'

'Perhaps my lawyer's wind may be stronger.'

'That's not a very fortunate phrase, Mr Toppin.'

Toppin stood up, perhaps more deeply wounded by the humour than by any of the previous insinuations. 'You already seem to have forgotten the explicit instructions of your Chief Superintendent, with whom I have developed a very close working relationship.'

McCadden shrugged. 'Mr Toppin,' he said, 'I have no interest in who you've developed close relationships with. The topic bores me. I'd much prefer to discuss a more engaging situation instead.'

'I have no intention of sitting here and—'

'It's purely hypothetical. You pursue me for harassment. I pursue you for assault. The boy's parents won't support my case. For his own reasons, the Chief Superintendent won't support yours. Not very satisfactory. Alternatively you could answer a few non-incriminating questions and we could both agree to *mutual* tolerance.'

Toppin had paled. Not from fear, McCadden thought. But from the horrors of personal choice. Standing there, confronted by McCadden's demands, he contemplated the death of either his ideological consistency or his hopes of election. As McCadden noted while staring at the exposed Rolex, the dilemma occupied the man for exactly sixteen seconds.

'What are the questions?' Toppin asked then.

'The boy knocked down a woman canvasser while running,' McCadden said. 'Is that correct?'

'Yes.'

'Had the boy been causing trouble earlier than this incident?'

'No.'

'Was he involved in the subsequent disruption of your canvassing?'

'No. Not that particular boy.'

'He went straight home after your, ah, encounter with him.'

'He left, yes.'

'Now,' McCadden said. 'Most important of all. Was he carrying anything...?'

twenty

At seven o'clock that evening, McCadden returned to the housing estate. He didn't travel alone. In one of the force's fortified vans, he went with Frank Ryan and three uniformed guards, one of whom was a dog handler with a trained Alsatian named Jess. Rose Donnelly, freed of the sling after intensive physiotherapy, also asked to join them, although her shift was due to finish in an hour.

They turned in along the third row. When the van stopped, McCadden went alone to the front door. He rang the bell. Tom Hayden himself answered. As always, he had his shoulders thrown back and his head and chest jutting outwards, ready for trouble.

'What do you want now, McCadden?' he demanded.

McCadden unfolded the document he was holding and showed its contents. 'This is a warrant to search the premises, Tom. We have reason to believe that there may be illegal goods or illicit substances con—'

Hayden tried to slam the door. McCadden placed a foot to stop it closing.

'Don't be stupid, Tom,' he advised quietly.

Simultaneously, he heard Ryan and Donnelly and the others hurrying from the van behind him. As they squeezed past into the narrow hallway and spread out to search the rooms, he said, 'If you have anything here, we'll find it, Tom. So you'd be better off letting us know now, before we start.'

'I haven't a clue what you're talking about!' Hayden protested.

'It's too late for the show of innocence, Tom. You should've tried it before closing the door.'

'What goods are you talking about? What illicit substances?'

'You tell us.'

'There aren't any.'

From the front room on the left, Rose Donnelly summoned McCadden uncertainly. 'Sir?'

Gesturing Hayden in front of him, he stepped in. Donnelly was standing with a uniformed guard a little to the right of the doorway, in front of the blank television screen. Neither had started to search yet. In a grubby blue armchair in front of the open fire, leaning forward with his elbows on his knees, sat a small, white-haired man dressed in the distinctive black soutane of the Christian Brothers' order.

The Brother turned his head without twisting his body. 'Ah, there you are!' he cried. And he laughed uncomfortably. 'Inspector McCadden, isn't it?'

'Brother Stevens,' McCadden responded. It was half a greeting, half an exclamation of surprise. 'Have we interrupted a pastoral visit?'

The man laughed uneasily again. 'Ah, no, no. I'm just in for a chat. Mostly about sport. Myself and Tom, you see . . . I used to train Tom at the hurling when he was a boy. At school. One of the best we ever had . . .'

'Right? So, do you call here often?'

Stevens stood up and made a show of warming his

hands at the fire. The gesture indicated that he was leaving shortly, that he was only storing up heat and energy for the cold evening outside. 'No,' he said. 'Once a month maybe. That'd be about it. Isn't that right, Tom?'

'When was the last time you were here?' McCadden asked.

'The last time? Let me see. That'd be last month. September. Just after school restarted. Tom's lad Nicholas . . . He's showing a bit of promise with the hurling.'

'Do you coach him in school?'

'Not officially, no. I still help out a little. And every little helps, as they say. Will you, ah, need me for anything else, Inspector? I was just ah . . .'

'It's not normal for anyone to be allowed leave during the execution of a search warrant, Brother.'

'I see, yes.'

'But if you're in a hurry and you have no objection to the guard there checking your person, we won't need to detain you.'

'What? Oh, no objection at all, no . . .'

McCadden indicated to Donnelly and the guard and turned back to Hayden himself while Stevens was being searched. 'Is your wife in, Tom?' he asked.

Hayden morosely shook his head. 'She's out at bingo.'

'Nicholas?'

'He's out playing somewhere.'

'Anyone else in the house?'

'No.'

McCadden nodded and took in the depressing poverty of the room while he was waiting. There was very little furniture. Two armchairs and a weak-legged table. The television and a dowdy glass cabinet. Both the floral wallpaper and the plain carpet were old and faded and the place had that distinctive smell of staleness that always suggested lack of effort and lack of hope to him.

Stevens's trembling voice cut in on his thoughts. 'I'll be off then, Inspector, if that's, ah...'

'Right. My apologies for the inconvenience.'

'Not at all, no. Goodnight then, Tom.'

McCadden, diplomatically ushering the guard in front of him, accompanied Stevens to the front door.

'Can we offer you a lift? Or are you driving?'

'No thanks, no. The little Opel Corsa out there is mine. The order's, anyway. Goodnight then, Inspector...'

'Goodnight.'

When the door was closed again, the guard shook his head at McCadden's raised eyebrows.

'Nothing, sir,' he said. 'A pocket diary. Some loose change. A few sports medals.'

'Winners' ones, I hope.'

The guard smiled. 'One winner's, two runners-up.'

'Right. We'd better go back.'

Hayden, uncertain where to place himself at first, had finally decided on the armchair Stevens had just left. He didn't look at McCadden coming back in and he didn't seem interested in Donnelly as she rummaged around him. Obviously, McCadden thought, there was nothing concealed either on Brother Stevens or in the room itself to particularly worry him.

But Hayden's whole body was still tense with anxiety. He started at every slight noise that came from the others searching upstairs. When he heard the Alsatian barking, he lifted the poker and nervously broke coals in the fire. And as the door behind McCadden opened and Frank Ryan came in, he twisted sharply, with the poker still grasped in his hand. The expression on his face flashed from fear to hope before crumbling quickly into a despairing acceptance.

Ryan was wearing plastic gloves and carrying a small white drawstring bag. He placed the bag on the scuffed surface of the mahogany veneer table and loosened the string to display its contents. McCadden came across to peer inside.

'Ecstasy tablets,' Ryan explained. 'There must be two to three hundred of them in there, Carl. We found them in a waterproof bag in the tank in the attic.'

'Do you want to tell us how they got there, Tom?' McCadden invited.

Hayden desperately shook his head. 'I don't know anything about them. That's the first time I ever laid eyes on them. You must've brought them in yourselves.'

'With that quantity, you're looking at possession for the purposes of supply. And a long stretch in prison.'

'I was holding them for a friend. I didn't know what was in that bag.'

'Come on, Tom,' McCadden pleaded. 'We know that the boy brought them in.'

'Hah?'

'Can't you see that the truth is your best bet? I'll even give you your defence. *I didn't know what to do with them, your Honour. I was frightened for my son's safety.*'

'I don't want the boy getting in trouble. He don't know anything about it.'

'Nicholas stole them from Ronnie Harris last Thursday week, didn't he?'

'He didn't steal them. Harris was after losing them anyway.'

'Whatever. Nicholas picked them up and ran straight

home with them, leaving the other lads to do the fool's work of slowing the blind man. He was in such a hurry that he got a clout from Bill Toppin after knocking down a woman. You patted him on the head, didn't you, Tom? You gave him a few pounds as a reward after patching up his injuries. He spent the money on cider, by the way. But what happened? Did your wife see the boy's bruises the next day?'

'The little fool dragged off his T-shirt right in front of her.'

'But you pulled her off hassling Toppin for fear of attracting too much attention and too many questions,' McCadden guessed. He sighed and gestured at the bag. 'Have you sold on any of these yet?'

'Naw. They're up there where you found them since they came into the house.'

'Does your wife know about them?'

'What do you think?'

'No. I don't imagine she does. When was the last time you were in trouble, Tom?'

'When was the last time I bought anything for the house, hah? Why don't you ask me that, McCadden? Look around you. When was the last time I bought anything more than food for the wife and kids? Because that was the last time I was in trouble, too.'

'If I was you, Tom, I'd give some thought to how the boy so easily recognized the tablets and so quickly saw his opportunity. I think he was watching Harris. I think he set up the snatch. I'd give some thought to that. And I'd worry about it.'

'What else is there for him, McCadden? Tell me that. He's not much good at school. And nobody wants him to be there, anyway. He'll be gone as soon as he's old enough. Stevens says he's all right at the hurling. But I was good at hurling. What did it ever do for me? Where's he going to get a job? What else is there for him? Tell me that!'

'I can't control the programming on the television stations, Tom,' McCadden said enigmatically. 'I can only turn the set off in my own house.'

He shrugged, gestured to Ryan and Donnelly and had gone back into the hallway before Hayden could work out a response.

In the company of the others, he allowed the disappointment to show on his face. He'd hoped for a lead to Jason Whittle, some connection between the drugs and the boy's disappearance. But it hadn't developed.

'Rose,' he said. 'Are you going off-duty?'

'No, I'm okay for a while, sir.'

'Right. When we get back to the station, I want you to co-ordinate and update all the reports on Jason Whittle. We're going to have to take a new line. I'll be in the Carnival Inn around nine. Can I see you there?'

'Yes, sir.'

Ryan held up the bag of tablets he'd taken with him. 'And these?'

'There's a section of the woods where Harris may have stored some more. No point trying to do anything about it now, in darkness. You can check it out tomorrow.'

'What's a blind man doing hiding drugs?'

'Who knows?'

'Are we charging Hayden?'

'With what, Frank? Stupidity?'

'For possession.'

McCadden shook his head and went back into the

183

front room after answering Ryan. He needed to repeat the response to Hayden himself. He said, 'They're gone, Tom. Your kid found them and brought them home. You didn't know what to do with them and you were scared. But after a long struggle, you told us. Now they're gone.'

Hayden stared at him suspiciously. 'I'm not doing any of your dirty work for you, McCadden. Not in return for this. You can put me in jail instead.'

'I don't want any payback, Tom...'

twenty-one

Orla Stanley was still sitting in one of the gloomy booths at the Carnival Inn. It was nine fifteen by then. And McCadden was more than an hour late. Left alone, with no one to talk to and nothing to do but ignore the blatant curiosity of others, she was now bored and resentful.

McCadden rushed in with apologies and explanations. 'I'm sorry. We had to serve a search warrant. I got delayed...'

What could she do? She couldn't afford to be peevish enough to complain immediately about the demands of his job. So she waited, looking for a better opening for her irritation.

McCadden ordered drinks. A pint of Guinness for himself, a gin and tonic for her. They chatted stiffly about neutral news. Every topic brought a minute or two of dull pleasantries before hitting another awkward silence. Neither could animate the conversation. McCadden was tired and dispirited. His mind was elsewhere, on more important failures. She was too irritated.

'So,' she asked finally. 'Did you find anything?'
'What?'

'What were you searching for? With the warrant. Drugs?'

'Oh, anything, really.'

'Anything?' she repeated. 'Early Christmas presents? Pictures of U2's last concert?'

'Anything illegal.'

'Had it something to do with this boy who's gone missing?'

'I can't really discuss that, Orla.'

'That was the boy's father who broke his wrist out at the hospital last Thursday, wasn't it? Joseph Whittle. Or can't you discuss that, either?'

'Not really, no.'

'I see. It's like that, is it?'

'No, it's not like that, if what you mean is—'

'You get here more than an hour late.'

'I told you, it wasn't my fault.'

'You didn't even ring to let me know. And when you *are* here, you can't even talk like an ordinary person.'

McCadden looked at her miserably, reminded again of his estranged wife. Ex-wife, he corrected himself. There were no physical similarities between the two women, and their personalities were sharply different. But the situation being created here had too many painful echoes for him. He knew exactly the ruts along which the argument, and ultimately the relationship, would run. And flounder.

He said, 'Maybe we should leave it for another night, Orla. It's just—'

She stood up immediately, before he was finished. Awkwardly holding her body to the shape of the curved space between the table and the seat, she worked her way out of the booth. 'I get it,' she said.

'No, you don't.'

'Do you think I'm blind or something?'

'Don't be stupid, Orla.'

'The stupid thing was waiting here for you in the first place.'

She turned and walked briskly away. She didn't look back. And McCadden made no effort to stop her. He didn't really have the energy. And he wondered if he had the interest.

Besides, he saw Rose Donnelly rising from a group of detectives in another booth and heading towards him to take the nurse's place.

'I assume you're free, sir?' Donnelly asked when she reached him.

He looked at her balefully. Usually, he complained that she was too deferential, too short on the self-confidence that her abilities and personality entitled her to. Usually, he would've been delighted to find her so mischievous and so chirpy. But not right now.

'Sit down, Rose,' he said wearily.

She put the drink she'd brought with her on the table and slid in along the imitation leather seat.

'Got anything?' he asked without hope.

She shook her head. 'Very little, sir. At this stage we've tried all the relatives and all the friends where Jason Whittle might've taken refuge. The hostels and guest houses in the city have all been circularized. People who might've spotted him leaving the city have been questioned. All blanks.'

'It was always a long shot, anyway. That he'd run away.'

'We've got one small lead on tracing his movements Tuesday night. There were very few children out playing on the street at the time, because of the kidnapping of Luke Brady. But a group of older teenagers saw Jason in the row in front of his own, apparently on his way to leaving the estate, around nine o'clock that night. That's the only sighting so far.'

'Has someone interviewed John Ryle?'

'Mr Ryle maintains that he was alone in his home all Tuesday evening.'

'Alone?' McCadden repeated. 'Where was his wife?'

'Visiting a friend.'

'Is that corroborated by a separate interview with her?'

'No. It's Mr Ryle's account.'

'Did she have the car?'

'She's injured, sir. She can't drive.'

'Yes, that's right. Did Ryle drive her or did her friend collect her?'

'She walked to get the bus.'

'She walked to get the bus,' McCadden repeated thoughtfully. 'So what was keeping Ryle so unhelpfully at home while his injured wife walked to get the bus?'

Donnelly shrugged. 'Did you know that Mr Ryle was once a Christian Brother, sir?' she asked.

'He was in their seminary, Rose, but he was never ordained. Why?'

'I was just checking something before I came out. You see, we agreed that I'd look at child abuse cases locally. But Ryle lived in Cork. And it occurred to me ... Do you remember the case of Timmy Line? He was twelve or thirteen as well, and he disappeared without a trace.'

'That was about ten years ago, Rose.'

'But it was in Cork city. And Ryle was living in Cork at the time.'

McCadden frowned. 'Have you followed this through?'

'No, it's just a thought. I haven't had time to check it. It just came back to me a little while ago. I was just after joining the force when it happened, you see.'

'You'd better do it in the morning, then.'

'Yes, sir. Oh, and talking about the morning, the Chief Superintendent wants to see you then.'

'About what?'

'Overtime applications, I think.'

'Right.'

'And have you talked to Harris and Cooney yet, sir?'

McCadden shook his head. 'No. No time.'

'They're being remanded in court locally in the morning and being transferred to prison in Dublin some time in the afternoon. If you want to get to them before that.'

'Maybe. I don't think so. I'll probably leave it to Frank.' He shook the last of his Guinness in the base of his glass. 'Fancy another drink, Rose?'

Something had undoubtedly happened in her personal life, he thought. Something positive. Uplifting, even. Other times, she would've pleaded the needs of her child at home. Now she stood up, smiling, and insisted on buying the round herself.

McCadden sighed.

He stared for a while at the beer mat under his glass, but then gave up trying to read the joke that was printed on it and went back to thinking about Ryle, the Christian Brothers and the education of working class boys. When a fresh pint was placed in front of him, he glanced up again and said, 'Rose, when you're . . .'

But it was Orla Stanley who was slipping back into the seat opposite him.

She had a wry, apologetic expression on her face, a look admitting that the effort was against her better judgement, but that she couldn't help herself.

'I met a sergeant,' she said enigmatically. 'I told you sergeants were less retentive.'

McCadden frowned.

'Frank?' she prompted.

'Frank Ryan?'

'That's it. He stopped me on the way out. He told me you'd been knocked on the head and suggested I should make allowances since you were even weirder than usual because of it.'

McCadden smiled. 'Frank,' he said affectionately.

She laughed. But she was still a little tense, still a little uncertain. She hadn't fully shaken off the earlier irritation. Her right hand held her drink too tightly. The other, lying on the surface of the table, was slightly clenched to make a fist.

McCadden reached across and covered it with his own right hand. Under his palm, he felt her slowly relaxing. And responding.

'You were right,' he said gently. 'I should've rung here to let you know I'd be late instead of leaving you dangling. My fault. I'm sorry.'

twenty-two

McCadden wasn't on duty the following morning.

A little after eight fifteen, he was lying on his back in the bed, his hands joined behind his head, his neck pillowed by his palms. He stared for a while at a pattern on the ceiling above him, worried it was dampness, but finally realizing that it was only a spider's web.

'No,' he said drowsily then. 'I'm going to stay on, get some rest, maybe have breakfast in Bewley's . . .'

He waited for a response. When none came, he glanced sideways. Orla Stanley was also lying on her back beside him. But she wasn't looking at him. Her eyes were closed. Her breathing was soft and regular. And she was obviously still asleep.

As he watched her, she frowned suddenly. Her lips moved urgently and she said, quite distinctly, 'There's no point even *shouting* before the shellfish, really.'

She talked in her sleep, he realized. And her earlier question about getting up hadn't been addressed to him at all, but to some odder figure from one of her dreams.

The trouble was, McCadden, attentive as ever, had woken fully to deal with it, expecting her to be lively as well. And he was too alert now to slip easily back into dozing again. He tried to mould himself against her for more comfort. But she held to an unyielding posture, as if she was doggedly defending a space. So he finally sighed, moved away from her again and swung out of bed.

He dressed, went downstairs and left the flat to buy the morning newspaper and freshly baked bread rolls in his local shop. When he came back he made coffee and bacon in the kitchen and had breakfast alone in front of the television, slightly exasperated that she was able to sleep so solidly through the sounds and the smells of his cooking. But still, he humoured himself, it was only pleasurable irritation, which was a different world from the bleakness of arguing with himself.

But his good form lasted only until the news programme he was watching on television carried a report on the disappearance of Jason Whittle.

The item delivered a bland, formulaic interview with Chief Superintendent Cody, and then seemed to deliberately contrast this with an emotional, wrenching appeal from Joey and Corina Whittle at a press conference the couple had given the day before. Perhaps the public display of feelings helped the Whittles to cope, McCadden conceded. But he doubted it. Or perhaps the higher profile would lure into the open some witness the investigation hadn't already reached. But he doubted that, too.

The whole feature, he thought, plucked quite cynically at instincts that couldn't avoid responding. Here, under the illuminating television lights, was the devastated family, distraught father hugging bereft mother. And somewhere out there, in the darkness beyond the studio, lurked the monster who might strike again. It was a fairy tale. As frightening and as imaginative as the stories people had always told each other. The only difference was, like everything else on television, it had no moral, no resolution, and it was told only as a warped form of entertainment. Even worse, it kept gasping loudly in horror at the grotesqueness of its own reflection.

McCadden, following his own advice to Tom Hayden the night before, switched off the set and settled down to finishing his coffee in comfort.

But the telephone rang.

With the coffee mug still held in his right hand, he left the small kitchen, picked up the receiver in the living room outside and walked with it to look out the front window over Manor Street as he answered.

It was the Chief Superintendent on the other end of the line. 'Good morning, Inspector,' he greeted crisply.

McCadden was wary, wondering if Toppin had already been in touch to add to his complaints. 'Morning,' he responded.

'I arrived in my office some time ago,' Cody confided, 'more than ever convinced of the wisdom of putting Jason Whittle's father under covert surveillance.'

It wasn't Toppin, McCadden realized. It was just Cody himself, trying too hard to make up for his own mistakes. 'I'm not sure that's going to be a cost-efficient use of manpo—'

'I've already done it.'

'Right.'

'And it has instantly borne fruit.'

The biblical imagery deflected McCadden for a moment. He couldn't manage a response.

'You'll be interested to know, Inspector, that five minutes ago, John Ryle left home with his wife, driving their white Honda Civic, and that they were immediately followed by Mr Whittle, in a red Nissan Sunny driven by an acquaintance.'

'But wouldn't that seem to indicate that Joey Whittle has lingering suspicions about Ryle, rather than that he himself is implicated?'

'We'll see.'

'Who's tailing them?'

'Sergeant de Burgh is on surveillance duty.'

'Where are they now?'

'Outside your front door.'

'Eh?'

Another man might've enjoyed the situation. Cody only frostily expanded on the information. 'They've all just pulled up outside a florist on Manor Street. I'm sure if you look out your front windows you'll be able to see them.'

McCadden craned to get a better view of the flower shop on his left. Actually, he saw, only the Ryles' white Honda, with Ryle himself at the wheel and the car otherwise empty, was parked in the bay outside the florist. Liam de Burgh was in a Ford Mondeo in a recessed bus stop behind, only a couple of doors down from the flat.

McCadden said quickly, 'I'm going to join Liam.'

'Yes,' Cody agreed crisply. 'Quite.'

McCadden's efforts to view the street below had overstretched the flex and left the telephone cradle rocking on the edge of the table behind him. He got back just in time to save it from falling. Leaving the unfinished mug of coffee on the table beside it, he bounded up the stairs to the loft and approached the bed.

Orla Stanley was still lying on her back. And still asleep. He shook her by the shoulder and called her name. She only moaned at him angrily and twisted her head away.

She was wearing a white T-shirt that had a coloured map of the world printed on its front. He took America and Asia between his fingers and gently brought them closer. It woke her instantly.

'Hey!' she snapped. Before recognizing his face, recalling the events of the night before and remembering where she was. But her smile didn't last very long, either.

'I've got to go out,' he told her.

'What time is it?'

'Past nine. Something's happening in the case. I'll contact you later.'

'Yeah, that's okay.'

She was already turning over, back into sleep, before he started descending the stairs. In the living room, he grabbed his leather jacket from the coat rack and went out, hurrying down the three flights of stairs and then along the ground floor hall to the front door. On the footpath outside, he kept his face lowered and concealed. He slipped into the front passenger seat of the Mondeo beside de Burgh, a small, compact man with a talent for steadiness that McCadden found astonishing.

'Where's Whittle?' he asked immediately.

'How are you doing, Carl?' de Burgh greeted him. As if that was more important.

'Fine, fine.'

'I haven't seen you for a while.'

'I'm fine, Liam. Where's Whittle?'

'They drove past and turned up the side road on the left. I suppose they're waiting there until the others move again.'

'What are they up to?'

'They're following the Ryles.'

'I know that, Liam. *Why* are they following them?'

De Burgh shrugged. He wasn't a man to guess when the answer wasn't obvious.

McCadden waited.

Five minutes later, when Miriam Ryle came from the florist, she held a mixed bunch of long-stemmed flowers awkwardly cradled in her left arm. The other arm, of course, was still strapped up and out of commission. The shop assistant held the door for her and then rushed across the footpath to open the car door as well. Miriam Ryle sat in without releasing the flowers, in obvious difficulty and considerable pain.

The little drama was interesting to McCadden. The devoted husband, he thought, would at least have worried about the flowers being crushed.

Ryle pulled quickly into the light traffic, before his wife had time to settle or to fix her seat belt.

A few seconds after the Honda had passed the junction, the red Nissan Sunny edged its nose out to follow. In the front passenger seat, Joey Whittle seemed to have gone to extraordinary lengths to tuck himself out of sight, underneath the dashboard and the windscreen. The only drawback to the subterfuge was that his plaster cast, jutting stiffly upwards, was now just as recognizable as his face.

McCadden had a clearer view of the driver. He was a worried, middle-aged man with thick untidy hair and a heavy moustache. A man McCadden had last seen chasing John Ryle through the grounds of the Regional Hospital the previous Thursday.

Ryle turned right at the next junction and drove up Johnstown and St John's Hill before parking outside a three-storey, bay-window house opposite the grounds of St John's College. Again he stayed sullenly in the car while his wife struggled out, handicapped by her flowers and her dislocated shoulder. He didn't even lean across to help her close the door. And as soon as she turned to approach the house to ring the door bell, he pulled away without waiting to see if she was admitted or stranded.

And the suddenness of his move caught everyone else by surprise.

'Do you want me to stay with the woman?' de Burgh offered.

'Let's see what Whittle is doing first,' McCadden suggested.

But Whittle had no interest in the woman. The red Nissan Sunny immediately followed Ryle.

'Okay, Liam,' McCadden said. 'I'll take the car. You stay here with Mrs Ryle. I'll be back in touch later.'

John Ryle only drove back home after dropping his wife, however. He went by the shortest route. Without stopping. And apparently without realizing that he was tailed.

At the turn-off to the estate, McCadden was slowed by oncoming traffic. By the time he reached the fourth row, the now empty Honda Civic was already parked outside Ryle's home and the red Nissan had pulled in tight behind it. Only the driver was still sitting in the Sunny.

McCadden slipped past and walked back after parking.

Wanting to keep an eye on the houses as well, he crossed in front of the Nissan's bonnet and tapped the glass on the front passenger window. The driver looked uncomfortably across at him and nervously licked his moustache with the tip of his tongue. McCadden knocked again on the glass. This time the other leaned over and wound the window down.

McCadden stooped to talk. 'You remember me?' he wondered.

'I do,' the driver said anxiously. 'I think, anyway. Yeah.'

'That's a relief,' McCadden told him. 'I was starting to doubt it myself. Who am I?'

'You're, ah, the Garda inspector. McCadden.'

'Right. Where's Joey Whittle gone?'

'Joey? He's gone into his own house.'

'I should've mentioned by the way. If you give me wrong information and something happens, you're an accessory. Do you understand?'

'I told you. He's gone into his own house.'

'Then why are you sitting up here instead of down outside *his* door?'

'I, ah, kind of overshot.'

'Stay there a while. I'm going to call at John Ryle's house. If I find—'

'He's gone round the back.'

'What?'

'Joey. He's gone round the back through the gardens.'

'After Ryle.'

'Yeah.'

'Have a little sense,' McCadden suggested then as he stood up. 'And go on home.'

He heard the car starting up behind him and

manoeuvring slowly out of the small space as he walked through the front garden of Ryle's next door neighbour and rang the bell. The woman who answered looked at him wearily, without surprise, and had obviously been watching him from behind her curtains.

'Mrs Long,' he greeted her. 'You might remember me from last week. I'm Inspector McCadden.'

'I know you, all right.'

'We have reason to believe that there may be an intruder in your ever popular back garden. Would it be possible for me to go through and check?'

'Oh, go on,' she sighed. 'Although I'm getting sick and tired of all this.'

'It's in a good cause,' he assured her. 'Believe me.'

Mrs Long had just hung her washing on the line in the back garden and no one had yet blundered through to spoil her whites. Standing by the dividing wall, McCadden could hear John Ryle humming to himself as he watered the shrubs and plants in the layered garden next door.

Ryle himself, it seemed, was therefore the fastidious gardener. Just as he was the amateur photographer. And the computer buff...

From beyond the line of washing, a low grunting broke through McCadden's thoughts as Whittle struggled to clamber over a wall. Obviously, the man had forgotten how awkwardly he was lumbered with the plaster cast. Finally, though, his head punched through the gap between two white sheets. He then stopped dead when he saw McCadden, with the sheets still draped in front of him, like the flowing contours of a clerical robe.

McCadden put his finger across his lips for silence

199

and gestured behind him with the other hand as he walked across.

'Get out of the fucking way, McCadden!' Whittle hissed at him when they met.

McCadden shook his head. 'You're already on parole with me, Joey,' he reminded him. 'No more favours. If you go past me now, it's assault on a Garda. If you get into the next garden, it's breaking and entering and—'

'And if I get my hands on Ryle, it'll be fucking murder!' Whittle predicted.

'Touché,' McCadden accepted.

'Hah?'

'You have a point.'

'Then get out of the fucking way!'

McCadden gently took him by the arm. 'Come inside, Joey. I need to talk to you.'

Mrs Long was already waiting for them in the kitchen, after watching their dispute through her open back door. 'Are you all right, Joey?' she asked Whittle anxiously.

'I'm sorry about all this, Betty—'

'Don't mind about that. Are you all right?'

'I'm okay, yeah.'

After that she went back out to finish hanging her washing and left them alone.

'I can guess at your feelings, Joey,' McCadden told him. 'I can't say I understand them or anything like that. But I can guess. I have an idea of your frustration and your lack of confidence in the guards. But I did think that you were happy enough that John Ryle might be out of the picture.'

Whittle desperately, violently shook his head. 'He's up to something, McCadden!'

'How?'

'He's got Jason! I know it in me bones!'

'What's he up to, Joey?'

'He's acting queer all day yesterday. I was watching him. He wouldn't stir outside the door once his wife was in there. She's not in work because of her shoulder. Once she's gone, though, he's out of the place.'

'He's there now. She isn't.'

'How do you know?'

'I heard him in his back garden.'

'How do you know he's not gone again?'

'Well...'

'One time yesterday he even pretended to go off, but then he hung around the main road outside and came back when she was gone and set off himself again. I wasn't able to follow him. I didn't have a car organized yesterday. But he's up to something he don't want her to know about.'

'Why should it be Jason?'

'Because he brings food with him. Every time he goes out, he has a bag of food and drinks with him. Ask Mrs Long there. She's kept an eye on him for me, too. Why have the food if he wasn't bringing it to someone?'

'It's a reasonable question, Joey.'

'Fucking right it is.'

'But how did you expect to get the answer from him?'

Whittle made a fist and beat it against the unyielding plaster cast. 'Like that! That's how!'

'Too risky, Joey,' McCadden cautioned. 'Too risky if you're wrong. You'll end up being convicted of assault. And much too risky if you're right. You might never find where Jason is.'

'So what the fuck are you going to do about it, McCadden?'

twenty-three

As it happened, apart from sending Whittle home and moving the Mondeo to a less obvious spot, McCadden chose to do nothing until twelve fifteen, because John Ryle himself stayed innocently at home until then.

The wait was almost two hours. During it, McCadden reported to the station, caught another lecture from the Chief Superintendent, but failed to raise Liam de Burgh, and then passed the rest of the time sinking a little deeper into boredom. There were no books or newspapers in the car.

When Ryle eventually left the house, it was without caution, without concealment, and without the fear of being watched. His mood seemed more morose than furtive. His posture was slumped and he kept his head down as he walked. His movements were slow and almost reluctant. As Whittle had predicted, he carried a food parcel with him to the white Honda Civic.

Putting the bag on the front passenger seat after sitting into the car, he strapped himself in and pulled away with only a casual glance in his rear-view mirror. At first he followed the same route he'd taken earlier that morning. But instead of finishing the return journey to pick up his injured wife, he parked almost immediately after turning into Johnstown. For a long time afterwards he sat stiffly in the car, staring vacantly through the windscreen. When a traveller couple came to beg at his side window, he either ignored the pair or failed to notice them.

It was almost one o'clock before he finally got out and walked back towards the junction of Manor Street and Johnstown. Again the traveller couple accosted him on the footpath. He stopped, baffled by their appearance, and then thrust the food parcel he was carrying into the man's outstretched hands before walking on. He turned right along Parnell Street and climbed the steps of one of the street's tall eighteenth-century buildings that was now being used as a budget hotel.

Behind him, McCadden waited a few minutes, entertained by the enraged cursing of the couple who had no use for the food they'd received. When Ryle didn't reappear, he jauntily took the steps himself and breezed inside, as if he was on other, more enjoyable business.

The narrow lobby was deserted. To his left, the reception had an enclosed counter and an open perspex hatch that was reminiscent of the government's public desks. A door at the back presumably led to an office beyond.

McCadden pressed the button that was mounted on the hatch's wooden frame. But even before the buzzer sounded, the shadow of a stocky man appeared behind the frosted glass of the office door. Distracted by a loud knocking on one of the upstairs doors, McCadden glanced behind and when he turned quickly back to question the clerk found himself staring into the stolid features of Sergeant Liam de Burgh behind the counter.

'The mirror there,' de Burgh explained, pointing

over his shoulder. 'It's two-way. I could see you from inside.'

Again, as if *that* was the really surprising thing.

'Right,' McCadden said. 'You haven't changed careers since early morning, have you, Liam?'

De Burgh solemnly shook his head. 'No, no. You see, it's just that I . . .'

But McCadden had already guessed. De Burgh was following Miriam Ryle. And Miriam Ryle, therefore, must also be in the hotel.

From upstairs, after more loud knocking on one of the doors, came immediate confirmation of his guess.

A woman's voice called sharply from within a locked room. 'What is it?'

'Open the door,' a man commanded.

'Who is it? Who's there?'

'It's John, Miriam.'

'What?'

'It's John.'

'Jesus Christ . . .'

'Open the door, Miriam. I have to talk to you.'

McCadden gestured. De Burgh raised the counter at the hatch. And they both went through to the office behind.

A sweating fat man sat at a round mahogany table over a ruined lunch of chips and sausages that had congealed from neglect. Beside the plate, held down by a thin teaspoon, there was fifty pounds in ten-pound notes.

'This is Tip Tooley,' de Burgh made the introductions. 'Inspector McCadden. Tip is the receptionist here.'

'How are you keeping, Tip?' McCadden enquired.

Tooley smiled painfully, leaving the answer uncertain.

McCadden gestured at the money. 'Did you get this from the man who came in here a few minutes ago?'

Tooley laughed miserably and nodded.

'Not for a room, though, was it, Liam?' McCadden asked de Burgh.

De Burgh shook his head. 'It wasn't heading for the till, anyway.'

'So what are you into, Tip?' McCadden wondered. 'A little extortion?'

Tooley paled and trembled. 'Ah, no, no. Nothing like that...'

'Have you seen a boy around?'

'What?'

'I'm looking for a boy. Thirteen years of age. Black hair. Hooded grey sweat top and blue jeans. Have you seen him around?'

'No. I haven't, no.'

'So what's the story, Tip? As crude and as fast as you can make it.'

Tooley swallowed. 'Mr Ryle found out his wife was using here and—'

'How?'

'Hah?'

'How did he find out?'

Tooley again looked pained. 'She used to teach me, you see...'

'She used to teach you,' McCadden repeated. 'So you recognized her and thought you'd coin a little extra silver with a bit of blackmail.'

'I just gave Mr Ryle the information, that's all. I didn't ask him for anything.'

'Did you ring him a while ago?'

'I did, yeah.'

De Burgh, who'd been keeping watch through the two-way mirror, called back quietly. McCadden walked across. Through the open frame of the hatch he saw John and Miriam Ryle reach the end of the stairs. Ryle's hand was on his wife's arm. She was struggling to shake him off. The expression on the husband's face was as dull and abstracted as before. But she was fighting to control her fury. Her clothes, McCadden noticed, were all in a fairly decent state. Neat. Uncreased. Revealing nothing. It was her sling that was in disarray and that betrayed her.

The food, McCadden realized then. It was Ryle's own lunch. While he sat in the car, waiting for his wife and her lover to finish, he brought a packed lunch to keep his strength up.

'What room were they in?'

'Twenty-four.'

McCadden and de Burgh climbed the narrow stairs after the couple had left. The door to number twenty-four was still ajar. Through the gap they could see that clothes were scattered on the faded purple carpet. Between the man's neatly placed shoes and his crumpled trousers, between his tidiness and his lust, lay the frilled pink panties that Miriam Ryle had left behind her.

McCadden pushed the door. And saw that the man still sitting on the edge of the unmade bed, naked except for his navy socks and his black-strapped watch, with his blond head sunk despairingly in his hands, was the familiar figure of George Ducy.

'Taking an early lunch, Mr Ducy?' McCadden asked innocently.

Ducy's head snapped upwards, his pride more hurt by the accusation of professional neglect, apparently, than by the compromise he found himself in. 'It's Thursday,' he reminded everyone mysteriously.

'So?'

'I have free periods either side of my lunch hour.'

'Right.'

McCadden and de Burgh stepped in. De Burgh closed the door behind them and stood guard beside it. McCadden strolled across to sit in the ragged wicker chair opposite Ducy.

'So your visit to Miriam Ryle in hospital last Saturday was more than the sympathy of one colleague for another,' McCadden probed.

Ducy shrugged. 'As you can see.'

'And her anxiety about her husband's absence the previous night was really ... what? Because she was frightened Ryle had already found out and abandoned her?'

'Something like that.'

'Why does she want a transfer to Cork then?'

'Miriam doesn't want to go back to Cork. That's just a story to explain her dissatisfaction.'

'Dissatisfaction with what?'

Ducy wearily shook his head, convinced at last that the caricature was accurate and that policemen really were irredeemably obtuse. 'Jesus!' he cried. 'You've met the guy. You've been in his house. I mean, what kind of lunatic would import designer styles into a poor working class housing estate? And this is what's wrong with him, you know. He's simply not in touch with the real world. He went into the seminary when he was fourteen or fifteen and never really shook off that sense of distance from the world that they're all afflicted with. It's unreal. The garden. The living room upstairs. Miriam is convinced his mind is fried from writing computer programmes.'

'And yet I'm told she poses for his photographs on a table.'

Ducy raised his head again. And the complex look in his eyes, half shameful and half triumphant, immediately revealed the truth.

'Ah!' McCadden realized. '*You* were taking the photographs!'

Ducy smirked a little. But only for a while. Because McCadden suddenly started into a suppressed laughter that he could neither release nor fully control.

Ducy watched him spluttering for a while and then said angrily, 'What's the joke? What is it? There's nothing to laugh at.'

'Ah, there is,' McCadden argued. 'You have to admit there is.'

As he shook helplessly with laughter, he thought of the lovers entertaining themselves with the husband's sophisticated but lethally faithful equipment. He thought of the absurd difficulties Miriam Ryle must have suffered while dressing herself again after tumbling nude from the table and breaking her collar-bone. And he thought of himself and de Burgh stalking the kidnapper of a young boy and managing to flush only a pair of furtive lovers from the heather.

A cul-de-sac, he accepted. Blocked off with farce instead of concrete at the end.

twenty-four

Sitting in the front room of the Whittles' home a little later that afternoon, McCadden wondered if the explanation of John Ryle's packed lunches and unusual movements was good or bad news for the family of the missing boy.

He didn't try to embroider or delay the truth. He said simply, 'John Ryle has nothing to do with your son's disappearance. My own opinion is that Ryle and Jason haven't seen each other for at least a fortnight.'

Both Joey and Corina Whittle were in the room with him. They sat apart, without a point of contact. Instead of bringing them together, the loss had driven a broader wedge between them. They blamed each other for the tragedy.

'What about the way he's been acting the past day or two?' Whittle demanded.

'He has his own problems, Joey,' McCadden told him. 'Nothing to do with Jason.'

'What about the photographs Jason was talking about?'

'We were invited to search his home by Ryle himself. I've just come from there. We found nothing incriminating.'

'That doesn't mean anything.'

'I don't think he's involved, Joey. There was a friendship between the two of them. But that's all there was.'

'So what are you saying?'

'I'm not in a position to say anything at the moment.'

'Are you saying you think that Jason just ran away? Is that it?'

'It's a possibility, Joey. Since you asked me, I have to say that I don't think so; but it's still a possibility. Could I ask a favour?'

'What?'

'I know other officers have been there already, but could I have a look at Jason's room?'

Corina Whittle laughed sarcastically. 'His room,' she sneered.

'I mean, where he slept, where he kept his personal things.'

'Come on,' Whittle invited.

Once they were upstairs, McCadden understood the mother's battered derision. The small bedroom slept four of the older boys. Jason and Joe, the next in line, each had a separate bed. The other two shared.

The room smelled badly, of old socks and unwashed clothes and bodies. The windows had been more recently painted than opened. The gloss paint from the last coating was still unbroken between frame and sash. Three-quarters of the wall space was crowded with Manchester United posters, stuck to the fading wallpaper with grubby Sellotape. The corner where the walls were bare was also the corner where Jason had slept.

Another deliberate gesture of rejection towards his old man, McCadden thought. And maybe a conscious separation from the more childish interests and attachments of his brothers.

Only one of the other boys was in the room at the time. Although he was named after his father, Joe took his appearance from his mother. Wispy fair hair and thin features and a small frame. He was curled on the bed, leafing through an album of soccer stickers. When he looked up as the others came in, there seemed to be a flicker of hope in his eyes, as if he was praying for news of his brother. It died, of course. Almost instantly.

What disappointed McCadden was the bareness of the room, the lack of any item of furniture, a locker or a chest of drawers, where Jason might've kept his personal possessions. There was a communal wardrobe with one of its doors hanging open and detached from the upper hinge. The boys' clothes hung along a rail inside. Their few toys were thrown haphazardly on the base.

'I realize you must be sick answering this one, Joey,' McCadden said, 'but is there anything left behind that Jason wouldn't usually go without, or anything he brought with him that he wouldn't always carry?'

The boy on the bed looked up again from his album and stared. His worried face *advertised* a knowledge he wasn't yet certain about sharing.

Whittle was saying, 'Look at all his clothes still hanging there in the wardrobe. Everything was left, the way it would be if he was just going out to play for a while. All his toys and stuff—'

'He took the medal,' the boy interrupted.

'What medal?' McCadden asked.

'Da's medal.'

'The Junior Cup winner's medal I got,' Joey explained.

'Remember we were talking about it in the hospital there last week. I told you I gave it to Jason. He's the eldest, so I reckoned . . .'

Jason, McCadden thought. A lad of many . . . Not confusions. Not contradictions, either. Both implied negative judgements. Complexities, he preferred. Jason respected only his father's authority in the house. And yet went out of his way to make it clear that he had no time for the man's most passionate interest. He refused any involvement in sport. And yet he carried his father's medal along with him. Although of course, his reasons for taking it that night were still just as clouded as his disappearance.

'Do you play yourself?' McCadden asked the boy on the bed.

'I play for Bohs Under-12.'

'He fancies himself as a bit of a striker,' Joey put in.

'I'm the leading goal scorer, I am.'

'Will you go away! The season's only started. Wait till the end.'

'I'll still be tops.'

'He thinks he's Eric Cantona, he do.'

'Oooh-aaahh . . .'

There was, McCadden saw, a genuine relationship between this boy and the father. Their bond was soccer. It was where they found their mutual respect. And both obviously felt that although the medal had been given to Jason, it morally belonged to Joe. He would've treasured it and in time tried to add to it with his own achievements.

'Are you certain Jason took it?' McCadden asked the boy.

'He kept it in his box in the wardrobe. It wasn't there

the night . . . the night he was gone. I searched everywhere. It's not around.'

'Have you tried under the bed?'

'Hah?'

'When I was a boy, I always kept my secrets between the mattress and the base.'

There were other reasons for McCadden's suggestion, but it would've been too insensitive to expand on them. In a house as untidy and neglected as this, there were certain areas where the dirt lay undisturbed. The floor around the beds might be cleaned occasionally. But under them would never be touched.

'Would you mind?' he asked Whittle.

But there was nothing at all between the mattress and the base, apart from a sweet wrapper so old that it was no longer even sticky.

There were no castors on the bed's legs any more, McCadden noticed. Walking to the head, he gestured Whittle towards the bottom. 'Could we lift it?'

The floor underneath was very dusty and covered with fluff and cobwebs. There was no medal among the dirt. There were two odd socks, some more sweet wrappers, a blue Lego brick, a small ball-bearing. And a book. *Alice's Adventures in Wonderland* and *Through the Looking-Glass*, by Lewis Carroll.

If it had been a children's edition or a standard edition of the classic, McCadden would've probably ignored it. But it wasn't either. It was an adult's edition, with a scholarly introduction and annotations, expanding on the author's complex puns and references. A Penguin paperback that McCadden himself had on his own shelves.

It had been slipped in there quite recently, he noticed.

Presumably to avoid the derision the boy would've attracted at home if it was spotted. Some fluff had adhered to its cover and its spine, but the book had none of the ingrained dirt that the other items under the bed were marked with.

McCadden picked it up and gently brushed it off. And as he held it and looked at Tenniel's illustration of Alice on the cover, he felt that tingling on the back of his neck and along the muscles of his shoulders that warned him of a buried significance his mind hadn't yet understood, although his instinct sensed the closeness of it.

He puzzled over it in silence for a while. Opening the book on its title page, he read the owner's signature and the date of purchase. *J. Ryle, Aug 1987.*

And so he thought he'd cracked it as he called Whittle back outside the bedroom, beyond the boy's hearing, and said excitedly, 'Remember Jason screaming about the photographs? Can you remember exactly what he said? How he said it? This is important. Did he say directly, *Ryle was taking photographs of me naked*? Or did he say, *Ryle something something*, and then quite separately, something about taking photographs of naked children?'

Whittle looked at him. And as he slowly absorbed and disentangled the questions, it was possible to read the answer in his eyes. 'Why?'

'Why?' McCadden repeated.

Because the author of *Alice in Wonderland*, with the permission of the relevant parents, had made a pleasurable, and perhaps an aesthetic pastime of photographing pre-pubescent girls in the nude. Because Jason, knowing that the association would suggest all the wrong things in the minds of the ill-informed, had taken the trouble to hide the otherwise innocent book to protect his friend and mentor, John Ryle. Because, waking up in Ryle's house with no clear memory of what had happened to him after crashing out on cider, Jason himself had feared that Ryle had taken advantage of him. Because, never admitting his suspicions to anyone but Luke Brady, the suppressed fears had exploded under stress the following week.

Because, because . . .

He thought he'd cracked it, with all his becauses. And yet the sensation of pins and needles along his shoulder blades still persisted and the sense of something deeper and something darker still niggled at his brain as he paged absently through the book in his hands.

Until Whittle, staring at him with bewilderment, said in a frightened voice, 'Are you all right?'

And McCadden started. 'What?'

'You look like you're having a heart attack or something.'

'I do?'

'You'd better stay on your feet, McCadden. We'll never get Jason back.'

McCadden nodded. 'Right.' He moved away. And came back again. A little disorientated. 'Joey,' he said, 'I'll keep in touch, okay?'

Whittle frowned again. 'Are you on to something?'

'Don't raise your hopes, Joey,' McCadden cautioned. 'I'll do my best.'

Still holding the book, he walked the fifty yards or so from the Whittles' to the Ryles'. John Ryle opened the door to him. The man looked downcast. And limp. And almost beaten.

'Would it be convenient to have a word with you?' McCadden asked.

'Yes, yes...'

Ryle led him into the front room, where the shelves were barer now than they had been. The books doused in petrol by the local vigilantes had obviously been lost and not replaced.

Not the only things, of course.

'Is your wife at home, Mr Ryle?'

'No, no... She's on sick leave, you see. Because of the injury. But right at the moment she's... out...'

McCadden offered the book. 'This is one of yours, isn't it?'

Ryle had already noticed the volume in McCadden's hands and his response was immediate. 'Yes. Jason Whittle borrowed it a few weeks ago. Like you said yourself, my library is an adult's. I think he found it interesting.'

'You know that Jason blurted something to his parents about you photographing him?'

'Yes, you told me that.'

'Didn't it occur to you, Mr Ryle, that some people might draw a simple straight line between the pastime of the author of *Alice in Wonderland* and your own recreation?'

Ryle nodded sorrowfully. 'Yes, I can understand that now.'

'But the mind doesn't work in straight lines, does it, Mr Ryle? It refracts, and twists, and goes off at tangents. We know that from dreams. Because it wasn't just the practice of photographing naked children that was deeply disturbing Jason Whittle.'

'No?'

'No. It was also the *profession* of the author of *Alice in Wonderland*. Lewis Carroll was a pseudonym. The man's real name was Charles Lutwidge Dodgson. The *Reverend* Charles Lutwidge Dodgson.'

Ryle stared. 'I'm not sure I really understand you now, Inspector.'

'You never told me that you joined the Christian Brothers as a boy, Mr Ryle.'

Ryle hung his head, but only ruefully. 'No. Perhaps it's something I'm not comfortable with. I mean, my failure to stay in there, not my decision to join.'

'You retain an affection for the order and its ideals, don't you?'

'Of course, yes.'

'And a certain loyalty to its members?'

'Loyalty? What does that mean?'

'I think that there are other things you've kept from me.'

'Such as?'

'Two weeks ago, Mr Ryle, when Jason Whittle stumbled in here drunk, looking for refuge, he talked to you before losing consciousness, didn't he? Rambling, maybe. Slurred. Disjointed. Mostly incoherent. But he talked to you. Unguardedly. Openly. Did he mention anything about a cleric?'

Ryle sighed. 'I do think, in the present climate, because of the well-publicized misdemeanours of a few rogue clerics, that the tendency to point the finger at every religious when the possibility of abuse is raised, is nothing short of reprehensible.'

'Did he mention anything about a cleric?'

'I got the impression that one of the Christian Brothers at the school was troublesome to him, yes.'

'Which one?'

'I have no idea, Inspector. When I asked him the same question, he laughed and reminded me that I was once one of them as well. Then he fell asleep. And the association and accusation obviously lodged in his mind, because when he woke again all he wanted to do was escape from me. At which point he phoned Luke Brady and waited for him outside.'

'Right...'

'You see how it goes, Inspector,' Ryle added bitterly. 'If you are now or were ever a Christian Brother, you must automatically be a sadistic brute. People conveniently forget the great service the order did this country in darker times. A partial view you yourself apparently share.'

'You should've criticized me a week earlier, Mr Ryle,' McCadden remarked. 'I think you might've saved a lot of trouble and a lot of suffering.'

twenty-five

From the car, still parked outside Whittle's house, McCadden called through to the station and then impatiently drummed his fingers on the steering wheel while waiting for the switch to put him on to Frank Ryan.

He glanced at his watch. It was two fifteen. In retrospect, he wondered why the boy, Joe Whittle, was still at home and not in school today . . .

Frank Ryan's booming voice on the radio interrupted his thoughts. 'Where are you, Carl? Rose Donnelly's been searching desperately for you the last hour.'

'I'll be in shortly, Frank. This is important. Have Harris and Cooney gone yet?'

'They left about half an hour ago.'

'Shit!' McCadden swore.

'They'll be back, though.'

'How do you mean, back?'

'They're only gone to court for remand.'

'Sorry, I misunderstood. I thought they'd been taken to Dublin. Are they applying for bail?'

'They're applying, but they won't make it. We're opposing on the obvious grounds of endangering the kid.'

'Right. Hold them for me when they get back. I need to talk to Cooney. Set up an interview room. And tell Rose I'll see her shortly.'

McCadden thought of calling again on the Whittles to ask the boy a new question or two. But he decided against it and pulled away instead, too concerned about the passing of time to risk wasting any more of it. Driving up College Street and Manor Hill, he thought then about dropping in on the Christian Brothers' school, but he passed that as well without stopping and kept on going until he reached the station on Ballybricken Hill.

It was two twenty-eight by then.

Frank Ryan was already waiting for him in the interview room, drinking coffee from a plastic cup. He said, 'I'll get one of the uniforms to bring Cooney up in a minute. They're back. Remanded to Criminal Court in Dublin.'

McCadden sat opposite the sergeant. 'Did you get anything out of them?' he asked.

Ryan laughed. 'You'll enjoy this, Carl,' he promised. 'Cooney's uncle was one of Harris's buddies way back in the old days. Richie Gale. He's doing time now in England for armed robbery. Cooney himself works as a minor trade union official here in Waterford. Part of his responsibility is the dock workers. Apparently, he's been bringing stuff in through the port for quite a while now. Someone must've decided he was easy pickings, though, or more likely, someone must've got pissed because he was working their patch. The lone operator against a gang. This is conjecture, but I reckon he buried the stuff when he was chased into the woods, intending to go back next morning and collect it.'

'It figures, yeah.'

'But he was watched and followed afterwards. He was desperate for funds. And the only guy he could trust was a blind man.'

'How did he contact Harris without fingering him as well?'

'He talks to a lot of people in his job. He's a union organizer. I suppose he passed off Harris as just another one of them. Harris was out a number of times in the woods, trying to locate the drugs. That's where young Hayden saw him and reckoned he was up to something profitable. We'll have to keep an eye on that lad, won't we?'

McCadden could only agree, although the story of the courier and the blind man, interesting in itself, was merely a distraction to him now.

When Cooney was brought up and Ryan had stood to let him sit at the interview table, McCadden, glancing again at his watch, asked without preliminaries, 'When you were standing over me with the branch in the woods, why didn't you follow through with the blow?'

Cooney wasn't a professional criminal. Not yet. After a few years in prison, he might graduate to it. But right now, like most of his type, he posed tougher than he actually was.

'I took pity on you,' he sneered. 'I'm like that. I've a heart of gold.'

McCadden shook his head. 'This has nothing to do with me,' he explained. 'And nothing to do with you. Your answer has no connection with the charges against you.'

'Why should I bother with it, then?'

'You might help save a boy's life.'

'Come on! Give me a break!'

'I think you intended to hit me,' McCadden persisted. 'But you were interrupted. Is that right?'

Cooney stayed sullenly silent this time, and the change in his response more or less confirmed McCadden's guess.

'Look,' McCadden said quietly. 'Let me put this in a way that you won't be frightened of incriminating yourself with. Apart from the two of us and Harris, there was another adult in the woods. Could you describe him?'

Cooney laughed derisively. 'So you can go and find him and use him as a witness against me! Are you crazy?'

McCadden finally lost his patience. 'For Christ sake!' he said. 'Get a bit of sense, man! We have the testimonies of a score of guards, including myself, to build a case on. We don't *need* any more witnesses. Don't you see that?'

'All right, all right,' Cooney snapped. 'There was some sort of cleric there in the bushes. Is that what you want?'

'That's exactly what I want. Now. Can you describe him?'

'No, I can't. He had white hair or grey hair or something. Other than that, I don't know.'

'How do you know he was a cleric?'

'I saw his black habit.'

'Was he tall? Medium? Low-sized?'

'I don't know. All right? I didn't see him. I'd tell you if I could. I heard him crashing around and I saw his habit through the bushes and I got out of there too fast to worry about checking him out. All right?'

McCadden nodded, sat back in the chair and gestured wearily at Frank Ryan.

Between the sergeant's departure with Cooney and Rose Donnelly's arrival, he had a few minutes to himself in the interview room. Mostly he wasted them, watching the clock. Sometimes he thought...

Stalking, he realized. That was the contemporary term. One of the Christian Brothers from the school had been stalking Jason Whittle. Following him at a distance when he played in the woods with Luke Brady and Nicholas Hayden, and when the three of them bought and drank the cider afterwards. Closing in when Jason left the other two to wander off by himself.

And McCadden hadn't been dreaming or hallucinating when he recovered consciousness after the fight with Cooney and imagined he saw a clerical figure receding into the cover of the woods again. That cleric had actually been there. That cleric, he realized, might even have saved his life.

He tried to recapture the scene now. But the details were blurred. As they had been then. There were no human features in the image. No distinct shape or size or build...

But the man must have driven from the school, he thought. When McCadden took Jason Whittle to the woods, the man must have followed behind in his own car...

Rose Donnelly bustled in just then, and clearly with exciting news of her own. She sat at the table opposite McCadden and hastily arranged hand-written notes in front of her.

'Sir,' she said. 'Remember you asked me to follow through on the Timmy Line case?'

'Yes, Rose.'

'Well, I've got the details. Timmy Line was also

thirteen years old when he disappeared. He was on his way home from school one afternoon in March. He never reached his home. Everyone was questioned. Hundreds of statements were taken. There were no clear leads. And he was never found. Now, sir. John Ryle was working in Cork at the time.'

As Frank Ryan returned to the room and stood by the door, listening to the account, McCadden shook his head. 'John Ryle had nothing to do with it, Rose.'

'I know that, sir. I was just going to tell you. The interesting coincidence is somewhere else, really.'

'Where, Rose?'

'Timmy Line was a pupil at one of the Christian Brothers' schools in Cork, sir. At the time, there were five Christian Brothers actually teaching at the school. Three of those, sir, were Brother Hennessy, Brother Stevens and Brother Traynor. It's the only other time all three of them were previously together in the one school.'

'Right. Sixty-four dollar question, Rose. Which one?'

Donnelly shook her head. 'All three gave statements, obviously. But none was ever suspected of any involvement in the boy's disappearance.'

McCadden sighed. 'Right,' he accepted. 'What about the rest of their careers? Any hints of anything dubious in any of the other schools they worked in?'

'I don't know, sir. I haven't had time to check that out.'

McCadden looked again at his watch. It was three o'clock. And he'd have to hurry, he realized.

'The Chief Superintendent in, Frank?' he asked Ryan.

The sergeant shook his head. 'No. Out for the afternoon. Pro-Am golf tournament for charity.'

'We'll have to move without him, then,' McCadden decided. 'I need you two, anyone else that's hanging around, and as many uniforms as you can muster. We'll ring the principal of the school. We'll get permission for uniformed guards to address each class on the dangers of talking to strangers. All that concentration of bodies, it might just flush something out. We need warrants. But we can't afford to wait. They can follow on. Get someone on to that, Rose. You lot nose around when we get there. I'm going to chat with the three Christian Brothers. And let's get going. School's out at four and our excuse will be gone by then.'

twenty-six

A tall middle-aged man, dressed in a heavy black jacket and a yellow hard hat, was turning in through the open gates as the crowded police van pulled up outside the Christian Brothers' school at three thirty. The placard he was carrying had a printed sign nailed to a length of plain wood, spelling out the name of his union and announcing the official strike. Obviously, he was on his way in to do his shift on the picket line outside the construction site.

Hearing the van braking sharply behind him, he swivelled nervously. When he saw the uniformed guards pouring out through the open doors, he took a couple of smart steps backwards, raised the placard across his body like a staff and dug his heels in at the entrance, ready to die defending his democratic rights if necessary.

McCadden slipped quickly out of the front passenger seat to calm him. 'Easy, man, take it easy,' he cautioned. 'We're not here to break up the strike.'

'Well, Jaysus,' the man swore, 'I don't suppose you're here to support it.'

'Other business. The boy from the school who's missing.'

'Oh, right you are. If there's anything we can do...'

'See if you can find anyone for me who was on the picket line on Tuesday, when the other boy was taken in the car. I might need to talk to them.'

'I'll ask around.'

McCadden watched as the worker walked across to explain things to his tense and curious comrades. It was the first time he'd seen the site clearly in daylight. Beyond the wire fence and the locked gate there was a half-finished building, with its piles of rubble and its exposed steel rods and its apparently broken concrete pillars.

'We're ready,' Frank Ryan announced from beside him.

'Right. I'm going into the living quarters, straight ahead. Once I'm in there, put a man outside the front door and another at the back. Just in case. Spread the rest around the school. Come back to me if you dig anything up.'

'Okay.' Ryan raised his voice as he turned away to address the others. 'Gather round, everyone! Here's what we'll be doing...'

No one watched him through the front windows of the red brick building as McCadden approached the living quarters. He rang the bell. Again, when Brother Hennessy opened the door for him a little later, he was surprised by the absence of a housekeeper.

'Ah, Inspector!' Hennessy greeted him.

His eyes flitted to his left, glancing over McCadden's right shoulder at the squad of guards marching across the grounds towards the school. But the eyes didn't register anything more significant than recognition. Although, McCadden thought, perhaps the very *absence* of surprise was significant in itself.

'Do you mind if I have a word with you, Brother?'

'No, no.' Hennessy stepped back and held the door wide open. 'Come in, come in.'

'I'm not disturbing you at anything?'

Hennessy laughed and held up the book he had in his left hand, pushing the spine outwards for McCadden to read. Boethius, *The Consolation of Philosophy*.

'Only dreaming,' he claimed ironically.

'Are Brother Stevens and Brother Traynor in?'

'They're both upstairs in their rooms.'

Hennessy led the way to the pine-floored living room where McCadden had previously talked to the three men. The fire was glowing. The television was off. And the curtains were drawn at the windows.

'Would you like a drink, Inspector?'

McCadden shook his head. 'No, thanks.'

'Ah,' Hennessy breathed. 'You must be on duty, then.'

He smiled to himself as he sat in what was obviously his regular chair, to the right of the fire and within easier reach of the bookshelves in the alcove behind him than of the drinks cabinet in the far corner of the room.

McCadden walked across to the nearest window and pulled back the curtain to look out. From there he could see the construction site more closely and, beyond and to the side of it, the guards starting to spread out through the school.

'Where are the bedrooms?' he asked.

'Oh, don't worry, Inspector,' Hennessy assured him. 'Brother Stevens and Brother Traynor can also see the strength of the force you've brought with you. All three bedrooms are directly above us. I've no doubt they're both sharing the same perspective as yourself right now, although with a better view.'

McCadden turned and shared a penetrating, unyielding look with this old man who seemed to derive sour satisfaction from knowing too much. Closing the curtain, he walked back slowly and sat in the armchair opposite Hennessy. He found the fire a little too hot and the air in the room a little too stuffy, but he tried to ignore the discomfort.

'In part,' he said, 'I really came here to thank you.'

'Is that right?' Hennessy responded dubiously. 'Why? What service have I done you?'

'I think you actually saved my life.'

Hennessy slightly raised his eyebrows. 'I presume you mean metaphorically. But do expand.'

'Do you hold a current driving licence, Brother?'

Hennessy slotted a bookmark between the pages and put *The Consolation of Philosophy* aside on the table to his right. He nodded. 'Yes.'

'Does the order have a car at its disposal here?'

'Two, Inspector. They're parked around the side.'

'Do you still drive?'

'Occasionally. It's not an experience I enjoy. Generally, I find the more enclosed and the more isolated you leave an individual, the more insensitive and savage he becomes. Locking him inside a weapon is fatal. Driving is essentially an anti-social activity.'

'You probably don't agree with our prison policy, then.'

'That's a more complex issue.'

'Wouldn't you say the same about your own community here?'

'In what sense?'

'Enclosed. Isolated. Out of touch.'

'And tending towards savagery?'

'I was following the lines of your own argument.'

'Well, well,' Hennessy approved sarcastically. 'A dialectical policeman. We're not quite an enclosed order, Inspector. We're not monks. We're teaching Brothers. A vital part of the community. With many outside contacts.'

'But there are severe limitations,' McCadden suggested. 'It seems to me that to force a community of males together and deny them the company of women—'

'It's not gender limitations that trouble me, Inspector,' Hennessy confided. 'It's the intellectual ones.'

'I like the company of women myself, Brother,' McCadden admitted. 'Don't you?'

'Men, women,' Hennessy said airily. As if there was no difference between the two. 'The mind is what matters to me.'

'Do you remember a boy called Timmy Line? In Cork. About ten years ago?'

'Of course I do, yes.'

'Did you know him well?'

'I taught him. He was very bright, very intelligent. Unusually, he had no complexes about accepting advice on books, despite the derision of his denser schoolmates.'

'Did you have a personal relationship with him?'

'Isn't that what teaching is about?'

'How well do you know Jason Whittle?'

'Are you labouring to draw connections between the two boys, Inspector?'

McCadden nodded. 'Yes.'

Hennessy looked at him unflinchingly. 'I asked Jason's English teacher to send him over to me. He came occasionally. I offered him advice on books and reading. He had the freedom to use the library here. What else is it for?'

'When I was here last Tuesday night, Brother, I asked some questions about your movements that day.'

'Yes.'

'I have some more now. Can you remember how you heard that Luke Brady had been snatched outside the school?'

'I met Brother Traynor on his way back in.'

'What did you do then?'

'I came over here.'

'Was anyone else here?'

'No.'

'Brother Stevens?'

'I didn't see him that afternoon.'

'Did you see Brother Traynor again afterwards?'

'No. Not until later that evening, shortly before you arrived yourself.'

'Did you use the car that day?'

'No, not that I remember.'

'Did you notice that either of the cars was missing at any stage that afternoon?'

'I'm sorry. I didn't notice, no.'

'A man I came across in the course of my duties was asking about you, incidentally. Possibly a former pupil. He now works as a trade union official here in the city. A small, stocky man, with long, wavy hair. Vincent Cooney.'

Hennessy looked baffled for a while, but then laughed and said, 'You believe I have something to do with young Whittle's disappearance, don't you?'

'I'm not a great believer, Brother, no.'

'*Suspect*, then. But what could you possibly base your suspicions on, I ask myself. Eh? Nothing, I can see. Can I perhaps *offer* you something, in that case? Do you suspect, Inspector, that there is a necessary consistency between a man's writing and his personal life?'

'I feel more comfortable *asking* the questions,' McCadden confessed.

'Of course you do, Inspector. People whose uncertainty troubles them always feel more comfortable asking questions. It appears as if they already possess the answers. Just as people who are weak prefer to bully and people who are stupid scoff to give the impression of deeper knowledge. Believe me, I wouldn't offer to help if I wasn't convinced you needed it. I think myself that only the timid and the unimaginative could possibly join an organization like the police force.'

McCadden smiled. 'Not greatly different, perhaps, to a religious order.'

'Did I ever claim intellectual courage or vigour or originality for myself?'

'Why *did* you join the Christian Brothers?'

'Why did you join the police force?'

McCadden sat back in the armchair. 'My father was a paratrooper in the British Army,' he said. 'He fought with distinction in Europe during the Second World War.'

'Ah,' Hennessy exclaimed. 'Then you must be a member of our minority Protestant community.'

'Not necessarily. As I think you know, many Irish Catholics served in the British Army as well. But in any case, we grew up with the notion of service to the people. My brother is also a Garda.'

'Only you had the misfortune to discover along the

way that such fine abstractions as Truth and Justice are merely empty words. Am I right?'

McCadden stared, realizing now that he was dangerously stuck with a fellow agnostic, and trapped by a man who was desperate for intelligent dispute.

'Why did you join the Christian Brothers?' he asked again.

Hennessy pointed across the room, to the corner opposite the drinks cabinet. 'In that glass-fronted bookcase over there, Inspector,' he said, 'you'll find three or four copies of the proverbially slim volume of poetry called *Kneeling at the Altar* on the bottom shelf.'

McCadden got up and walked over. Opening the glass door of the bookcase, he took out a copy of the book. *Kneeling at the Altar*, by J. K. Hennessy.

'Is that you?' he asked.

'Yes.'

The volume had been published twelve years before by a small poetry press in Dublin. Inside, the permission of various newspapers and magazines to reprint was acknowledged.

'Go to page thirty-four,' Hennessy suggested. 'I recommend it as an infallible guide to the worth of any book. Read page thirty-four first. It's well past the author's freshest goods at the front and not yet quite close enough to be tainted by the disappointment of the ending.'

McCadden leafed through the book and read the poem on page thirty-four.

>   ***Lorcan's Song***
>   *I must –*
>   *must I? –*
>   *bury my dead . . .*

'You may keep it,' Hennessy offered. 'If you wish. I got ten free copies. I have . . . how many are left?'

'Four.'

'And one in my bedroom upstairs. In my entire life, I have met five acquaintances I thought capable of reading it.'

'Six,' McCadden corrected.

Hennessy laughed. 'So now, you might consider answering my question. Is there a necessary consistency between a man's writing and his personal life?'

'Obviously, a writer can posture. But in a large body of work the underlying sympathies and prejudices always come through.'

'What, then, does that make me?'

'I better wait until I read all of this.'

'Ah, but then it might be too late, mightn't it? For young Whittle.'

'Have you published other books?'

'No.'

'Do you still write?'

'No.'

'Why not?'

'Every poem since 1830, Inspector, including my own, begins with the first person singular of the personal pronoun and rapidly descends to whinge. *I fall upon the thorns of life! I bleed!* Every boy I ever taught is therefore a poet as well. And I'm an elitist at heart.'

'I get the feeling,' McCadden hazarded, 'that you never found a proper expression for your talents in the Christian Brothers.'

'People who write poetry are individualists, Inspector. If the poetry is considered very good, they're lauded as geniuses. If the poetry is very bad, they're simply

234

delinquents. Either way, an organization is unlikely to satisfy their tendencies.'

'So why join?'

Hennessy smiled grimly to himself. 'Fifty years ago, in the gloom of post-war depression, I sat in class in a Christian Brothers' school in Galway. We were all poor. V-neck sweaters unravelling at the hems. Short trousers crisp with unwashed grime. Sandals torn and flapping. It was the greyness that was intolerable. Everyone looked the same. Poor, working class boys. Going nowhere. One day a recruiting Brother came to our school, peddling vocations. A simple man. He offered us a choice between blissfully serving God and being a good rich man. We all knew that both were stupid fictions. And no one joined. Another came. Very naive, or very cynical. In that grey classroom with the rain slanting miserably outside from overcast skies, he held out the exotic promise of the missions. Sunlight in Africa. Tropical forests in South America. Wilderness in Australia. It still meant nothing to me. It wasn't until the following year that I was hooked. The third man. Each time you open a book, he told us, you enter another's world. The Christian Brothers as the sponsors and protectors of learning. Which is where our founder, Edmund Rice, originally started, here in Waterford in 1802. That was what lured me in.'

'Why didn't you subsequently leave?'

'Because the man was telling the truth, Inspector. Every book is another world. And most of them were at last available to me, along with the time to study them.'

'But then?'

'The second part of my duties as a Brother. That was what ... *Teaching* the books. Not to boys as eager as I had been myself, but to the poor, the ignorant, the prejudiced, the uninterested. Can you imagine what it does to a line of Shakespeare:

> *Let me not to the marriage of true minds*
> *Admit impediments. Love is not love*
> *Which alters when it alteration finds,*
> *Or bends with the remover to remove:*

to have to explain every syllable in dead prose to every dim-witted grubby-faced boy in every classroom, every day for every one of your forty years' teaching? Can you imagine what's left of the mystery? Of the poetry?'

'You don't like children, Brother,' McCadden observed.

'I see one or two in every generation, Inspector, who have the same love of words I once had.'

'And you like to guide them away from your own mistakes?'

'If my example could be of help to them, yes.'

'Was Timmy Line one of those?'

'Yes, Timmy was, yes.'

'And Jason Whittle?'

'Jason, too, yes.'

'They seem to pay a high price.'

'Yes. There's something almost darkly biblical about it, isn't there? As if this myth that plucking the tree of knowledge leads to death actually had some truth in it.'

twenty-seven

McCadden carried Hennessy's book with him as he climbed the wide oak stairway to the upper bedrooms. He climbed slowly, hoping to unsettle those who were waiting for him with the pace and unevenness of his movements. Halfway up he stopped, then turned and came back down again.

He waited at the bottom of the stairs for a minute. When no one appeared to check his position, he ambled down the corridor to look into the other rooms on the ground floor. He had no search warrant, of course. But he doubted if anyone was going to risk objecting. Nor had he any real hope of finding anything. It was just a faint optimism. Another ploy. A little breathing space to allow him to reflect on Brother Hennessy's strange existence...

On the way back, he knocked on the living-room door and opened it gently. Hennessy was sitting again in his armchair, calmly reading his Boethius once more. He turned his head at the noise.

'There's something I forgot to ask you,' McCadden said.

Hennessy slightly raised his eyebrows. 'Yes.'

'Where exactly are the bedrooms?'

'Oh! Turn left at the top of the stairs. Brother Stevens is the second door, Brother Traynor the, ah, fourth.'

'Thanks.'

Stevens was waiting for McCadden.

'Come in!' he cried, almost simultaneously with the knock. His voice was high-pitched and a little cracked.

He seemed nervous. He was sitting at a small writing bureau in a far corner of the room, with a silver Parker pen poised over a sheet of writing paper. A very impressive display of absorption in other duties. Except that the ball-point wasn't yet exposed at the bottom of the pen.

'Am I disturbing your letter-writing, Brother?' McCadden wondered.

Stevens flipped the cover back over the writing pad, as if he was concealing something more intimate than a blank page. 'What? Oh, no. Just a note to my sister. She's in New York. She's coming home for Christmas.'

'Where's home?'

'Here, for myself. It has been for the last few years. I suppose it'll be the last one now.'

'I mean, the family home.'

Stevens's small, rounded face expressed a childlike regret. 'There isn't one, Inspector. Not any more. We owned a hardware store in Thurles, in County Tipperary. But when our parents died, with Mary in the States and myself in the order ... I believe it's a video store now.'

'Your order's founder, Edmund Rice, was a merchant here in Waterford, wasn't he, before he established the Christian Brothers?'

'That's right. His wife died from the fever that was

sweeping through Europe in 1789 and the tragedy changed his life.'

'He was married?' McCadden wondered innocently.

'Oh, yes. And entirely devoted to his wife.'

'And yet he founded a celibate order.'

Stevens laughed uneasily. 'It's a question of total dedication, you see . . .'

'Right.'

McCadden had been taking in the character of the room while talking. Its most distinctive feature was the vast collection of framed photographs literally covering the walls. All of them shared a sporting theme. Most were team photographs or action shots from inter-school hurling matches. Stevens, always in his clerical habit and never in a tracksuit, featured as coach and mentor in the majority. Usually, with what seemed like a dogged perversity, he happened to be standing in the back row beside some tall teenager who towered above him.

Gaelic football and handball were also heavily featured in the collection. The range of Gaelic sports, as McCadden knew, that was traditionally promoted by the Christian Brothers. And often, in the past, to the exclusion of everything else. There were no photographs of soccer or cricket, both of which had been damned as alien, corrupting, and all too liable to dilute the native purity with foreign influence.

Although there was nothing on horse racing or greyhound racing, either, McCadden had his suspicions. He'd never known a sporting cleric like Stevens who wasn't also fond of gambling. They didn't publicly admit it in school, for fear of leading their pupils astray.

And with such small evasions, they hoped to form the characters of the boys in their care.

McCadden made a point of studying the photographs. 'No car racing, Brother?' he said suddenly.

'Car racing?' Stevens repeated, obviously surprised by the angle of approach.

'Formula One,' McCadden expanded. 'Stock car racing. Rallying. The Circuit of Ireland usually passes through Waterford.'

'No, I don't have a great deal of interest in—'

'Do you drive yourself?'

'In races?'

'On the road.'

'I do, yes. The car.'

'That's right. You had it at Nicholas Hayden's house the other night, didn't you?'

'We have a school bus, as well. Otherwise it might be a tough job getting from match—'

'Do the other Brothers here drive?'

'They both do, yes. Although Brother Traynor . . .'

'What?'

'It's something that's on your files, anyway, I suppose, so there's no real point in concealing it, is there? Brother Traynor lost his licence for a while a few years back. Over the limit. Drink, you see.'

'Has he got it back?'

'I'm sure he has.'

McCadden placed Hennessy's book on the bed, with its cover showing. Stevens looked at it, but didn't comment.

'I actually came in to thank you, Brother,' McCadden said.

Stevens looked up at him. 'Oh? For what?'

'Well, we've got some guards in on the invitation of the principal to talk to the boys about personal safety. That's my official reason for being here. But I thought I'd drop in while I had the chance.'

'I see.' Stevens glanced at the closed notepad on the bureau and then pulled slightly on his lower lip with his left hand. 'But what did you want to thank me for?'

McCadden had drifted away. He was standing in front of a photograph of two boys challenging with raised hurleys for an aerial ball in a competitive match. He seemed distracted.

'Eh?' he enquired. 'Oh! For saving my life. I saw you as I regained consciousness.'

'I think you must be mistaking—'

'Did you know a boy named Timmy Line, Brother?' McCadden interrupted. He tapped the glass covering the photograph. 'Cork. Ten years ago. About the time this photograph was taken.'

'I did, yes. It was a very sad case.'

'Still is, I suppose. For the boy's parents and family.'

'Of course, yes.'

'Did you know Timmy well?'

'I taught him History. He was in second year, I remember, in our school.'

'I see a photograph of you here coaching the hurling team. Same year, isn't it? How did you do?'

'Beaten by a point in the semi-final of the cup.'

'You've a good memory.'

'I, ah . . .'

'Did Timmy play?'

'No, no. Timmy was an academic boy. I don't remember him being accomplished at sports.'

'But you would've taken him for games, wouldn't

you? I mean, it was a compulsory part of the curriculum, even for the unenthusiastic.'

'I was never hard on those with no ability, Inspector. What's the point? Apart from a little healthy exercise. No, the tough work was for the ones with the drive.'

'Only the best,' McCadden muttered.

'Sorry?'

'It's a theme that keeps cropping up in accounts of the Christian Brothers. Only the best at sports were given the attention needed to improve. Only the best academically. Only the best socially.'

'I think that's a very unfair notion of our contribution to Irish education.'

'Maybe. It's not my view. It's a distillation of the views of others. Most of them past pupils.'

McCadden allowed a pause. But Stevens never went back to wondering how he had saved the detective's life. Maybe he was too disturbed by the carping analysis of his order's worth to deal with anything else . . .

'Do you still coach, Brother?' McCadden asked then.

'I'm officially retired,' Stevens told him. 'The school has paid coaches now. But I help out when I can.'

'Jason Whittle. The boy who's missing. Any good at sports?'

Stevens shook his head. 'Not that I know of, no.'

'His father was a very good soccer player.'

'I've heard that, yes.'

'Do you meet him much?'

'The father?'

'Jason.'

'I occasionally take the boys for PE classes when the need arises. Teachers absent or ill or anything like that. Sometimes it's Jason's class.'

'Have you ever seen him over here? In the library downstairs?'

'Not that I remember, no.'

'Brother Hennessy, it seems, is particularly friendly with him. Are you aware of that?'

'You'll have to ask Brother Hennessy about that, I think.'

Turning from the photographs, McCadden walked across to the bed and tapped the book that was still lying on the covers. 'Have you read this?' he asked.

Stevens grimaced. 'I'm not a great one for poetry, Inspector.'

'But you know that it was written by Brother Hennessy?'

'He reminds us occasionally, yes.'

'What do you think of the title? *Kneeling at the Altar.*'

'I hadn't really thought about it at all. Why do you ask, Inspector?'

'Because I think myself that it's either a very unfortunate mistake, made out of ignorance, or a very sick exercise in cynicism.'

'I don't understand.'

'No?'

Stevens suddenly abandoned the Parker pen he'd been playing with in his right hand all the time. He turned fully towards McCadden, pulling again on his lower lip. In the silence, he clearly struggled to decide whether he should stay sitting or stand up. Without rising, he shook his head and said once more, 'I don't understand.'

'The apparently devout phrase, *kneeling at the altar,*' McCadden explained, 'is also American prison slang. It means *to fellate.*'

Stevens became restless, although he seemed too

243

weakened by the crude blow to actually stand. He looked quickly from the hard stare in McCadden's eyes to the book on the bed to the photograph of the hurlers on the wall, before finally settling on the neutral space along the floor by his own feet.

'My God!' he groaned. 'You're surely not suggesting that Brother Hennessy...'

'Do you remember last Tuesday evening when I visited here?' McCadden shifted breezily.

It took Stevens a while to adjust to the change of topic. 'Tuesday?' he echoed faintly.

'You opened the door for me and were kind enough to serve me some of your excellent whiskey.'

'Oh, yes. Tuesday. Of course.'

'What did you do after I left?'

'I chatted with the others for a while and then came up here.'

'Did you leave the house at any stage?'

'No, I was here all the time.'

'Did either of the other two Brothers leave?'

'I don't think so. I couldn't be certain. Why?'

'Did you hear either of the cars starting up?'

'No.'

'You've got a good, clear memory of events, Brother. And a very quick recall.'

'Yes. You see, I—'

'Maybe it's all the sports, is it? Sharpening your instincts.'

'*Mens sana in corpore sano*, perhaps.'

'You believe that?' McCadden wondered.

'A healthy mind in a healthy body? Why not? I believe that games are excellent for discipline. I believe they're vital for a boy's physical health. I believe they are a great bulwark against impurity and moral degradation, which are not very fashionable notions these days, I accept.'

'I don't think those are the reasons people play sport, Brother.'

'Maybe you're not a man who was ever much involved in it yourself, are you?'

'No, I've had my moments,' McCadden admitted modestly.

'And I suppose virtue and morality wouldn't be any of a modern policeman's concerns,' Stevens sneered, stung a little by the assault on his convictions.

McCadden shrugged. 'One man's purity is another man's boredom. Morality. Virtue. Justice. I'm more comfortable with rules than with principles, Brother. It's why I like sports. And why I'm a detective, I suppose.'

'You must lead a very pragmatic life, Inspector.'

'Are *you*, by the way?'

'What?'

'Comfortable with rules. Poverty. Obedience. Chastity. It's a very personal question, I know, but as we're discussing personal topics ... Are you comfortable with celibacy, Brother?'

'I've spent almost fifty years in our order, Inspector, without severing my vows.'

'But are you comfortable with it?'

'Yes, of course I am.'

'Is that so?' McCadden enquired. 'I would've thought that all the best saints went through hell struggling with temptation instead of being untroubled by it.'

Stevens paled. His hands trembled slightly on the

writing surface of the bureau. But whether the response was anxiety or anger, it was impossible to tell. 'Inspector, I have never claimed to be a saint or a—'

'Can you remember, incidentally, how you heard last Tuesday that Luke Brady had been kidnapped outside the school?'

'Luke Brady? Brother Traynor told me.'

'Where were you?'

'It was after school. I was in the sports hall, putting away equipment after a session with the seniors.'

'Anyone else there?'

'No, I was by myself. Until Brother Traynor came in.'

'What did you do afterwards?'

This time, Stevens made a point of reflecting, of pulling the details more slowly from his memory. 'Let me see. I finished tidying. That was Tuesday ... Yes. I had to travel to Stradbally in the county to pick up a batch of hurleys from our supplier, Shay Griffin. One of the very best in the country, you know. I have his phone number here for you ...' He rummaged in the bureau's compartments, plucked out a mud-stained business card and handed it across. 'I was just after getting back, in fact, before you called that evening.'

'Yes, I remember. So you must've taken one of the cars from outside?'

'Only the small one was left there. The big Ford was already gone. That's the one I'd usually use for collecting gear.'

'Any idea who was using it?'

'I was in too much of a hurry to worry about that.'

'Why? Did you have to pick up the hurleys at a particular time?'

'Well, it's a journey of twenty miles or so along the coast. I'm not fond of driving.'

'Right. You said you had a sister in New York. Any other family?'

'No, only the two of us. Very small for an Irish family at the time, but I believe my mother was unable to give birth again after Mary.'

'What age were you when you joined the Christian Brothers?'

'I was fourteen.'

'Why did you join the order, Brother?'

Stevens no longer liked him, McCadden noticed. Or maybe he'd never liked him and just didn't bother concealing it any more. Every question was now taken resentfully. Every answer tended more and more towards dismissiveness.

'I had a vocation, Inspector,' he said sharply.

'Same question, really,' McCadden suggested. 'It's just that it strikes me as unusual. In normal circumstances, the only son would have inherited the business.'

'I never saw myself as a merchant.'

'Even at fourteen?'

'Not at any age, Inspector.'

'And your sister?'

'Mary also became a teacher in New York. She had no great talent for business, either.'

'What age was she when she left home?'

'She went to America when she was twenty-four.'

'Right. But what age was she when she left home?'

'I think . . . I'm not sure, really. I was in the seminary.'

McCadden was wondering about the circumstances and the personalities that could drive two teenage children from a family business in the nineteen-forties, when the electric school bell rang outside and set off a chain reaction among the whooping students. He glanced at his watch. It was four o'clock.

When he looked back at Stevens, it seemed as if there was a slight smile of quiet triumph on the Brother's face. It was as if the man had come through a punishing fight against incredible odds and was relieved to hear the bell that ended the contest.

McCadden took Hennessy's book from the bed covers. He held it in his right hand and tapped it lightly against the raised thumb of his left.

'A mutual acquaintance of ours was asking for you, by the way,' he said. 'A stocky young man with long curling hair. He works as a trade union official here in the city. Vincent Cooney.'

Stevens frowned. 'Is he a past pupil?'

'You tell me,' McCadden invited.

Stevens slowly shook his head. 'I don't know, Inspector,' he said sadly, 'what you think you're trying to do here...'

twenty-eight

Walking along the corridor after leaving Stevens's room, McCadden was inclined to agree with the little cleric.

He knew what he was *trying* to do, of course. He was trying to flush out Jason Whittle's abductor with pretence and pressure. He was trying to persuade the culprit that he had seen him in the woods and that he was now only giving him a decent chance to confess before publicly exposing him. He was trying to get the man to reveal, simply and quickly, exactly what had happened to the boy.

But what if none of them crumbled, he wondered now. What if they all took the same range of questions and insinuations with the same puzzlement and calmness? What was he going to do then?'

He didn't know.

He stopped outside Brother Traynor's room and knocked on the door. As he waited, he wondered if he had made a mistake with his calculations. There was no answer. No one opened the door. And no one called to invite him in or curse him away.

He went back to the top of the stairs and counted again to the fourth door as he returned along the corridor. He ended up at the same room. He didn't knock this time. He listened. And from inside, he heard that distinctive, tinny sound that comes from the speakers of a cheap television set.

Trying the handle, he found that the door was unlocked. He pushed it open and stepped in.

The bed, unmade and angled crookedly, was to his right. On his left, over by the curtained window, Brother Traynor was sitting in a deep armchair with his back to the door. The only parts of him that were visible were his black shoes and black crossed trouser legs. Beyond him, against the dark curtains, was the television. And what he was watching, McCadden finally realized, was a video tape of the comedy series *Father Ted*.

McCadden walked across and sat back against a sideboard that was placed against the wall, about midway between the screen and the viewer. Traynor didn't even glance at him. The big man, raw-boned and red-faced and with his sparse grey hair wild from a recent walk, just sat stolidly in the armchair, grasping a whiskey glass with two melting ice cubes in his right hand. The only movement along his entire body was in that right hand. It was trembling slightly. And the ice cubes were tinkling gently.

The man had been dour in company, McCadden remembered. And he was obviously impossible when alone.

McCadden looked at the television screen. On it, the scabrous, demented alcoholic named Father Jack was screaming uncontrollably for booze.

'There but for the grace of God, hah?' McCadden remarked.

However else they protect themselves by blindness, failures always have antennae for irony. Traynor turned his drooping eyes towards McCadden.

'What do you want?' he growled in his thick rural accent.

'I need to talk to you,' McCadden told him.

'About young Whittle, I suppose, is it?'

'Yes.'

'What about him?'

'Could we turn the tape off?'

Traynor peered into his glass and found only water. He put it down by the side of the armchair and picked up the remote control instead. He stopped the tape and switched the television set to standby.

'Would you like a drink?' he offered.

'No, thanks. I'm on duty this time.'

As Traynor stood up and reached across to a nearby table to pour himself another whiskey, something about him struck McCadden. Some difference between this man's movements and those of Stevens and Hennessy. He had a speed and a vigour that the other two lacked.

'How old are you, Brother?' he asked.

'Old?' Traynor repeated. He had to think a little about it, calculating a sum that hadn't been important for quite a while. 'I'll be fifty-seven this November.'

'Didn't you say you were retired?'

'I don't teach any more, if that's what you mean.'

'Why did you retire so early?'

Traynor laughed. 'Do you take me for a fool or something? You're only trying to catch me out, aren't you? When you already have the answer. Well, there's no reason to hide it any more. Why should I? Everyone else knows about it. They won't let me teach because I gave some young pup a lesson he'll never forget.'

'Where was this?'

'Down in Cork.'

'Was it Timmy Line?'

'What are you talking about?'

'The boy you assaulted. Was it Timmy Line?'

'I said a young pup, didn't I? Are you listening or aren't you? Timmy was a respectful little lad.'

'Did you teach him?'

'I had him for Maths. God help him. Poor Timmy.'

'I'm told he was very like Jason Whittle.'

Traynor shook his head. 'Whittle's a bit of a pup. Oh, he's bright enough, the same fellow. But he'd want to run with the hare and hunt with the hounds. He's into too much trouble, he is.'

'Have you much contact with him?'

'Me? I don't have much contact with anyone these days.'

'Did you ever notice him over here?'

'I did. Hennessy had him. Wasting his time trying to knock some sense into him.'

'You don't like him very much, do you?'

'I wouldn't give you tuppence for the same fellow.'

'This other lad, you assaulted—'

'Don't make me laugh!'

'Sorry?'

'Thirty or more years ago it was, spare the rod and spoil the child. You weren't anything if you didn't beat the living daylights out of them young pups. No one had any respect for you. That was how you were judged as a teacher. Then all of a sudden you're a monster for doing your job. Hah? And no one even told us they'd gone and changed everything. Assault? Is that what you said? It used to be called discipline.'

'Did drink have anything to do with it?' McCadden wondered.

Traynor didn't answer.

So McCadden was left to imagine.

This big, awkward country man, he thought. Goaded in a cage-like classroom by street-wise city kids. Knowing he was being mocked, but half the time not even understanding the jibes they threw at him. Out of place. Maddened. Frustrated.

He should've spent his life on a farm, McCadden knew. Stacking hay. Looking after the calves and the foals. Roughly ploughing the land.

Instead, he drank to cope with his loss. And the booze only exaggerated his inadequacies. And probably released that terrifying strength of his in terrible destruction.

He had a tendency to feel sorry for this one, McCadden realized, in a way that he hadn't experienced with the other two. And he had to check it.

'I've been asking the others,' he said, 'why they originally joined the Christian Brothers.'

'Is that a fact?'

'Maybe you'd let me know your own reasons?'

'Well, there's no great secret to that,' Traynor said. But he paused. And then seemed to erupt again in the middle of a totally different topic. 'They think they know what hard farming is around these parts!' he cried. 'They don't have the first idea! Not an idea! Throw a stick down in a field in the evening and 'tis covered with grass by the next morning. That's how rich the land is here!'

'Where are your own people from?'

'Kerry. Beautiful scenery, don't you know. All lakes and rocks and mountains. And damn all to feed a goat on. My father had a small farm. Big enough for one of us to work and come into when he died. But I was the third son. And that's how I ended up joining the Christian Brothers. Because the second son was already gone to the priesthood.'

'Is the farm still there?'

'I wouldn't know, to tell you the honest truth. And I wouldn't care, either. It's past now. Dead and gone. Like everything.'

'Last Tuesday,' McCadden said then. 'Do you remember the incident outside the school?'

'I do.'

'What did you do after I left with Jason Whittle to follow Luke Brady?'

'I was going to give Mr Ducy a hand getting the names you asked for. But sure, he didn't want it. They don't have any time for you any more, the young teachers. No one does.'

'Did you go back into the school?'

'I had to go in to see Brother Stevens about something. He was in the sports hall. I met Brother Hennessy on the way, before I got there.'

'Did you tell the two of them about the incident?'

'I did, the two of them.'

'What did you do then?'

'You wouldn't have any interest in that at all.'

'You're wrong, Brother. I have all the interest in the world.'

'I went to see a man about a dog, Inspector.'

'What man?'

'He wouldn't want me telling his name or his business to the likes of you.'

'A small, stocky man, with long flowing hair?'

'No.'

'He said he'd be looking out for you once he's free again.'

'Hah?'

'His name is Cooney. Vincent Cooney.'

'Do you know what you're talking about, Inspector? I hope you do. Because I don't.'

'I'm talking about you saving my life.'

Traynor laughed. And it sounded genuine. 'Me?' he cried. 'How would I manage that? I can't even save myself.'

'Someone drove away from here on Tuesday afternoon after I left with Jason Whittle,' McCadden explained. 'The same man probably drove away again on Tuesday night after I'd been here. Did you notice either Brother Stevens or Brother Hennessy using a car during those periods?'

'I'd be a fool to say I didn't, I suppose.'

'Did you?'

'I didn't.'

'Did you use the car yourself?'

'I lost my licence a few years back,' Traynor said. He raised his whiskey glass and nodded at it. 'Something else I have to thank our friend here for.'

'That doesn't answer the question. You can drive without a licence.'

'I haven't driven a car ... not in the last month, anyway.'

'Right,' McCadden said.

Maybe he actually *was* closer to the truth than when he'd arrived about an hour ago, he thought. But he didn't really *feel* any closer.

He had one more stick to brandish.

He said, 'You're not thinking of going anywhere for the rest of the afternoon, are you? We have a warrant to search the premises and the grounds, which we'll be executing shortly. If you have anything concealed here, we'll find it. So you'd be better off letting us know immediately.'

Traynor laughed. And reached for the remote control to turn the television and the video recorder on again.

twenty-nine

McCadden, stopping on the way back to give the same notice of an impending search to Brother Stevens, was desperate enough now to open the door without knocking and step inside without waiting for an invitation.

The little man was still sitting at his writing bureau. He seemed to have made a start to his letter and was already halfway down the first sheet of notepaper.

'I understand,' he said quietly.

'Did you have any plans for going anywhere this afternoon or this evening?'

'No, I won't be leaving here.'

McCadden went downstairs and into the living room, interrupting another sentence from Boethius to pass the same information to Hennessy. Hennessy looked back at him with arched eyebrows, with a certain sense of *confirmed* superiority.

'I'm afraid you really have no idea, do you, Inspector?' he said. 'You think that one of us is responsible for young Whittle's disappearance, don't you? Did you imagine you could read guilt and innocence in our faces?'

McCadden didn't directly respond. 'Did you intend leaving here at any stage today?' he asked.

'No, Inspector. In our enclosed lives, the opportunities for live theatre are so rare that it's essential not to decline any.'

Outside, Frank Ryan was waiting for McCadden in the hallway.

McCadden looked at him eagerly. 'Well?'

Ryan shook his head and simultaneously spread his arms in a hopeless gesture. 'Nothing. And you?'

McCadden signalled towards the open front door. 'Let's go outside. Get some air. I'm getting a headache in here.'

They walked on to the gravel driveway, past the uniformed guard at the door. Ryan lumbered straight ahead. McCadden turned sharply right.

'Christ, Carl!' the sergeant complained. 'Hang on, will you!'

They turned around the corner of the red brick building. On the gravel by the gable wall, the order's two cars were parked. A black Opel Corsa and a Ford Orion of the same colour behind it.

'Are you certain we're in the right place?' Ryan wondered. 'Because if we're not, we're going to look a bit cheap, coming down like this on three old men from a religious order.'

'You're starting to think like a chief superintendent, Frank,' McCadden muttered.

'Give us a break, Carl!'

'Chief superintendents always start their sentences with the phrase, *if we're wrong here* . . .'

'Well, we might be.'

McCadden shook his head. 'In one of those cars,' he said, pointing at the pair in front of him, 'one of the

Brothers followed Jason Whittle and myself to the woods last Tuesday when Luke Brady was snatched.'

'Why?'

'If I knew that, Frank, I'd also know which of the Brothers it was. Jealousy? Protectiveness? Fear? The point is, each of them knew I was with Jason. And none of them saw either of the others leaving.'

'Come on, Carl,' Ryan encouraged. 'I know you better than that. How do you read it? Which of them took the boy and what did they do with the kid?'

'Hennessy has the motive,' McCadden proposed. 'Stevens the opportunity. And Traynor the temperament.'

Ryan sighed. 'Great.'

'Hennessy peddles a strong line in arid cynicism. Most of it is a pose. But he's actually quite embittered. Intellectually. He feels himself condemned to living with asses. He'd both encourage and resent the prospects of intelligent working class boys like Timmy Line and Jason Whittle. He was one of them himself once.'

'*Yet each man kills the thing he loves.*'

'You surprise me, Frank. A sergeant quoting Oscar Wilde? But more or less.'

'So you incline towards Hennessy?'

'I'd be more inclined if he'd published a second volume of poetry.'

'I haven't a clue what that means, Carl.'

McCadden held up the poetry book he was still carrying. 'Hennessy published a volume with an ambiguous title. You know the slang?'

'Jesus!'

'If he had done it deliberately, he'd probably have followed it up with another. If it was a mistake that was later pointed out to him, his bruised ego would've kept his face out of the limelight afterwards.'

'Right. Stevens, then. And opportunity.'

'Stevens is much more mobile than the other two. He drives kids to sports events all the time. No one would hesitate about getting into the car with him. But . . .'

From beyond the cars, around the back of the house, a red-faced, sweating uniformed guard appeared, jogging along the gravel. He carried his cap in his right hand and waved it when he saw the others.

'Sir!' he called breathlessly. 'Sir!'

McCadden looked up and watched as the guard made his way along the gravel between the gable wall and the cars. 'Yes? What is it?'

'I thought you were in the house, sir. But you weren't. They said you'd left, so I thought—'

'All right, all right,' McCadden said impatiently. 'Now that you've found me, what is it?'

'Detective Donnelly is looking for you, sir. Urgently.'

'Where is she?'

'At the back here, sir. I'll show you . . .'

Behind the house, Rose Donnelly was standing at the edge of the gravel walkway, staring fixedly into the long grass that stretched down to the wall at the bottom of the grounds. Refusing to shift her position, she didn't even turn as she heard the footsteps approaching her.

'What is it, Rose?' McCadden asked.

'I was coming back from the school, sir,' she explained, pointing to roughly indicate her movements. 'As I was passing by the construction site, I saw something being thrown from one of the windows at the back of the house. It landed in the grass somewhere around here.'

'What was it?'

'Something small. The size of a coin, a keyring, nail clippers, a penknife. That size.'

'Did you see who threw it?'

'No. I couldn't actually see the back of the house or the windows themselves. The way I was approaching, I was kind of level with the wall. I just saw the object itself.'

'It wasn't just something blowing off the roof, was it, Rose?' McCadden wondered.

'There's no wind, sir,' Donnelly reminded him testily.

'You know what I mean, Rose. Something dropped by a bird. Something disturbed by a seagull up there. Bits flaking off the gutter.'

'If it had fallen, I wouldn't be interested in it.'

'I know that, Rose, but—'

'And I wouldn't be looking for it out here. It was the trajectory of the thing that made me suspicious. It was such that it could only have been thrown by someone trying to get it as far away as possible. And it could only have come from the upper windows.'

'Fair enough.'

Ryan, standing beside him, gently tapped McCadden's elbow with his hand. When McCadden looked across, he saw that the sergeant wasn't uselessly studying the heavy grass like everyone else. He was staring back towards the house, his head tilted, looking at the upper bedroom windows.

McCadden swivelled to follow his example. Above them, at their bedroom windows, each of the three Christian Brothers was standing, holding more or less the same pose, with their hands tucked into the pocket slits of their soutanes, and looking back down.

From McCadden's left, they grew in stature. Stevens,

in the second bedroom, was barely tall enough to reach above the central sash of the window frame. His round little face was neither pressed against the glass nor drawn back into the shadows. In the room beside him, Hennessy stood, no doubt deliberately, in a shaft of light from a lamp to his left-hand side. Lit like a hood or a private eye from a film noir, he made the most of the illumination to display the indulgent disdain on his face. In the fourth bedroom, Traynor, his gigantic frame filling almost the entire window, seemed to stoop to peer out properly. And the effort of holding the posture made him look even darker and more gloomy than usual.

McCadden didn't consider the other two separately. He expected their presence. But Hennessy, he thought, must have speed-read Boethius and left the living room to climb upstairs almost as McCadden and Ryan were leaving the house by the front door.

'Right,' McCadden said decisively. 'It looks like you've tumbled something, Rose. And it looks like we have an interested audience, too.'

He glanced at his watch. It was four forty-five. Early in October, sunset was about six thirty. They had more than an hour of good light. And nothing better to do.

'Right,' he said again. He turned to the uniformed guard who'd summoned him. 'Bring the others round the back here. Make it quick.'

When the guard left, the three detectives, their heads bowed and their hands joined, considered the grass in front of them. As if they were praying by a graveside.

'You play golf, Rose?' Ryan asked finally.

Donnelly looked across at him dubiously. 'No. Why?'

'Frank spends his time on the course driving into the rough, Rose,' McCadden explained. 'He's used to locating misplaced golf balls. I think he's wondering what you used as a marker to judge where the thing landed.'

'There's no marker. I couldn't, at the angle I was approaching it. I just tried to keep my eye on where it had fallen. I had to wait here until someone else came along before I could manage to call you.'

'You realize we're standing directly opposite Traynor's bedroom, don't you?' McCadden observed.

Donnelly shook her head. 'I don't know one of them from the other, really, sir.'

'Well, we are. Did the object come straight out or at an angle?'

'Again, because of the way I was approaching it, I couldn't really tell.'

By then, the uniformed guards had gathered on the gravel behind. There were eight of them, McCadden counted. The ninth was still standing guard at the front of the house.

'All right,' McCadden called out his instructions. 'We'll be searching this long grass in front of us. One straight line. Four of you each side of Detective Donnelly there. Single arm's length. You're not going to be able to see anything except grass while you're still standing, so this is a hands and knees job, with every blade of grass turned over. Use the gloves the sergeant has here for you.'

'What are we searching for, sir?'

'We're not too sure, to be honest with you. So take out everything you find.'

Twice McCadden looked back up towards the bedroom windows while the search was in progress. Twice he was confronted by the same range of expressions on the Brothers' faces. Stevens remained tight, and perhaps a little tense. Hennessy held that slightly superior curl to his lips. Traynor glowered.

Each time, McCadden used an object brought to him from the search to try to rattle the three. A rusted lid from a tin can. A page from a prayer book. He had no idea how much detail the Brothers could distinguish. But if they were moved or disturbed by any of the finds, they did a wonderful job disguising it.

Although he'd learned to respect Donnelly's judgement and instinct, McCadden wondered if they weren't wasting their time. He wondered if they'd have enough light to complete the search. Sinking a little into cynicism, he wondered if the discarded object wasn't just a black joke by Hennessy or a clever decoy by any one of the three. And as the bits and pieces that were brought back were stacked by his side, he wondered at the amount and variety of human debris a small green area could conceal. Writing instruments, bolts, rotted food, an unused condom ...

'Sir!'

The call caught McCadden's attention wandering. For a moment, he had no idea who had made it or where it had come from. He looked up, along the rows of trodden grass the searchers had made in front of him. The uniformed guards were all looking sideways, half of them to their left and half to their right. In the centre, only Donnelly was staring downwards.

McCadden's shoes slipped across the rough pebbles of the gravel walkway as he tried to move quickly. He didn't ask what she'd found. He didn't have to. As he reached her, he followed the line of her pointing forefinger.

The small, round silver object was lying almost on its side, with one of its points embedded in the earth and its back resting against a thick blade of grass.

McCadden pulled on plastic gloves and stooped to pick it up. It wasn't a coin that Donnelly had seen being thrown from one of the windows above, he saw. It wasn't a penknife or a keyring. It was a sports medal. And according to the lettering inscribed on the back, it was an FAI Junior Cup winner's medal. Won by Joey Whittle in his healthier youth. And given by the man as the only gesture of love he could manage to his eldest, most mysterious son, Jason.

'Wednesday night, Rose,' McCadden said. 'Out in Tom Hayden's house. The guard who searched Brother Stevens before we checked out the house itself. It was Gifford, wasn't it?'

Donnelly stood up, wiping blades of grass from the knees of her jeans. 'Yes. Why?'

'Is Gifford here?' McCadden called out, searching quickly along the line of uniformed guards. 'Come on, man. I saw you earlier.'

'I'll get him, sir,' one of the other guards volunteered. 'He's around the front.'

While he waited, McCadden gently closed his fingers over the medal and stared thoughtfully at his fist. He didn't want to look up again at the windows until he was certain. If he could eliminate Stevens, he was left with only two to pressurize. If he could eliminate the other two...

He heard the footsteps running towards him across the gravel.

'Are you looking for me, sir?' Gifford reported.

'Wednesday night,' McCadden reminded him. 'You searched Brother Stevens at Tom Hayden's house. What did you find?'

'Ah...'

'Pocket diary,' McCadden hurried him along. 'Loose change. Medals. One winner's. Is that right?'

'Yes, sir.'

'The winner's medal. Describe it.'

'Well...'

'Soccer or hurling? Old or new?'

'Soccer, sir. Very old. The shine was well gone off it—'

McCadden opened his fist to display the medal lying flat on his palm. 'Was it that?'

'One the very same as that, sir. But I couldn't say if that was the exact one.'

'That'll do.'

Only then did McCadden look back up to the bedroom windows. His expression of mild triumph didn't find the audience it sought, though. Hennessy and Traynor were still staring down at him. But the window in Stevens's bedroom was now empty.

'Who relieved you at the front door, Gifford?' he asked. Calmly. Without anxiety. Assuming that the simplest, most basic of procedures would've been followed automatically.

But the silence that met his question started to worry him.

And when he glanced at Gifford to hurry the answer along, he saw behind Gifford's right shoulder the pained, embarrassed face of the younger guard who had enthusiastically rushed off to summon his colleague and, in his eagerness to be of service, had neglected to replace him.

thirty

McCadden ran.

Stevens had only just left the house, he calculated. With Gifford guarding the front door, he'd had no opportunity to slip away before this. And no reason to. The rare medal he'd taken from Jason Whittle hadn't yet been found. And even when it was located, there was nothing to tie it directly to himself. Fingerprints? But he'd probably been clever enough to wipe it and use gloves when throwing it from the bedroom.

It was only the sudden appearance of Gifford at the back of the house that had put the desperate idea of flight into his mind. The memory of Gifford already seeing him with the medal. Along with the realization that the front of the house was now unguarded.

McCadden was hoping to head him off before he reached the cars. But as he ran along by the gable wall, his shoes slipping from under him on the loose gravel, he heard the engine of the Opel Corsa in front already starting up.

For a moment, he thought the gravel that hindered him was also going to work to his advantage. The Corsa's wheels dug into it and skidded. But he didn't fancy slipping between the Corsa's boot and the Ford behind it to risk getting crippled if Stevens reversed. And he had even less of an appetite for rounding the bonnet and being driven over. He kept going until he reached the front door on the passenger side.

The door was locked. As he raised his right arm and smashed his crooked elbow into the window, he had a glimpse of the fastest of the uniformed guards arriving at the driver's side. The glass cracked but didn't break. The guard grasped the handle, but didn't manage to open the door. And the car's wheels suddenly found some purchase on the ground under the gravel.

'Let it go!' McCadden shouted as the Opel jerked away.

Pebbles and dust were thrown up at him. The stones that hit his legs didn't trouble him. But one jumped higher than the rest and caught his cheek as he was falling after losing his footing. When the cloud of dust had thinned, he saw from the hand he brought down from rubbing his face that he was bleeding a little. But it wasn't his cheek that had been cut. It was the palm of the hand itself, where he'd been clenching Joey Whittle's medal so tightly that it had punctured the flesh.

Across from him, the uniformed guard was being helped to his feet by others. His clothes were coated with dust. His cap, lying on the ground in front of him, had so many small stones in it that it seemed as if he'd been using it to collect them in.

'Are you all right?' McCadden asked.

'Yes, sir. I'm okay.'

Others had run past, towards the open gates, to watch the Corsa's route. Rose Donnelly was at the front of them. The driver of the van they'd come in was already back behind the wheel, with the engine running. The van's side door had been rolled back and was now being held open.

'Left down Manor Hill, sir,' Donnelly reported when McCadden reached her.

'Two stay here,' he ordered quickly. 'No one in or out. Rose, come in front with me. Frank, take charge in the back.'

Even under pressure, he found a little time to think of his own small comforts. And the prospect of enduring a high-speed chase while squashed beside the sergeant's bulk in the front of the van didn't appeal to him.

'Has this thing got a siren?' he asked the driver as they pulled away.

'Yes, sir.'

'Put it on. Get on the radio, Rose, and let's have some more cars around.'

After the recent snatch of Luke Brady and the disappearance of Jason Whittle, their presence at the school had already brought neighbours to their doors. They sped down Barrack Street as if on a race track, between two solid lines of spectators.

Turning left down Manor Hill, they could see the Corsa at the base of the hill breaking a red light at the junction of College Street and Cork Road as it swung right. Most of the cars coming against it managed to brake in time. One was slower. It had to swerve violently to avoid contact and then swerve again as it mounted the footpath and made for a terrified old lady with a shopping trolley.

'He's heading for the woods,' McCadden guessed.

And he seemed to be right.

All the way out the Cork Road, past the estate where Jason Whittle lived, they kept the Corsa in view ahead of them. Not particularly gaining on it. But not conceding to it, either. On the series of bends beyond the estate, they lost sight of it for a while. But they'd expected that. They weren't worried. Until the road straightened again and they saw nothing ahead of them now except a white Garda patrol car speeding towards them from the opposite direction.

The car and the van stopped abreast of each other for the drivers to consult. And no, the two officers in the car hadn't been passed by a black Opel Corsa.

'Go back,' McCadden ordered.

They turned on the road where they'd stopped. The patrol car waited, and then tagged on behind.

'Next turn right,' McCadden instructed. 'It's the old road, little used. It has the derelict cottage where Luke Brady was held. Another cottage beyond it is owned by an elderly woman. The road loops back on to the main road. He didn't take that turn because we would've seen him.'

The driver indicated and swung down the narrow, pot-holed road.

'What's Stevens up to?' Donnelly wondered. 'He's trapping himself.'

McCadden twisted to look into the rear of the van. 'Which one of you nearly killed himself trying to stop Stevens back there?'

'He stayed at the school, sir.'

'Right. I was wondering if Stevens had changed his clothes. Did anyone else manage to see him?'

'No, sir . . . No.'

Halfway down the road, they found the Corsa. A hurried attempt had been made to conceal it. Stevens had driven it across the old front garden of the derelict cottage,' into the overgrown bushes to the side. They might've passed it by. The light was fading. Very little of the car's rear was actually showing. And its black colour was almost merging with the darkness. But the ground was still churned and muddy from the recent siege and the tyres had sunk deeply into it, leaving an obvious trail behind.

The Corsa was empty now. Footprints leading away from it headed for the woods before disappearing in the grass. It was possible, of course, that Stevens could've doubled back and run in the opposite direction. But McCadden didn't think he'd had the time to risk it. Even if his intention had been only flight, and only escape.

McCadden allocated two more guards to the patrol car and sent it back to the main road to seal off the exits there.

'These woods are shaped like a crescent,' he explained. 'There are only two ways out. This road. And the main road on the other side. Spread out just inside the fencing. Stay there. Don't go into the woods. We'll flush him out from this side.'

Once the car had left, McCadden now had Frank Ryan and Rose Donnelly and five of the uniforms to himself.

'Four of you to my right,' he ordered. 'Three of you to my left. We've got to cover the length of this road. A small man. White-haired. Don't look for clerical clothes. He may have changed. The pathways run diagonally through the wood. Don't follow them. Cut across them in a straight line. Use your torches. I'm giving everyone two minutes from now to get into position. Let's go!'

Dusk closed in quickly after they'd set off. To McCadden's right and left, the torch beams swung back and forth in the gloom like mobile searchlights. He wondered briefly what Mrs Whelan was making of it all if she was at home. Crossing a rough footpath and knowing that the clearings where he'd fought with Cooney and where Stevens must've followed Jason Whittle two weeks before were close on his right, he wondered if either was where the Brother was now making for. But he couldn't deviate to check. Those were someone else's responsibility now. And he had his own patch to look after.

For fifteen minutes, they searched without results. No one at all seemed to be in the woods apart from themselves. Maybe it was now too late for the casual strollers and the dog owners, and a little too early for the cider drinkers.

But then, as they were approaching the main road on the other side, as their straight line was being bent to an arc with the shape of the woods, McCadden heard a call.

'Hey! Hey, you! Stop! Gardai! Stop!'

It came, he calculated, from the second man on his right.

He broke into a sprint. The trees impeded him. Now that he'd changed the angle of his own movement, their lines were different. He had to adjust.

But in less than a minute, he came on the drama.

Stevens, still wearing his black clerical trousers and jacket, but without the soutane that would've slowed him, was standing just beyond the fence, in the grass margin on the edge of the road. Three uniformed guards were converging on him. One from behind. One from either side. And a car, with its headlights on, was speeding towards him from the city.

McCadden knew instantly what the cleric intended.

He tried to time his intervention to throw off Stevens's timing.

'Stevens!' he called. 'It's McCadden!'

But Stevens's concentration was too intense to be deflected. With a perfect judgement that must have served him well, despite his size, when he was a young sportsman, he threw himself in front of the oncoming car, so that he was hit while still in the air.

It was the bonnet of a grey Volvo that collided with him and tossed him savagely up and to the right.

And even if he'd survived the contact, McCadden thought, he couldn't possibly have come through the sickening landing, when he hit the road head first.

McCadden was right. Stevens was already dead by the time he reached the scene. Two uniformed guards were bending over the body. One had turned slightly away and was shaking his head, half in communication, half with shock and nausea. Behind them, the rest of the search party were spilling from the woods.

'Two of you go down the road on this side, two of you on the other,' McCadden ordered. 'Slow the traffic down. We don't want any more accidents here. But keep them moving. Filter them through the lane that's clear. You, call in to the station. Get an ambulance out here. Rose? Where are you, Rose?'

'Here, sir.'

'Look after the driver of the Volvo, Rose.'

Frank Ryan, heavier and slower than the others, was the last to arrive on the scene. He came up to McCadden's side, breathing heavily, and looked down at the mangled body of the cleric.

'Shit!' he swore.

McCadden knew exactly what the big man meant. It wasn't an accident victim that Ryan saw lying there lifeless on the road. It was a kidnapper. A kidnapper who couldn't tell now what he'd done with the boy he'd taken. Who couldn't explain where Jason Whittle was concealed. Who couldn't even reveal whether the boy was dead or alive. And who couldn't confess whether he'd led the police to the woods here out of compassion or malice, as an act of mercy or even deeper cruelty.

'Cover him up,' McCadden ordered despairingly.

thirty-one

McCadden and Frank Ryan travelled back in the ambulance with Stevens's body. Their presence unsettled the paramedic who was on duty. They sat on the bench opposite the corpse, both leaning forward and staring intently at the casualty. As if the man wasn't really dead. As if they were waiting for him to regain consciousness and be questioned.

Stevens hadn't yet been wrapped in a body bag. He was lying as they'd strapped him on the stretcher. Most of his small frame was shrouded, but the covers had slipped away from his upright feet. Only one of his shoes was still on. The other was knocked off in the collision with the Volvo and had been collected at the scene. It was now lying beside the stockinged foot, upside down, so that it kept rocking back and forth with the motion of the ambulance. Its movements and the noise it was making were starting to irritate McCadden. But just as he was about to reach out and adjust it, Ryan spoke to him.

'You reckon he did Timmy Line as well?'

'It's probably safe to assume it, yes.'

'Same suffering all over again for the parents. And still no certainty.'

'Nothing we can do. Unless . . .'

'*Why* did he do it? Why now? Why then? Why ten years apart?'

McCadden shrugged. He'd already sketched an outline of Stevens's life for Ryan. But there were no answers in the account. Only further questions.

He said, 'Maybe there was some entangled, personal conflict with Hennessy. A twisted resentment of Hennessy's influence over kids he himself desired. Maybe he was ramrod straight. Maybe Hennessy *is* homosexual. Maybe Stevens was perversely trying to protect the kids from corruption. Maybe it's buried deep in his own childhood. He ran away from home to join the Christian Brothers and dragged his problems with him. Abusers are usually abused. Maybe it was a combination of all those things.'

'You think the boy is still alive?'

'I don't know, Frank. Since he disappeared, I've worked on the feeling that he's still alive. But now I don't know. Sometimes I think that Stevens leading us to the woods and then committing suicide is a hopeful sign. The bastard was malignant enough to try and throw us off the scent with a false trail. Other times I think it's a bad sign, that he was really indicating where the grave was before he said goodbye.'

'Maybe it was just panic. Desperation.'

'Maybe. I've been trying to work out when Stevens decided to go for Jason. What triggered his actions? There doesn't seem to be any one outstanding event. I know Stevens followed Jason in the woods a fortnight ago. I imagine he tried to assault him when Jason was drunk. Probably, he was disturbed by others in the woods. The boy had blacked out and was left only with the feeling of terror. He made the mistake of blaming the wrong man when he woke up in Ryle's house.'

'Stevens couldn't have known that.'

'I'm not too sure. Not the details, I suppose. But Stevens would've pumped Nicholas Hayden for information, or got it indirectly, through Hayden's old man. He reckoned he was in the clear.'

'Until you brought Jason to the woods on Tuesday.'

'And he was scared enough to follow.'

'Then, when you called Tuesday night...'

'That's when he made his next decision. I told him that all three of the boys had seen a Christian Brother. He calculated that it was only a matter of time. It was, too. The clerical author of *Alice in Wonderland*. The naked children. It was all coming together for Jason.'

'Sounds like they met halfway.'

'That's what worries me. I'd be happier if I knew *where* they'd met. Did Stevens go looking for Jason last Tuesday night after I left? Did he find him in the estate? Or did Jason finally have his suspicions and head towards the school to find out for himself? If we knew, we'd be closer...'

'But we don't.'

'No.'

'And we can't ask the bastard.'

'Well, we can *ask*.'

They fell silent.

Looking out the back window of the ambulance into the darkness, McCadden saw that they'd just turned on to the ring road to the hospital in the east of the city. He wondered where Orla Stanley was. He hadn't had time that morning to ask about her duty hours. So much had happened since. And he wanted to talk to her, as easily and as lengthily as they'd talked through half the night before.

Jenny, of course, would complain that his behaviour was typical of men. After years of inflicting silence on her in a strained marriage, he'd casually found a younger and a more impressionable ear to bend with his troubles . . .

The thought suggested another to him.

'Rose Donnelly, Frank,' he said. 'Is she, ah, in good shape?'

'Rose? What about her?'

'She seems jauntier lately. More confident.'

'Oh, herself and the husband are back living together again.'

'Right.'

'He decided he couldn't hack it by himself. Wasn't half the misunderstood, unappreciated genius he thought he was. He's come down to live here in Waterford. You might've noticed that her hours had a bit more flexibility the last few days.'

'I'm happy for her.'

'I'm not. He's a gobshite. How's your wife, by the way?'

'Ex-wife.'

'Doesn't matter. How is she?'

'Jenny's getting married again.'

'To someone else?'

'She's an intelligent woman, Frank, and willing to learn from her mistakes, so I think the answer is yes, to someone else.'

'How's the nurse, then?'

'The nurse is fine, actually. Thanks to you. I owe you a pint.'

And after that, there didn't seem to be anything more to say.

In the silence, McCadden again became aware of the odd shoe that was rocking back and forth at the base of the stretcher, now one way and now the other, and never quite toppling over to settle on its base. Again he reached out to adjust it. And again he was detained.

Not by Frank Ryan this time, though. By a creeping sensation along the back of his neck.

As if paralysed, he stayed for several seconds with his arm outstretched, staring at the shoe.

'Are you okay?' Ryan asked him.

'Hey!' McCadden addressed the paramedic. 'Can you communicate with the driver?'

'Yeah, sure, I—'

'Tell him to turn this thing around. We're going back to the school first. Barrack Street.'

The paramedic gestured at the corpse. 'What about—?'

'He won't mind,' McCadden said with conviction. 'Just drop us at the school. You can take him on the rest of his journey then. Do it, man! Quickly!'

Ryan, having realized what McCadden had fixed on, was also staring at the shoe now. He saw everything that McCadden saw. The new black slip-on shoe. The mud from the flight through the woods. The harder grey deposit under the softer mud in the ridges on the sole. But he couldn't see any of its significance.

He didn't ask, knowing that he wouldn't get an answer. He waited.

Outside the school, when the ambulance pulled up, McCadden jumped out first, taking the odd shoe with him. It was now almost eight o'clock. The two uniformed guards he'd left there earlier were still on duty.

'Come with me,' he ordered. 'Frank, get on to the station. We'll need some more men out here.'

He led the way, across the gravel driveway in front of the Brothers' quarters, glancing over only once to see what rooms were illuminated and finding the place in darkness. At the locked gates to the construction site he stopped. The discarded placards had been left lying against the wire fence by the men on strike.

'We need to get in,' McCadden said.

Ryan glanced at his watch. 'We'll have to phone the building contractor or—'

McCadden shook his head. 'No. There's a gap in the wire somewhere. You two go that way. We'll go this, Frank.'

'Hang on, Carl! We need lights and—'

'Can't wait.'

'We'll never find anything in this darkness . . .'

But it was Ryan himself, still complaining about the conditions, who came across the opening in the side of the fence. A gap, large enough to crawl through, concealed by crates and bricks on the ground.

They summoned the two uniforms and all four went in together. They were at the side of the unfinished building. A wall of fifteen or twenty feet rose in front of them. They went right and quickly found themselves in a narrow dead-end blocked by rubble. Turning back, they came out at what would eventually be the front of the building. A theatre, McCadden remembered the project being described as.

The entrance door and front windows were only gaping holes. Inside, the joists for the floor were in place, but the boards hadn't yet been laid. The basement underneath was exposed.

'Down,' McCadden ordered.

They couldn't immediately find a stairway and had to jump. Only their torches illuminated their landings amid the dangerous rubble.

Frank Ryan was suffering physically. 'Are you certain of this, Carl?' he wondered.

McCadden shook his head. 'Only guessing. This part, anyway. It might be somewhere else on the...'

But his guess was accurate.

In the furthest section of the basement, under what would eventually become the stage, beyond a doorway hastily blocked with sheets of plywood and sloppily cemented bricks, they found Jason Whittle.

The boy was alive.

His mouth was gagged to prevent him calling out. His hands and feet were tied with heavy rope. Fastened by more rope, he was secured to a ring that had been fixed to the wall in a corner.

He was blinded by the lights of the torches, unable to see who was approaching, and at first his eyes were bright and wide with fear.

But McCadden called, 'It's Inspector McCadden, Jason! You're okay! You're okay!'

When they took the gag from his mouth and released the ropes, the boy was shivering and crying uncontrollably. He tried to stand. But he must've been trapped in the one position for a long time without movement. The blood wasn't circulating. His muscles were weak.

McCadden crouched beside him and put his arm around the frail, heaving shoulders. He tried to balance the need to get him quickly out of this traumatic hole against the need to give him a little space to recover himself.

The boy struggled for control. 'It was Stevens!' he sobbed. 'Brother Stevens!'

'I know,' McCadden told him. 'We have him. Did he harm you?'

'He hit me. I came up here to see Brother Hennessy on Tuesday night. I thought it was him that was after...'

'I know, I know. But did Stevens harm you? Apart from hitting you.'

'No, he didn't do nothing. Not to me. He did it to the other boy.'

'What other boy?'

'There was another boy. Stevens said there was another boy. He did things to him because he wouldn't promise to stay away from Brother Hennessy. He said the same would happen to me if I kept on being friendly with Hennessy.'

'When was this, Jason?'

'I don't know, I don't know. He said the boy had to fast, he couldn't eat, because of his sin, he had to fast, and then he died, because he wouldn't give up his sin, and he starved. He said the same thing would happen to me, unless I gave up the sin. I don't know what he was talking about. He said the boy died in Bishopstown. I don't know where. Under an old primary school, he said. He said I was going to die under a school as well if I didn't give up the sin...'

The boy was crying and shivering violently again. McCadden, who had let him run on, now hugged him again to quieten and comfort him. The 'other boy' was Timmy Line, he guessed. Bishopstown was a suburb of Cork, where the abduction had occurred. The information would lead not only to extensive searches in the area, but also to the re-opening of the case and of the public agony of Timmy's parents.

'It happened a long time ago, Jason,' McCadden said. 'He was talking about something that happened more than ten years ago. We already knew about that. What's more important now is what happened to you.'

The boy breathed noisily through his blocked nose and struggled to get calm again. 'Nothing,' he said. 'He didn't do nothing. He just tied me up.'

'Are you sure? There's nothing else wrong with you?'

'I'm hungry.'

McCadden laughed and hugged the boy again. If Jason was aware of hunger, he guessed, he was probably telling the truth about being unharmed.

'Right,' he said. 'We're going to get you out of here. Okay?'

'Okay.'

'You go with this guard here. You won't be able to walk, so he'll carry you. You won't mind that, will you?'

'No, it's okay.'

'You'll be brought to hospital. Just for a rest and a check-up and to get some food. The other guard there will go and tell your parents you're all right.'

In the shadowy light from the deflected torch beams, he thought he saw disappointment and anxiety on the boy's face. He reached into his jacket pocket, took out the Junior Cup winner's medal, and offered it to Jason.

'Here,' he said. 'I got that back for you. When your dad comes to visit you, show him that you still have it. And tell him I said the name of the sweeper on the losing side in the final was McCadden.'

'Was it you?'

'No. My brother. But make sure to show him that you

still have it, all right? Your dad didn't give you that because he didn't want it himself, you know.'

Words and gestures, McCadden thought sadly as Jason was brought out. He had no great faith in their power to change the smaller relationships in life. Come Christmas, Joey Whittle would still have a problem with drink. Corina Whittle would still be incapable of rising much above neglect in her attention to the family. And Jason, if he was lucky, would again be taking guidance from Brother Hennessy and John Ryle and setting his sights on the education that would lift him away from that family.

Frank Ryan, standing by his side in the darkened basement, cut in on his pessimism.

'So,' Ryan said. 'What's with the Cinderella act?'

McCadden started. 'Cinderella?'

Ryan shone his torch on McCadden's left hand. 'The shoe.'

'Oh! Right! You know what Ruddell, the principal here, said to me a few days ago? He was quoting one of the Brothers, although he didn't mention which one. He said, *The foundation of a good school is its worst pupils.*'

'Very black,' Ryan agreed. 'But the shoe?'

McCadden turned the shoe over and flicked the mud from between the ridges to expose the hard, grey substance underneath. 'That's cement, Frank,' he explained. 'Stevens told me on Tuesday that he'd just bought the shoes that morning. He went to the trouble ... You know those little clusters of pebbles held together by cement that you get on building sites?'

'Uh-huh.'

'One detached from his shoe and he threw it on the fire. It should've bothered me more than it did at the time. You don't throw stones on an open fire. Anyway, the site has been closed by the strike, as you know. He couldn't have picked the things up accidentally, while inspecting the site. And as you'll notice, the cement has set in his shoes. All the cement on site would've been dry for a week or more. So he must've been mixing the stuff himself ... Were you educated by the Christian Brothers, Frank?'